THE HOUSE ON FINDLATER LANE

HELEN GOLTZ

For Bev, I'm so glad Dad found you.

The characters and locations in this book are entirely fictional. Any resemblance to a location, or person living or dead is purely coincidental, and a bit of a worry really given the quirky cast in this novel!

THIS IS HOW IT BEGAN...

*I*t was love at first sight.

Admittedly, Holly Hanlon's expectations were high and rose in accordance with the gear shift change as they drove up the steep slope and followed the oceanside esplanade to the very last house before the road turned and began its descent.

The house at the top of the esplanade, or lane as it was known, was perfect – unlike everything else in Holly's life. Holly knew from experience that when you know, you just know, and she could see herself happily ensconced within the walls of this little village "cottage".

Holly and the young man next to her alighted from the car. She breathed in the salty air and turned to admire the ocean view. He stood by, waiting patiently; it was his job. Holly then turned to admire the house that would soon be her home for the next six months.

While its neighbours were a mixture of glass beachfront homes and modernised white brick rendered cottages, this house looked like it had come through the last century untouched. It was a two-storey white timber cottage with enough distance from its neighbour to feel remote. At the front of the house were enormous bay windows on both levels and a delightful little cottage garden.

'The light and sea view will stream into the house! You are just what I need – *Findlater House* on Findlater Lane,' she said in a low whisper. Holly smiled, forgetting for just a moment about the real estate agent standing beside her.

'Sorry?' he asked.

She jumped slightly. 'I love it.' She turned to face him. 'I'll take it.'

'But you can't take it...' he stammered.

'Why? It's for rent, isn't it? The sign says so.' She glanced at the sign, then back to the agent. 'Is it taken? Why are we here then?' This was not going to end well if he was a time-waster.

The real estate agent ran his tongue over his lower lip – a nervous gesture. Holly noticed he did this regularly... more so since they arrived at *Findlater House*.

'Yes, yes, it's for rent,' he assured her, 'but you haven't seen inside. I can't rent it to you until you see inside, it's our company policy, Ms Hanlon.'

'Really?' she doubted that and her voice betrayed her.

Damien Flat (truly his name) was tall, thin, dressed by catalogue, and lucky to be a year out of high school; his parents owned the real estate agency and he was working in the family business. There were so many properties for rent in the small seaside village during the non-tourist season that Holly expected her announcement that she would rent the cottage would be met with great enthusiasm. She expected Damien to immediately pull the papers and a pen out of his stylish leather shoulder bag and point at the "sign here" line with glee.

Let's face it, she thought, *Findlater House* was not going to appeal to everyone. It was old-fashioned, it looked like a good gust of wind from the ocean would topple it and the garden was a shambles. She was desperately hoping that the bathroom and kitchen were at least modernised.

Fortunately, the house was high and slightly back off the road, so, like a voyeur, you could sit and watch everyone walking past but not be obvious to the street. Holly liked the fact that she could live unseen and no-one would know how many wines she had at cocktail hour! *Heaven.* But if she wanted people contact, which occasionally was necessary for human survival, she noted the small area in front of the garden where she could sit and wave to those walking by on the footpath, or make a bit of small talk about the weather.

'C'mon, I'll show you around,' he said, fishing in his pocket for the key. 'I've got another four properties to show you, we've only just started.'

Holly squinted at Damien in concentration. She had just realised what was going on – Damien Flat was bored stupid. It was mid-morning on a Wednesday, she was probably the first person he'd seen all week and it was his chance to get out of the office.

She took pity on him. After all, it wasn't the city, there wasn't a queue to rent the house and she could cut him some slack.

'Good-oh, let's go then. We'll have a look here and then go see the other four,' she said with enthusiasm, for Damien's sake, 'and please, call me Holly.'

'Sure, great... Holly,' he said, buoyed, and headed up the garden stairs with an improved attitude.

Holly followed him up to the front of the house, stopped at the top stair and turned around to observe the vista. It truly was the perfect location... two streets from the village, across the road from the drop to the ocean and suspiciously cheap. Her Aunty Kate was right... ghost or no ghost, who could resist?

～

In a flash of consciousness, Damien stopped just before he turned the door handle to *Findlater House*. Holly almost ran into him, not realising that he wasn't moving forward.

'There's something I need to tell you,' he said and cleared his throat. 'Legally, I don't have to tell you, but we're a very upfront real estate agency with integrity.'

'Okay then, please tell away,' she said, waiting for it... she knew what was coming but Damien Flat didn't know her connection with this house.

'It's got termites?' she ventured.

'What? No, no termites,' he said, looking put out that she would think such a thing.

'Oh well, that's good,' Holly said. 'You've put the rent up then?'

'God no,' he declared, 'it's hard enough to rent as it is,' he said, and then realised the error of his ways. He shouldn't have said that, now she might negotiate! He cleared his throat again, pulled at his tie as if it was tightening around his throat there and then, and looked her in the eye. 'I think you need to know that... um, this property is what we call a... well, a stigmatised house,' he said, finally.

Holly burst out laughing, and Damien looked affronted.

'A stigmatised house!' she repeated, and laughed again. 'It sounds like the house needs therapy. Stigmatised... that's great! Are you talking about the portrait of the Sergeant? The ghost?'

'Yes,' he said, his eyes widening. 'You know? How do you know about the portrait?' He sighed. 'Who am I kidding? Everyone knows... it's even part of the local history walk.'

They were still standing at the front door and all she wanted to do was go in and sign the papers, not necessarily in that order.

Holly shrugged. 'Long story, but to make it short and quick...' She began her rave at super speed. 'My grandmother, Lily, owned this house and her children – my father Joseph and my Aunty Kate – they inherited it and the portrait and the ghost, on the basis they didn't throw the portrait out. I think Loopy Lily, sorry Grandma Lily, quite liked it and the ghost. My Aunty Kate bought out my father – he was pleased to be cashed up and rid of it I suspect, so now she owns it. She won't sell it because she's sentimental like that. You see, my grandparents – her parents – have both passed away. As you manage the property for Aunty Kate and she was complaining to me that she wasn't having much luck renting it out long-term, I decided I really needed a sea change. With me so far?' Holly asked, stopping for breath. Damien gave an unconvincing nod.

Holly continued. 'Mm, well, if I told Aunty Kate that I wanted to stay, she'd offer me the house for free. But I might want to stay long-term... longer than six months and I don't want to take advantage of her, so I'd like to rent it under my married name because she won't remember that name. And yes, I'm very familiar with the portrait, but I'm sure the Sergeant will be in it when we go in!' Holly finished, looking rather pleased with her abridged version of history. Bet he's glad he asked, she thought.

'Right, just so I have this straight... you know about the portrait and its, uh, subject, and you still want to see the house and maybe rent it?' Damien asked, his mouth slightly ajar.

'That's the gist of it,' she agreed. Holly wondered if he had heard anything she said.

'She was just here, you know, the property manager, your aunty Kate. She did a few renovations and stayed in the village while it was being tweaked. She left this morning,' Damien said.

'Oh, I had no idea. It's a shame I missed her,' Holly said. *Aunty Kate was in town? Phew, that was close.*

'Will your husband be living here, too?' he asked.

'No, just me. Shall we go in?'

'Sure,' he said looking relieved that he'd done the right thing by her and now she was sure to take this property off his books. She could tell that coming here terrified him and a long-term rental would be no doubt be a godsend.

INTRODUCING THE SERGEANT

*S*ergeant Alexander Austen froze... if a ghost could freeze. He heard the rattle at the door as the house key went into the lock.

'Sod's Law,' he said, aloud, as he raced down the hallway to take up his position in his portrait. 'You would think by now the presence of a sinister bleeding ghost in the house would be enough to keep that wet real estate agent away.'

He could see through the window the young agent unlocking the door. Beside him, a petite, attractive blonde looked keen to enter. He scoffed – *that'll be easy*. He adjusted himself into the portrait frame to watch their entry.

The door opened and the agent stood aside to allow her to enter first. She inhaled and smiled, apparently pleasantly surprised.

'Mm, the smell of fresh paint and not at all musty,' she said.

The agent looked around nervously. The Sergeant smirked; he liked to put the wind up him. Damien's gaze ran up the hallway to the ceiling and then as soon as the woman moved out of his way, he looked straight to the portrait that was one of three on the living room wall. Two were landscape paintings and the third was of a good-looking young man in a military uniform.

From his lofty position on the wall, the Sergeant watched as the woman turned to Damien.

'So white and bright,' she said and followed the agent's gaze towards the Sergeant's painting. 'If that is our ghost, he's definitely framed.'

He heard the young agent breathe a sigh of relief.

'Yes, that's him and of course he's framed. You don't want to be swayed by those silly village stories,' Damien said, in a tone that implied he expected nothing less. The agent continued: 'Anyway, as I said, Kate decided the house was all a bit tired, which it was, so while she was here she got it repainted inside, bought new linen for the beds, crockery for the kitchen, and replaced the rugs. It's like new.'

'It is... and clutter-free, I love that,' the woman agreed – the Sergeant was yet to hear her name. 'Lucky me!' she said.

The Sergeant turned his attention to her. She was young... mid to late twenties, wearing white sneakers, a white T-shirt, jeans, and a black jumper with some sort of a hood on the back. A black bag was slung over her shoulder.

She turned around slowly, taking in the room, and smiling.

'Oh, I love it. I love the space and the view,' she said. 'These big windows are gorgeous.'

The Sergeant's eyes followed her as she turned to study the rooms. In front of her, a staircase curved its way up to the floor above and she glanced to the ceiling.

'Ah, I know enough from my house renovation to recognise this was once a couple of rooms before it became open-plan,' she said to Damien. 'A big improvement. The beams along the ceiling give it away.'

'Must have been poky in the past,' Damien said, taking in the beams.

'Codswallop... it was perfectly fine as it was,' The Sergeant said, but not for their ears. He crossed his arms but they didn't notice. 'Although it is better now,' he conceded, seeing it from her point of view.

The woman stood in the living room which took up the entire front of the house. On one side was a small dining room table for four, and on the other side was the couch, coffee table, television, and a black marble fireplace. She moved closer and looked at the Sergeant's portrait again, this time with more concentration, and then moved to the painting of the ocean next to him.

'That's clever, isn't it?' she said, observing the painting, then looking out of the window at the view which was mirrored in the painting. 'It really does draw in the eye.' She then returned to study the Sergeant. He was sorely tempted to raise an eyebrow at her.

'I can see the attraction to the portrait,' she said, her voice softening. 'I'd want to keep it there, too. Quiet striking, very handsome. Did he ever live here? I can't remember the story.'

The Sergeant stopped short in his tracks – or would have, had he been out of his frame. He studied the woman with more scrutiny. The agent still hadn't said her name and the Sergeant sure as hell didn't recognise her.

'Who are you?' he muttered, trying to place her. He could swear he had never set eyes on her before, but how did she know about the portrait and its story? And who was attracted to him? Who was she talking about? Surely not Lily. Dear, sweet Lily, old enough to be his mother and then his grandmother by the time she died.

'I think he did live here,' Damien said, fussing with his folder before returning to stare at the portrait above the fireplace. 'That does ring a bell. The locals are mostly ancient around here and they love to share a story. I think one of them told me that,' he said, rolling his eyes. 'You can ask them yourself. They'll be over with scones as soon as they see a removal truck. Come and have a look upstairs, Holly.' The agent invited the woman to take the stairs before him.

'Holly,' the Sergeant repeated her name. 'Nope, I don't know anyone called Holly.' He waited until they were halfway up the stairs, and then moved out of his frame to follow them. Holly led the way, with the agent reluctantly in tow. The Sergeant raced up and went past them towards the main bedroom, past the bathroom and two other rooms, and waited for her on the square landing of the main room. He chose who could see him and when, but unfortunately everyone could see the empty frame if he wasn't in there.

'Thank goodness,' she exclaimed and turned to the agent. 'It's a modern bathroom! Old houses are best when they've been brought gently into the current century.'

Damien nodded and glanced in through the bathroom door and then quickly around the rooms.

So nervous, the Sergeant noted, *poor young Damien.*

'We've had it up for weekend and holiday rentals for a few years now so you've got to offer all the mod cons. Prior to that, I don't think it had had a facelift since the Sixties!' Damien said.

And what a rocking time that was, the Sergeant thought, amusing himself.

The agent continued talking as he led her down the hallway. 'Not that we got many holiday rentals... you know, word of mouth about the g-h-o-s-t.' He spelled the word out.

'Speaking of which,' she said and looked around, 'are we likely to see the Sergeant, or do we only feel or hear his presence?'

The Sergeant's mouth fell open, and he abruptly closed it. *What a cheek. She's heard of me and is here for a show. Sorry to disappoint you, love, but I don't perform on cue.*

'He's totally unpredictable,' the agent was saying. 'I've never seen him, thank God,' he said, lowering his voice. 'But I've heard him groan a few times and once I heard him say "Get out". I was terrified, so was my client – she didn't take the place after that.'

'I'd be freaked out, too,' Holly said. 'So you've never seen him in bodily form?'

'No,' Damien shook his head, 'but as we left – and we left in a big hurry, I can tell you – he wasn't in his frame... it was just black.'

The Sergeant saw the woman shudder, and he felt it, too – she was genuinely nervous. *Odd*, he thought, that connection – why did I feel that? The Sergeant didn't like surprises and she apparently was one.

If you are scared by that, then why are you here? The Sergeant studied her with more interest. *Perhaps she's on a dare or been sent to write a story.* She didn't look like a journalist, but then again, it was a tourist town... casual attire was in. He watched her enter the main bedroom and she gasped.

'Wow! A balcony and what a view!' She took in the large bed adorned in white linen, the blue suede chaise chair in the corner, and the huge bay window with a seat perfectly placed to appreciate the ocean view. She clapped her hands together.

'I love it,' she said. 'I could dive in amongst the bed's white linen and look at that ocean all day.'

Damien blushed and so did the Sergeant; he raced downstairs before them and took up his place in the portrait. He noted that they both glanced towards it as they resurfaced on the lower level.

'This living area will make a great office for me, and it has a lovely, homely feel. I can put my desk in front of the window and enjoy the view,' Holly said.

Homely! How did that happen? The Sergeant stood flummoxed. *Homely! Well, that's just not on.*

She wandered over to the fireplace and turned to the big front window where she intended to set up her office. Then a small rectangular-shaped piece of black plastic sticking up in the carpet caught her attention. She bent to pick it up – it was a name tag with a business logo on it for none other than Damien Flat!

'Yours?' she asked, handing it over.

'Wow, thanks. I lost that months ago, I didn't know where,' he said, taking it and pinning it on the front of his suit.

Holly shrugged. 'Well, it is *Findlater House.*'

Damien scoffed. 'So, do you know why he sticks around?' he asked, with a glance to the portrait of the Sergeant. 'I mean, should we tell him to go to towards the white light or invite a priest to visit? I saw that work on a few television shows... I'm just putting it out there.'

The Sergeant laughed and saw both heads turn towards the portrait. *Uh-oh*, he thought, *did I do that out loud?*

The woman frowned. 'I was about eleven when Grandma died, so I never heard the story directly from her and we rarely came here for holidays, she came to stay with us. But Aunty Kate said it was something about him and his wife living here before he died, and he died in suspicious circumstances. Now he's waiting for her to join him.' She then sighed, and said, 'so sad.'

The Sergeant felt a stab of pain. That was *his* story... not a soap opera to be shared. He muttered: 'Sad? It's bloody tragic! So, she must be Lily's granddaughter?' He studied her to take in her features, comparing them to what he remembered of Lily who had joined him on the other side about fifteen years earlier.

'I wish she'd sell it,' Damien said, cutting off the Sergeant's thoughts. 'Someone would buy it. It's been hard trying to rent it out and Kate won't remove the portrait. Sorry, I don't mean to criticise your clan, it's their place so they can do what they like, of course,' he added.

You got that right... how ungrateful! the Sergeant said, but not so they could hear.

'That's cool, and yes, I knew some of that,' Holly said. 'But it will be good for your agency to have a long-term tenant... if I take it.'

'You can say that again,' he agreed, 'but don't let that sway you, we've got a few more to see. Besides, every now and then we get someone who wants to live with a ghost, so everyone is happy.'

'Not everyone,' the Sergeant muttered.

'Mm, well, I don't really want to live with a ghost, or anyone at the moment for that matter,' Holly said, moving closer to look through the large window at the cliffs in the distance, seeing the waves crashing against them, the sea spray rising high in the air. 'Thanks for showing me, through. C'mon, let's see the other places you wanted to show me.'

Damien Flat wasted no time opening the front door and making a quick exit. The Sergeant moved away from his portrait and to the window to watch the pair depart.

Well, good riddance, I doubt you'll be back, the Sergeant said, watching her stop again on the stairs in the front garden, turn, study the house as though she had heard his thoughts, and then depart.

Very curious indeed, that one. He turned to face the sitting room and remembered a time when the fire was lit, and his beautiful wife was brighter and warmer than the fire could ever be, and this was his home. But that would never be again.

HOLLY SIGNS THE RENTAL LEASE

'*Y*ou know,' Holly said, as she followed Damien up the stairs of the next potential rental property, 'I read the reviews that *Findlater House* had on your holiday rental site. There's very few who talk about the ghost.'

'True,' he said. 'My folks and I have reviewed this before ... *Findlater House* attracts three types of people,' he said, sounding very authoritative. 'Those who want to see the ghost, those who want to stay there and are terrified of seeing him, and guests who flat out don't believe.' He opened the door to the next home and Holly followed him inside. She continued to ask about *Findlater House* as she inspected each room.

'I thought the Sergeant had long gone and the rumours about his presence were just the product of guests' imagination with some added dramatics,' she agreed, 'but not so, according to some of the reviews. And you are right,' she grinned, 'it seems those who didn't want to see the Sergeant invariably got the fright of their life.'

Damien laughed. 'And you? Do you want to see him?' he asked, as they reached the front door again after the tour.

'I was glad he didn't appear during our inspection and that I didn't feel his presence,' she said and shrugged. 'At heart, I'm a scaredy-cat.'

He grinned. 'Yeah, me too, to be honest. Next one?' he asked, reaching for the door to lock it.

'Yes please,' Holly said and exited.

As she wandered back to his car she thought about the Sergeant. She didn't want to see him, hear him or feel him, but her desire to escape the city life to *Findlater House* and her need to put some space between herself and her soon-to-be ex-husband outweighed the fear of the Sergeant dropping in... or so she thought in her bravest moments. Besides, she could afford *Findlater House* at the current rental rate.

They got back in Damien's car and drove about one street before he stopped again.

'We could have walked,' he said, seeing her expression, 'but sometimes, after you've seen a few places it gets a bit exhausting.'

'I'm sure,' she agreed. She hadn't been swayed yet. *Findlater House* was still top of her list although this little one level place was cute.

'Are you close to Kate?' Damien asked, keeping up the small talk as they exited the car.

'I am. I spent a lot of time with her when I was a kid especially during school holidays. Dad travelled a lot for work and Mum liked going with him. Me not so much, so I stayed with Kate. I wished I'd caught up with her.'

'She was a twin, wasn't she?' he asked.

Holly looked surprised.

'My parents told me. Everyone's history in this joint is shared. He drowned thought, didn't he?'

Holly nodded. 'Yes. Sam was his name, he was ten. It was a family tragedy never spoken about again. If you check out our family tree there's a trend of not living long lives. Anyone who got past sixty-five was bucking the trend and Grandma Lily who owned *Findlater House* had done just that, living to seventy-one.'

Holly was amazed she could match Damien for rambling small talk; it wasn't her speciality.

'What about your clan?' she asked.

'God no, we stick around ... longer than wanted in most cases,' he joked.

Holly laughed. She was warming to Damien Flat and he was warming up and letting his guard down. She followed him on a tour of the next house while thinking about her family line. The Hanlon name was soon to be extinguished... reproducing didn't seem to feature highly in their genes. Aunty Kate never had children of her own, Holly's parents had only produced her, and if Holly took a future husband's surname, it was all over.

'This is a nice feature,' Damien said, pointing out the garden.

Knowing her mind was made up, she agreed and then dutifully followed Damien Flat into the remaining procession of rental houses, feigning her interest, and then into the final house he wanted to show her.

'That's it then,' he declared as he locked up the fourth house and headed back to his car with Holly in tow. 'What grabs you?' He opened the passenger car door for her and she slid onto the seat and waited for him to come around to his side, enter, belt up and start the car.

'Okay, I have to admit that so far the houses all have good things about them and some negatives, too,' she said, with a glance to the fourth house as they departed. 'This house is too far away from the beach and too close to the village traffic.'

Damien nodded. 'It is a high traffic area, but some of our

clients like that… they like the atmosphere, so that's why I thought I'd show you. Mind you, it's only busy in peak season – about three months of the year.'

Holly nodded. But it was on the main street of the village and walk-by traffic could look right in. She didn't like drop-ins and the fourth house seemed to encourage that. It would be a downer in the high season, given she would be visible sitting at the front in her office window for a good deal of the day.

'I like the third one, it would be my back-up choice,' she said to Damien.

'There are more properties if you're undecided… but those four properties met your specification list more so than all the others,' Damien said.

He drove his car back to his office, where Holly's vehicle was parked and the paperwork waited for whichever house she decided upon.

'Thank you for doing your homework for me,' she told him. 'You are absolutely right… you know your stuff. But… the second place was way too big for me. I'd feel empty there,' she told Damien. 'Like I should have produced kids to fill every room and there's no sign of that happening any time soon.'

Damien gave a nervous chuckle, not sure if it was a joke or a tragedy.

'The third place… well, it was lovely and modern, but I'm not a modern house girl. I'm a vintage girl. I like chair rails or picture rails, ornate ceilings, vintage light fittings and a cottage history. But the location was great.'

'So?' he asked, and Holly heard his breath hitch. She felt like she was choosing a box in a television game show, and half expected a spotlight to come on and someone to ask her if she was sure, before a beautiful woman appeared and turned the panel to reveal her choice!

'I'd like to take the first house we saw – *Findlater House* – it's me,' she said, pronouncing the verdict.

Damien exhaled and, frowning, he asked, 'So you're saying you want the ghost house? Just clarifying... the ghost house for six months.'

'Yes, please,' she said, with a firm nod. '*Findlater House* for six months.'

'Six months... right then. Commencing when?'

'How about if we start the lease from today? How soon do you think I can get water and power connected?'

'They're connected... we keep it on for the short-term holidayers,' Damien said.

'Great. So, let's sign the paperwork and you have a new tenant!' she said and clapped her hands together. So easy, meant to be... Holly always believed in that.

Holly walked out of the agency with a set of keys and debated whether to let her aunty know that she had rented the house for six months, or let her believe she had a bit of income from a good tenant. No doubt her mum would spill the beans anyway, as soon as she knew.

Holly returned to her own car with the keys to *Findlater House* in her bag. She turned on the ignition but, for just a moment, she sat letting it idle.

'I'm really going to do this,' she said aloud. 'I'm really going to leave the city and move here for six months.'

Long enough, she thought, for her soon-to-be-ex-husband to get his finances in order, buy her out of their home and get the divorce started. Long enough to be away from the scene of the pain. Not far enough away to feel totally isolated; it was only three hours' drive back to London to catch up with family and friends – not like she was going into the Argentinian rainforest on a scientific mission with the possibility of no return. She was just moving down the road... a long road.

She put the car in drive and decided to celebrate with flowers as they would brighten the house. She drove to a nursery that she had spotted just a few streets from the esplanade – everything was only a few streets from everything else in this village – to grab a bunch of flowers from the buckets she saw out the front. Once upon a time, she would have felt guilty buying flowers, or, as her soon-to-be ex-husband would say, 'wasting money on flowers.' But now she thought, *What the hell! Stop and smell the roses... or flowers!*

She drove along looking for the entrance to the nursery and, spotting the sign well in advance, swung her car into the venue. It was a huge nursery, and she made a mental note to do some work on *Findlater House's* garden while she was in residence... in its current state, it would scare a ghost away – most ghosts, anyway!

Narrowly missing a female driver of around her own age who was too busy looking in her rear vision mirror to look forward, Holly steered to a car park out the front and, within moments, was selecting a mixed bunch of colourful blooms. As she pulled the flowers out of the bucket of white, a glimmer caught her eye. She reached in and pulled out a chain with a heart on it. *How lovely*, she thought. Turning it over, she saw the heart had one word inscribed into it – *Forever*.

A pleasant, thin and distinguished older man came to assist her – probably the manager, she thought – and Holly showed him the delicate chain.

'Finders keepers, I think,' he said, introducing himself as Alfred.

'Oh, I couldn't,' Holly said. 'Someone might be pining for

it. Perhaps if none of your staff owns it. You could put a FOUND notice in-store.'

He smiled. 'Very thoughtful. We'll do that, and if it isn't claimed within three months, let's declare it yours then!'

He offered his hand and they shook on it. Holly left her business card, paid for her flowers and then, returning to her car, headed to a small grocery store that she had spotted and picked up some fresh milk, crackers, bread and cheese – a toasted sandwich would do for the first night until she officially shopped. Next stop, *Findlater House.* She felt a surge of excitement as she accelerated up Findlater Lane, navigated her car into the tight carport and cut the ignition.

'I'm home!' she said aloud, and smiled.

Right then, get to it. Holly coaxed herself out of the car. She had arrived with survival luggage, as she called it – the bare essentials – the rest remained in a small storage garage in London. Luckily, her new abode was furnished.

Grabbing a suitcase from the boot of the car and the bouquet of flowers, Holly went to air out *Findlater House* and start the next chapter of her life.

INTRODUCING LUKE MAYER – HORTICULTURIST

*L*uke Mayer put the last of the bright blue agapanthus into the rear space of Juliet Spencer's car and dusted off his hands. He had spent ten minutes discussing whether they were purple or blue with Juliet; he knew she was stalling. He closed her car's rear hatch door, stepped back and gave her a wave. She started the car and headed off, glancing back more than was necessary... about six times more than was necessary.

Watch the road, he thought and winced as Juliet narrowly missed another driver coming into the nursery. He sighed. Most of his clientele were more interested in a dinner invitation than gardening advice.

Luke knew he was a bit of a rarity in the village... thirty, single, fair-haired and just hitting six feet when he stood straight, a businessman, and yes, as mentioned, single. He was eligible bachelor material for the local ladies who, like him, had not chosen to leave for the city or had since returned disillusioned and wanting to settle down to the life they knew, to marry and raise their own families. Juliet was a prime example... he can't imagine what she did with the number of plants she bought.

Luke was always getting ribbed by his brothers and friends for never leaving the village, but he had never wanted to leave. His family had owned *How Does Your Garden Grow?* nursery for two generations; he was the third. With his mother deceased and his father semi-retired, the business was his. He managed four staff – several of whom had been with the business before he was born – and took commissions for special projects like a Remembrance Garden for the village botanic garden display. That's how he preferred to spend his days.

And he was open to love, he just hadn't found it yet and he knew why. Luke took after his father; he didn't get the charm gene, he was better at talking with plants than people. He got plants, but as far as people... women... were concerned, he ran out of conversation after 'hello'. Juliet might be attractive, but her inane banter about fashion, her social media accounts and whatever reality TV program she was into was absolutely lost on him. Like his father, he was often accused of being gruff or abrupt, whereas his two brothers took after their mother, chatty and charming, and were now married with kids and living far away from the family business.

So, he'd wait for that nerdy type of girl who took more of an interest in nature than her appearance. Who, similar to Luke, liked plants and botany, reading, hikes, staying in and cooking dinner at home. Yep, good luck with that.

It was then he recognised the low hum of Jessie Petrach's 4WD. She swung the vehicle in next to the driver that Juliet almost wiped out and gave him a wave.

Crap, he muttered, returning the wave – *Juliet and Jessie both in one day.* Luke turned just in time to see Alfred suppress a smile. Alfred was his father's first employee and now managed the business for Luke, getting his hands dirty when he wanted to, but mostly he supervised and greeted customers, put in the orders, and managed the paperwork; he was a godsend. He was also serving a woman that Luke hadn't seen around the village before.

Luke didn't want Alfred to retire and Alfred wouldn't know what to do with himself if he did, so they were both happy. Luke gave him a quick smile and rolled his eyes.

Yep, it was Friday and all his "groupies" were facing a date-less weekend and thought they'd drop in for some gardening advice and the hope of a date before they had to swipe their dating apps, or go to the local clubs pretending to like the music. He knew how they felt, but he wasn't the settling type.

MOVING-IN DAY

'Creedence time', the Sergeant said, reaching for the record from the cottage's vinyl collection. 'I need some *Bad Moon Rising*'. When he was truly melancholy, Alexander would play *Have You Ever Seen The Rain*. He didn't know how to use the small modern music box in the corner or those little metallic records... CDs, or whatever they were called. He was keen to use the WiFi – the password was written on a scrap of paper stuck to the fridge with a magnet – but he didn't know what to use it for, so he stuck to the record collection. He liked the sound of the needle following the groove of the music.

'Vintage', some of the short-staying guests had called the vinyl albums and laughed about it.

'Vintage... bullocks,' he'd mutter. 'Not every change is for the best. You just wait and these will come back into vogue. Cassettes will, too! Then again, maybe not, they were always getting stuck in the machine.'

He looked around, enjoying being alone again. 'Better,' he muttered, 'much better.'

If he had to choose a tenant – and only if he had to choose on the threat of death, which, given he was already dead, was not much of a threat – the single female would be better to have staying in the house than those happy, romantic couples or families who disrupted his misery and solitude with their perfect lifestyles. He might allow a long-term rental from someone quiet and moody, but then he'd have to get out of their way and minimise his own lifestyle... if you could call it that. No, that wouldn't work, either. What he wanted was his wife to visit, just once. In the nearly four decades she had lived after him, not once had Meg returned to the house. *Why?*

'Meghan Austen.' He spoke her name. He smiled when he remembered how she was keen to take his name when they married, even when all her feminist friends were burning their bras and carrying on. He remembered, the year before he died, that awful song that came out and was a big hit – *I am Woman*. God, he hated that song.

He thought – hoped – Meghan was a sentimentalist, a romantic, but she hadn't even visited the town or driven past; he'd know, he'd feel it. Nope, nothing. If she could just come back and stay overnight, for old times' sake. Stay a weekend, stay a week. Sit where they used to sit, walk where they used to tread... but not once. Why? Did it mean that much to her or did it mean that little?

He lowered himself into a green, dimpled leather chair and closed his eyes, letting the lyrics roll over him. They danced to this once, he and Meg, in this very room. If he had to call it, he'd say she was most like Ali MacGraw... *Love Story*. A soppy movie that he managed to avoid by death, but Meg had wanted to see it. She looked like Ali... petite, that long, dark hair, the big eyes. He sat up alert; he'd heard a car out the front, turning off the engine.

'You've got to be kidding me, she's back!' The Sergeant

raced to the record player to turn Creedence off. He moved from one window to the other to watch Holly fussing at her car. She was lifting a large bouquet of flowers from the back seat, locking up and heading to the front door with a suitcase in tow.

'She's bringing me flowers?'

He watched as she stopped, observed the house again and then, searching for the correct key, unlocked the front door. By the time she had entered, he was back in the portrait, taking up his position.

The first thing she did was look his way. He could sense her tension. *She's a little scared, she'll be worse tonight,* he thought and softened. The Sergeant thought of his own wife and wouldn't want her to be frightened... Meghan had changed him, she was still changing him.

He watched as Holly placed the flowers on the table and worked her way around the room, opening all the windows in the living areas. She flung the front and back doors open; in poured the warm air, breathing life into the house. He could smell the heady mix of salty air and fresh flowers. Then she ran her finger over the screen of a palm-size phone and, like magic, a song came through the speaker box in the corner. Clearly, she knew how to use that new-fangled thing. It was jazz... *I've Got You Under My Skin* and, for just a moment, he thought he might like living with this other woman.

She smiled and danced just a little as he watched her from the frame and tried to resist smiling. She reminded him of his Meghan – a blonde Meghan, but she had the same small face and pointy chin, the same mannerisms at times – the way she put her hair back behind her ears and cocked her head on the side as she studied things around the house, returning to adjust the flowers again. He inhaled her perfume; lovely.

∾

'Better,' Holly said, and smiled. 'Much better. Okay, Sergeant,' she addressed him, and turned her eyes to the portrait. 'If you are going to appear tonight and scare the living daylights out of me, do you think perhaps you could do me a favour and just get it over with now? I'd appreciate it. For old times' sake?'

For old times' sake? He frowned.

She waited and nothing happened. 'We're almost related, you knew my grandmother, Lily. She lived here with you. Well, you didn't live together in that way... but you both lived here at some point and time and together... you know what I mean. Anyway, want to talk about it?' Holly turned in a circle, looking for him in case he was elsewhere in the room and not in the portrait. She liked to be open-minded. 'I think you met my grandfather, too, and my Aunty Kate... no?'

She turned back to the portrait. 'Okay then, please be a gentleman and don't scare me unnecessarily. I'll do my best to respect your space, once I know what this is.' She sighed.

She closed her eyes, willing him to appear and tried to feel him; feel some change in the energy in the room. Almost with dread, she slowly opened her eyes... nothing. She breathed a sigh of relief.

'Maybe you're not really here at all and that's just fine by me,' she said. 'Right then, time to explore.' Holly had no idea that she was being watched as she began to wander around the house, opening and closing cupboards, running her hand over surfaces and checking out the furniture.

'Nice,' she whispered, looking at the chair rails and fittings. She sat on the couch and wiggled. 'Mm, that'll do nicely.' And then she spotted a good-size table against the wall in the dining room. 'That's perfect for my desk. Guess you're no good at carrying things, Sergeant?' she said.

Holly went into the kitchen and returned with four tea towels which she wedged under each leg and then slid it into the best spot for her work and the ocean view... *who needs a man,* she thought.

For the rest of the afternoon, she set up the house how she wanted it, stopping once to make a cup of Earl Grey tea. Then, heading upstairs, she tried the bed, moved pieces of furniture, unpacked her belongings and made the house her own, at least for the next six months. To finish, she plodded back downstairs and put a small sign in her new office window:

Missing Me – Lost, Found and Broken
Holly Hanlon
Professional finder
Enquire within or visit www.missingme.com
Certificate III in Investigative Services, Diploma of Counselling

'I'm done,' she said to the Sergeant in his portrait. No reply. She listened, but all she could hear was the breaking waves and the latest CD of the eighties hits that she had put on when the jazz CD had run its course.

She straightened the sign and wondered if anything would be lost or anyone would need her to find something in this little village. Holly had always been a finder... some might call it weird, but it started so young and became so matter of fact that friends and family never gave it a second thought.

Things would just find Holly. Hats blown away in a storm, missing pets, lost jewellery, missing keys... Holly's mother, Jackie, once despaired of it and became quite impatient with people who bought into the idea, until she had lost a few items of her own and Holly retrieved them. Most convenient.

As the years passed and Holly progressed through school

and college, it got so that people would let Holly know when they had lost something, as they expected it to appear in her company in the imminent future. Mrs Tait rang when her favourite spotted scarf had gone missing on her train trip back from London; Holly found it tucked between the seats on her school excursion one week later. Her third best friend, Aimee, lost a silver ballerina charm from her bracelet which Holly sat on one lunch hour on the school lawn. There was such an endless stream of pets, that Holly's father enclosed the yard to ensure they were safe until their owners arrived to collect them. She just had the gift... like a living magnet, her father would say. Holly smiled at the memory. She wondered if there would be enough clients to keep her financially afloat in this village.

Heading up the stairs again, Holly checked out the closets, hallway nooks and crannies, and the main bedroom. which she fell in love with the moment she opened the doors onto the balcony and the fresh, salty air streamed in. The queen-sized bed looked delicious; she couldn't wait to head to bed with a good book.

She went into the second room; it too had a lovely little Juliette balcony with a sea view and an inviting double bed made up with clean white linen and scattered with pale blue cushions. There was nothing in the cupboards, on the wall or under the bed.

'I think I'm going to be very happy here,' she said and smiled, 'even if I have a housemate.'

'Thanks, love,' she heard a deep voice behind her say, and she spun around in fright, dropping the pillow she was currently fluffing.

There was no-one there.

HOLLY'S FIRST VISITOR

*T*he Sergeant was waiting for Holly to freak out – that was usually the reaction he got – but she stood stock still, frozen like a statue, her hand on her heart.

Well, this is new, he thought. *Lord, I hope she hasn't had a heart attack and will fall over dead in a minute. That's all I need. The bloody ghost hunters will be here in force.*

Do I say something else or just wait for her to react? Bloody hell, it's so much easier when no one lives here!

Then he heard a knock at the front door and a female voice called out Holly's name. It seemed to snap her out of her frozen state and she stepped back and looked around.

'I forgot the front door is wide open,' she said, as if to both of them. 'I would never have done that in London.'

He watched as Holly took her hand off her heart and spoke in the general direction of where she had heard his voice.

'This isn't over yet,' Holly said.

'You can be sure of that sweetheart,' The Sergeant responded, but not so that Holly could hear him.

She continued to talk out loud to him. 'And don't even

think about appearing to me tonight in the dark and scaring me to death,' she warned. 'Don't even think about it... you're supposed to be a Sergeant, so be an officer and a gentleman!'

He could tell she was putting on a brave face and was full of bravado, but he suspected it was an act. She made a *hmph* sound and put the pillow back on the bed.

The Sergeant remained out of sight, touched his heart and smiled. 'Ah, officer and a gentleman – low blow,' he muttered to himself. 'She's good, this one!'

The female voice called out again. 'Holly?'

'Coming,' she called and exited the room quickly to meet the guest at the front door.

'Crap,' he muttered. He had to beat her downstairs and get back into his portrait.

Holly skipped down the stairs surprised by the interruption. It can't be a client already, surely, I've only been here a minute, she thought.

At the ajar front door stood a face she recognised.

'Aunty Kate!' She stopped in her tracks, a smile of delight sweeping her face.

'Holly, it's you!' Her aunt's eyes were huge with surprise.

Holly raced to embrace her. 'I thought I'd missed you... Damien said you'd left town. You look wonderful,' she said, taking in the sight of her slim, sophisticated, fifty-nine-year-old aunt.

'It's you,' her aunty said again, pulling away to look at Holly. 'How wonderful! I knew it was a Holly renting the place, the agent told me, but he didn't say it was *my* Holly! This is terrific! What are you doing here? You can't pay rent, I refuse to let you! Don't you look great! Does your Mum know you are here?'

Holly laughed and pulled her aunty into the living room.

'I'll answer every one of those questions! Let's have tea and talk. I'm so pleased you are here, can you stay?' Holly asked, hoping that now she wouldn't have to spend the first night alone... alone with a ghost!

'No... well, yes. I was leaving this morning but got delayed with business in the next town. Then Damien rang and said he'd rented out the cottage for six months and that the tenant had already moved in, so I swung back and thought I'd meet the tenant, see if they needed anything... and it's you! Why? What's happening?'

'Stay with me here tonight, or for a few days,' Holly pleaded.

'I've got to be in London tomorrow night, so I can only stay one night. But I can get a room. I don't want to cramp your style and on your first night,' she said, with a wave of her hand.

'Don't be crazy... please stay with me, you're a sight for sore eyes,' Holly said, and tried not to tear up. For the first time that day, she realised how fast she had been running away from everything; *too* fast.

Kate hugged her again. Pulling away, she said, 'Forget the tea, I've got a lovely bottle of wine in the car. What do you think? It is cocktail hour, after all.'

'Bring it on!'

'Oh, by the way, I've lost the spare set of house keys to this place... I suspect they'll find you,' Kate said, with a wry look to Holly. 'I'm a bit surprised they haven't already.'

Holly laughed. 'I've only been here a minute, but I'll let you know should they return home!'

'*When* they return,' Kate said, and went to fetch her overnight bag and the wine. While she was gone, Holly found two wine glasses and, from her own meagre supplies, placed the crackers and cheese on a plate, and set them up on the table near the window with the ocean view.

From his vantage place on the wall in the middle of the room, Alexander watched the two women catch up, his arms folded across his chest, less than impressed.

Kate returned and as they sat and sipped, Holly updated her aunty on the misadventures that had drawn her to *Findlater House*.

'And so, I'm here and I insist on paying rent,' she finished.

Kate narrowed her eyes. 'Hmm, well we'll talk about a nominal rent later.' She lowered her voice and asked, So... you're not scared, are you? Have you seen him?'

'A little scared, and no, I haven't seen him, have you?' Holly asked.

'No and I don't know why he's back. When Lily died he left for a while, supposedly. There were no reports of him visiting for about a decade. So why now?'

'Bored, or unfinished business maybe,' Holly said. 'Did anyone else in the family ever see him?'

Kate smiled. 'Your mum rarely came here and Edward never did – not that your uncle believed in that sort of thing, anyway. But your Grandma Lily used to talk to the Sergeant all the time when she stayed here. She told me once about one of their conversations like it was the most natural thing in the world.'

'I hear she was a bit eccentric,' Holly said. 'And perhaps the Sergeant only speaks to those who are open to hearing him.'

'Maybe. She was quite eccentric and a little introverted,' Kate said, musing on her mother. 'You look a lot like her, you know – you only knew your grandmother when she was in her later years, but if you look at photos of her as a younger woman... she was a little thing and fair, too. You may have more in common with her than you thought.'

'Did Grandma Lily... well, find things?'

'Not that I knew of. Not like you, if you are wondering if you inherited that skill. But she did find the courage to start again when Dad died – seventeen years she had without him,' Kate said. 'She threw herself into volunteering and making a new life... so I guess you could say she found herself.'

'Hmm, well done, Grandma Lily!' Holly finished off her glass of wine and then continued: 'It's weird that I've never heard of Sergeant Alexander.'

Kate shrugged. 'Not really, when you consider the only time you saw Grandma Lily was usually when she visited you and your parents at your house, and the Sergeant would have stayed here, I imagine.'

'True,' Holly said, placing her hand across her glass so she didn't get a third red wine refill. 'When? What did he die from? How old was he?'

Kate glanced to the portrait. 'Perhaps you should ask him. But from memory, it was sometime in the Seventies... one of the locals told me when I was visiting. They ran a small story in the local paper about him because he'd lived here for a few years with his wife. They rented this place from Grandma Lily for a while... I think he was in his late twenties when he died.'

'Not in this house?' Holly looked horrified. 'He didn't die here, did he?'

'No. There was an incident...'

Holly shuddered. She hadn't sensed the Sergeant or felt his emotions and she didn't want to. Often, because of her business name, people assumed she was a clairvoyant or had the gift, but that was a gift she didn't want. She was an investigator, not a spirit hunter.

Her aunty stood. 'Well, I'm hungry. I know a very good little restaurant in the village we can walk to, if you like?'

'Wonderful, let's do it. But first I'll show you to your room, *m adame* and we could put your overnight bag there,' Holly said, with a grin.

Kate laughed and grabbed her bag. Holly led the way up the stairs to the bedrooms.

'You take the main room, Aunty Kate,' Lily said.

'Absolutely not,' Kate said, placing her bag inside the door of the second bedroom. 'I'm the guest and I'll go into the guest room... besides, it's fabulous!' She laughed. 'Come on then.'

They made their way back downstairs and as Holly locked the front door behind them, she glanced at the Sergeant's portrait – all was as it should be.

MY KINGDOM FOR A DATE

*I*t was a beautiful Saturday morning – blue skies, a crispness in the air and a good number of customers at the nursery. Luke loaded several bags of bark chips into the back of Jessie's 4WD, assured her they would do the trick for the area she had to cover, and wiped his hands on his jeans, glancing at Alfred for rescue before the inevitable Saturday night plans discussion began.

'Hello there, Jessie.' Alfred gave her a nod. 'Luke, I need your help please, son, as soon as you can.'

'I'm on my way. Well, thanks Jess, see you again soon,' Luke said, and started stepping backwards towards Alfred. He sighed with relief as Jessie realised her opportunity had passed, and she climbed into the driver's seat of her vehicle and started it up.

Alfred grabbed a spade and indicated the wheelbarrow to Luke, who dutifully grabbed it and followed behind.

'You know, we can't afford for you to get hitched,' Alfred said, teasing him and enjoying Luke's discomfort. 'Your admirers are spending a fortune.'

'God, I hope that's it for today. It's nearly five, isn't it? Let's close up and have a beer.'

The two men locked the tools into the shed, and went through their usual evening lock-up checks and routine.

'You don't think you're too fussy perhaps?' Alfred asked. 'I hate to see you alone. I'm not saying you're unhappy, of course, but it would be nice to know that you're going back to a well-lit home with a warm hearth.'

Luke grinned. 'Well, when you paint the picture like that, I hear what you're saying... Juliet and Jessie, they're both good-looking, and smart, but...' Luke shrugged.

Alfred let the subject go until they sat down overlooking the gardens with an ale. 'What about that young lady you took out last month?'

'Isabella,' Luke said. 'She blogs about shopping... that's all she talked about. Just kill me now.'

Alfred laughed.

'I don't want to settle just so I've got company,' he said. 'I've got my work, friends,' he said, with a nod to Alfred, 'a TV and it might be time to get another dog soon. It's been a few years since Rufus passed.'

Alfred nodded. 'I understand, Luke, I really do, it's just that – well, I guess your father and I would both like to see you as happy and settled as we were. When I met Audrey, God rest her soul, that woman had me the moment she set her blue eyes on me.' Alfred smiled at the memory. 'That honey hair, those blue eyes that could level you and love you in the same glance... ah, she was a grand girl. Beautiful, fun, compassionate... she taught me how to care about things, I looked at everything differently when she came into my life.'

'And that's exactly what I'm looking for... that is what I want.'

Alfred smiled. 'But I was a good catch, too, of course. Goes without saying, really.' He grinned.

'Still are!' Luke said, and laughed. 'Been beating those old girls off with a daisy?'

'Something like that,' Alfred agreed and the men chuckled.

'Who was that woman you sold the flowers to today? Haven't seen her around before,' Luke said, finishing his beer. 'A tourist?'

'Ah, that lovely young lady. No, she's here for a bit. Her name is Holly and she has just rented *Findlater House* for six months. She wanted some flowers to make it feely homey,' Alfred said, with a sly smile in Luke's direction.

'*Findlater House?*' Luke set his drink down and turned to Alfred. 'Seriously?'

'Seriously,' Alfred assured him.

'Do you think she knows... you know, about its history?' Luke asked.

'Can't say. We had some garden plans drawn up for that cottage once... a long time ago. If I remember rightly, Lily, or was it her daughter...' he paused to think of her name, 'Kate! That's it. Anyway, one of them wanted to do something with the front garden and your dad obliged with plans. I don't remember if they ever went ahead with it, though,' Alfred said.

Luke shrugged. 'I don't know, either. Before my time, I guess. Wow, I can't believe she's taken a six-month lease on *Findlater House*,' Luke said, still shocked by the news. 'I hope the agent was upfront with her. It's with the Flats' agency, isn't it?' Luke asked.

'Yes, young Damien's running the show this week, his folks are away. Anyway, Holly said she'd be back to talk plants – whether your dad did the work or not, it needs some sprucing, apparently.'

'Yeah, well, with the sandy soil around here, I hope she likes pot plants,' Luke said.

'I suspect you'll have to visit her place and check out just what the soil's like,' Alfred suggested. 'A budding garden, a budding romance!'

'She's bound to be swept away by my charms,' Luke said.

Alfred nodded in agreement. 'Especially if she likes the gruff type.'

The next evening, having bid her aunty farewell earlier that afternoon, Holly turned in for the night – the second night in her new abode and the first night on her own. Closing the bedroom door, she slipped beneath the sheets of the double bed. The room was lit by the small bedside lamp on the chest of drawers beside her. Normally, she would read for a while, but tonight, she lay staring at the ceiling, thinking.

'Here I am,' she whispered. 'I'm twenty-six, separated, starting again.'

She breathed out, feeling the pain in her chest. She felt lonely; even the house felt lonely. Most of the time she didn't miss James, especially if she kept busy and only thought of the grief he'd brought into her life. But late at night and in the early hours of the morning when her guard was down, she missed him. She had loved him from the first moment she saw him. Before that, Holly had never believed in love at first sight. But he was strikingly handsome to her... his dark hair and green eyes, moody and private, the square jaw... they were made for each other and for the first few years they were so inclusive that, in retrospect, she suspected it wasn't healthy.

She thought of the perfect moments, then stopped herself and filed the images away. But then Holly didn't want to stop.

She was safe here away from him and no-one was around to hear her, so she opened the file in her mind and let the images pour over her. She found herself remembering the time she lay beside him one morning as the rain fell outside and, for a small window of time, their love overwhelmed her... she felt like they were the only two people in the world. She remembered how he sent her flowers anytime he was away on business, to remind her that he missed her. She smiled at the memory of their first Christmas together when she told him how she missed the Christmas tree from her childhood, and he had bought and set up the most perfect Christmas tree she had ever seen. Then there was the time he did a deal with his chef friend to open the restaurant just for the two of them on their anniversary, and the first night she came to his house in a darkened street and he had turned all the lights on to guide her down the street to find him... it went on and on.

Holly had a thousand memories like this. And for every wonderful memory, there was a corresponding bad memory: the ex-girlfriend that was always on the scene, always meeting with him; the way he would call off their plans at a minute's notice if he got a better offer from his mates; his inability to say the words 'I love you', unless she was leaving him; the late-night meetings that were not in the office like he claimed; and the cruelty he displayed with his pleasure at her miscarriage, telling her he decided that he didn't want children anyway. The beginning of the end.

No, it was time for a new start with someone who had similar values and wanted the same things out of life, even though James once said he did. A tear rolled down her face and she breathed in deeply.

Let it go, she coached herself, *let it go*.

Holly took a deep breath. 'Enough now,' she said. 'I'm not shedding one more tear over him. No, tomorrow is a new start and I'm in an exciting little cottage in a new village. I'm open to new work, to new love... eventually, and to my new life.' She repeated her prepared affirmation.

'I am a finder, and I will find love again. There, things are looking up, already,' Holly said, and forced herself to smile.

Holly couldn't see the Sergeant watching her from the corner of the room, or see him lower his head and fade from the room. He wouldn't be appearing to her tonight.

The ghost was the last thing on Holly's mind as she switched off her bedside lamp. But as soon as the room went dark, she felt a little afraid and snuggled down further into the bed, pulling the sheet up around her face and muffing her ears to avoid hearing and analysing every unusual noise. She silently prayed she would get through the night without an unwelcome visitor.

HOME ALONE... OR NOT QUITE

For a ghost, Sergeant Alexander Austen had a reasonably good baritone voice. For the last hour he had had the place to himself, which was just how he liked it. He didn't know where Holly had gone and he didn't care, just as long as she was out of his space. But if he had to hazard a guess, well, he did see her grab some grocery bags and she muttered something about finding a library, so he figured he had a good few hours on his own – and so, Alexander was enjoying his usual selection of vinyl records.

If he were being truthful, he was just a little peeved with the new tenant. He'd wanted to give her a good fright last night and send her packing, which up until now had worked very well with other guests, thanks very much. But there was something about her that reminded him of his Meg... she was just a bit vulnerable, clearly still in some pain, and he didn't have the heart to do more damage. He wouldn't want someone treating Meg like that... it was just bleeding frustrating, he thought. But he hadn't given up on the idea of getting rid of her, it was just the right plan he needed.

He was rifling through the albums looking for another one to put on when he saw the Johnny Nash record. 'Ah, been a while,' he said, aloud. *'I can see clearly now*, yeah that was a big hit just a few months before I died, I remember it well.' He read the lyrics on the album sheet... 'Mm,' he mused, 'Johnny was seeing clearly now the pain was gone... good one Johnny, and not a bad message for her ladyship, either.'

He dusted the vinyl, put the album on, and moved towards the window singing the lyrics, when suddenly the door opened and Holly stepped in.

He hadn't heard the car... *Bugger!* He wasn't prepared to reveal himself right this minute... he wanted a strategy for that, or even to enjoy it. He faded and hurried to the frame to take up position before she glanced towards it.

In the background, Johnny continued to sing something about it being a bright, beautiful day.

Holly froze.

She couldn't see him, but a record was playing in her house; an album that she had not put on. Without moving far from the doorway, she slowly put down on the floor the bag of groceries, her handbag, and two books from the library. She didn't move; her heart was thumping.

There's someone in the house.

Do I go back out and call the police, or do I look around?

Why would someone come into the house and put a record on?

Has the real estate agency double-booked with a holidaymaker?

Is there anything obvious missing? The furniture's still here.

If I call the police, will they come, or just dismiss it because it's the ghost house?

Is it the ghost, the Sergeant?

What if it is an intruder and they've got a knife or something?

Nothing was moving, the house was still and quiet – no bumps, no sounds of anything opening or closing, or floorboards creaking – just the record player playing an "up" song. She glanced towards the portrait and the Sergeant was there in his usual stance. She cleared her throat and waited. No one rushed down the stairs and past her out of the front door; not that she was really expecting that to happen. She just wanted to let whoever might be in the house know that they were no longer alone.

She opened the screen on her mobile phone, punched in the number for police and emergency, ready to hit the call button if needed, and slowly made her way down the hall. She stayed close to the wall, hesitated and glanced into the rooms near the stairs; nothing. Holly breathed out and, with a glance to the upstairs rooms, came around and took the stairs slowly towards the bedrooms. She glanced in each, under the bed, in the cupboards and on the balconies, finally satisfying herself no-one was in the house.

It was then that the lyrics of the song came to her.

Was this a message?

Was someone, maybe the Sergeant, telling her to buck up and hang in there?

Had he seen her crying?

Which would mean he was in my room last night, she thought. I was naked for a while... between taking off my day clothes and putting on my pyjamas! Oh my God!

Holly didn't know whether to be violated because a man had seen her naked, or a ghost had seen her naked, or both.

Nope, it was time to lay down some ground rules! She took to the stairs and went back to the living area.

No-one, still.

Holly walked to the record player and took the record off, slipping it back in its plastic hood and then the cardboard case.

Cool and calm, she told herself. Nothing has happened, no harm has been done, except for a break-in and a record being played. Actually, there might not have been a break-in, either, technically.

She flicked through the records, and found a "classic" her mother would love... Carly Simon. Holly pulled it out and, placing it on the turntable, put the needle in place and waited for the dulcet tones of Carly to fill the room.

Perfect.

She returned to the open doorway, picked up her bag and books and settled them on her desk. She returned, closed the front door, grabbed the bags of groceries and put them away in the kitchen. Then Holly walked to the middle of the living room.

'Ahem,' she cleared her throat. 'Sergeant, we need to talk.' Holly waited.

The Sergeant didn't move.

Holly waited. Nope, not one twitch from him in his framed portrait. She looked around for him in case he was standing behind her in some other form. No, she was alone, so continuing, she returned her gaze to the portrait and folded her arms across her chest.

'We need to establish some boundaries, Sergeant. As we haven't met yet, I'm not sure what areas are strictly yours, but my bedroom is out of bounds. I'm not saying you've been in there while I'm in there...' she said, again glancing around.

The portrait twitched as Alexander tried not to smile.

She continued, trying to sound tough and firm. '... but I'm

just saying that's where I need some privacy. Not that I'm looking to... well, entertain...' she felt herself redden and hurried on, 'but I will be getting changed in that room. Oh, and my bathroom is out of bounds, too. The rest of the house... well, do your thing. If you want to tell me your exclusive areas or leave some signs about what you want, I'll respect that, too.' She looked at the record player. 'Or you could tell me with a song, if that worked.' She shrugged. 'Whatever. So that's it, talk over.' She narrowed her eyes at him in his portrait and then returned to the kitchen and flicked the kettle on.

How coy, Alexander laughed to himself... *entertain! You mean have sex, get amongst it, have a bollocking good time! Yep, good meeting, Holly!*

He watched her as she prepared a mug of tea for herself and as she walked back to her desk and turned on the computer. She was a brave little thing, he thought.

Should I introduce myself or not? Might ruin all the fun.

HOLLY GETS A CLIENT

The next morning proved to be fruitful. At around 9 am, there was a sharp rap at the front door; just two quick knocks as if someone was very busy and on a mission. Holly breathed a sigh of relief that she had got up early, exercised, showered, and looked a bit respectable if it was a business enquiry.

She straightened her dress, and answered the door to find a neat, slim woman no taller than herself standing there. Her grey hair was whipped back in a bun and she was tidy... that's how Holly's grandmother would have described her – a pale blue pantsuit, a floral scarf, sensible shoes and a tan handbag. Beneath her arm was tucked a grey-coloured folder.

'Hello, may I help you?' Holly asked.

'My dear, you look surprised to have potential clients knocking on your door. I gather I'm the first then,' the tidy lady said, with a nod to Holly's sign in the window.

'Yes, you're right. You are my first client in the village,' Holly said, delighted. 'Please come in, I'm Holly Hanlon.'

'Thank you. I'm Esther Bohmer,' she said, wiping her feet on the front mat and observing the room as she entered.

'I've just made a pot of tea,' Holly said, with a quick glance around; the room was clear. 'Will you join me, Ms Bohmer?' She led the way to the kitchen and offered her potential client a chair.

'Please call me Esther and tea, white, no sugar, would be delightful, thank you. Were you expecting someone?' Esther asked, noting the two cups and saucers. 'Were you expecting me, perhaps?'

Holly gave a small laugh. 'No, I'm not psychic... I find real things, not otherworld things. The two cups... well, I'm a bit embarrassed to say.' Holly blushed.

Esther sat opposite Holly at the table, placing her folder beside her, as Holly remained standing to pour.

'At my age, dear, I've heard it all. I'm sure you won't surprise me,' Esther said.

Holly smiled. 'Okay then...' She lowered her voice. 'I'm trying to coax the Sergeant to appear... you know, the resident... well, ghost. And I thought if I made tea for two... I'm not saying ghosts drink tea... it's ridiculous, I know,' Holly said, realising how daft she sounded.

Esther smiled. 'I think it is rather a charming idea. You know tea solves all problems, and I've heard he can be a problem ghost.'

'So, you know of him, the Sergeant?' Holly said, her interest piqued.

Esther reached out and accepted the cup of tea with a curt nod. Holly grabbed a plate and an unopened packet of short-bread biscuits (supplied thanks to Aunty Kate) and returned, sprinkling a few on the plate for the two ladies to share. She lowered herself into a chair.

'Never too early for shortbread,' Esther said, helping

herself. 'Thank you. The Sergeant ... yes, there are a few tongues already wagging in the village about you and this house. They're saying that you are quite brave. I'm gathering you know about its history then?' she asked, diplomatically.

Holly reached for a biscuit and gave Esther a nod.

'Yes, I actually am part of its history. My grandmother, Lily Hanlon, once owned this house and her daughter, my Aunty Kate, owns it now.'

'Is that so?' Esther said, her eyes widening with interest. 'Well, that is wonderful. I knew Lily... even though I look far too young to have known her,' she teased.

Holly laughed but not too much, as the joke required.

Esther continued: 'Lily moved away some time ago, didn't she?'

'Yes, she had friends in London and she went back there to live in a retirement village. She died about fifteen years ago, she was quite old – seventy-one. Oh, sorry, that might not be that old!'

Esther smiled. 'Well, I'm eighty-eight and I don't feel a day over eighty-seven!'

Again, Holly laughed. She liked this old girl.

'I always liked Lily, and your grandfather, Matthew, and I do remember their children as well. There was Kate, and two boys – one who died in an accident... a terrible time it was...' Esther frowned as she trawled through her memories.

'Yes, that was my Uncle Sam, Aunty Kate's twin brother,' Holly confirmed.

'Yes, the twins, they were delightful. Young Sam was a very good runner, but the water took him if my memory serves me well.'

Holly nodded. 'He drowned when he was ten.'

Esther shook her head. 'Life is a strange bag of experiences, isn't it? The other lad was a surly fellow... quiet and moody, good academically but always in the shadow of the twins, I thought. So, whose daughter are you? Kate's?' Esther asked.

'My father, Joseph, is that surly fellow,' Holly said, and smiled.

'Goodness! I won't be winning any diplomacy awards this morning, will I?' Esther chuckled.

'Don't worry, he is surly,' Holly said, assuring her. 'You wouldn't be the first to say that, but he's a big softy at heart. And did you meet the Sergeant when he lived here?'

Esther looked over at his portrait and smiled. 'Yes, he was an agreeable young man and his wife was delightful. Now, what was her name... Margaret, Mary... No, it was Meg, that's it.'

'Meg,' Holly repeated after her.

'But something tragic happened to that young man, the Sergeant. He was killed in the line of duty, leaving behind his beautiful young widow.' Esther sighed.

'So why is he still here then?' Holly asked, looking at the portrait.

'Here as in on the wall, or here as in spirit?' Esther enquired with interest.

'Hmm, maybe both.'

'That I don't know, but they were happy here. Maybe he feels his death was unjust. Maybe he's waiting for Meg to join him in the afterlife, if she hasn't already?' Esther asked.

'I'm not sure,' Holly said. 'So she obviously didn't stay on here?'

'No, she left within weeks of the Sergeant's death. Must have been too painful for her to stay here.'

Holly nodded and they paused for a moment and reflected on life and all its ups-and-downs.

'I'm sorry. You have come here on business. What can I help with?' Holly came back to the here and now.

'Yes, right you are, down to business. Now, young lady, I'm hoping you can find a necklace for me. I believe it is in England and... it's been missing for over fifty years.'

Holly paused, the biscuit halfway to her mouth. 'Wow! Well, there's a challenge. Most things find me before I find them. Wow... fifty years!'

Esther nodded. 'If you're interested in helping me, I'll tell you the whole story.'

'Please, yes,' she sat back and pulled her teacup closer. 'Oh, I should take notes.'

'No need, I have detailed it for you here,' Esther said, pulling some pages from her handbag, 'if you're interested in taking the case.'

'Thank you,' Holly said, suppressing a smile. Of course Esther had it all detailed, and probably cross-referenced as well. She seemed very organised, Holly thought.

'I came to England when I was seven, in 1939. Have you heard of the Kindertransport?'

Holly shook her head. 'No. What is it?'

'It's German for children's transport. Just before the outbreak of the Second World War, a lot of Jewish children were rescued from Germany and Britain took us in, about ten thousand or so. I was one of them.'

'Just children?' Holly asked.

Esther nodded.

'How terrifying for you,' Holly said, placing her hand on her heart.

'It was. Thank you for saying that. I was an only child and my parents sent me away for my own safety. We arrived at the Port of London and a lovely couple fostered me and brought me to this little village, I was very lucky. After the war, I found out my mother died in a Bergen-Belsen concentration camp in 1943, and I never found out what happened to my father.'

'Oh Esther, that's horrific,' Holly said.

'It was... it is,' she agreed. 'Some people say that we should move on now, not pursue those Nazis still alive because they are so old, or forget what claims we have to justice, but then I ask them... if your parents or children were killed by Nazis, would you eventually say, "Don't worry about it, everyone is too old now?" Of course not,' Esther answered her own question.

'I'd pursue them while I had breath in my body,' Holly said.

'Thank you, my dear, and that's why I know you'll be the perfect person for this job. Even if I die, Holly, I would like you to see it through.'

'Are you dying?' Holly asked, lowering her voice.

'No, but I'm old, you never know,' Esther said, again with a sly look.

Holly smiled and shook her head. 'I suspect you have a wicked sense of humour, Esther, I'm alert to that now.'

Esther laughed. 'Oh dear, I won't get away with anything then! So, let me tell you about the job. I'm chasing a very special piece of jewellery that my parents owned. It was made with love, and when they were taken away by the Nazis it was confiscated by a German family. I'd like to have it back before I die, so that I can choose to leave it with someone I love.'

A GARDEN, A CLIENT AND A RARE
PINK DIAMOND

*L*uke took a juice from the office fridge, unscrewed the
lid, and stood over his desk.

So, *Findlater House* has a new tenant, he mused.
He thought about Alfred's comment. If plans were drawn up
for a garden they'd still be on file somewhere. His father must
have done them because Luke had no memory of designing
anything for the "ghost house", as he and his school friends used
to call it.

Pulling out the chair, he sat down in front of the laptop,
logged in and went to the *Work in progress* files. He searched
using the cottage name, then the address – nothing.

He found the plans for his own garden which he had been
designing for close on ten years... yep, no time like the present,
he thought. But, after working all day, he just didn't have the
energy to do his own home. Not a good business card, he knew
it. *One day*.

He opened the file marked *Archive* and did the searches
again; three files appeared with *Findlater House* file names.

'That's more like it,' he said, to no-one. He straightened in his chair, opened the first file and let out a low whistle. He recognised his father's signature at the bottom of the design; it was beautiful. Tiers of plants and flowers embraced both sides of the entrance, arranged in rows of pots and curving around to the foot of the front stairs. A small topiary graced each stair on both sides.

'Beautiful,' Luke said. 'Cost a bit, too'. He opened the second file and found the quote... *yep, not for the fainthearted.* Opening the third file, he found all the original photos of the cottage and the existing yard. The photos were circa 1960–1970s – small, square shots that must have been scanned in and put online when they converted all their paper records to the system.

Who was the client – Kate or her mother? Luke wondered. He waded through the photos until he came to a shot that actually had people in it – a couple. He went back to the quote and saw it was made out to Sergeant Alexander Austen and Mrs Austen. Odd, he thought. Luke knew enough history to know the place had always belonged to the Hanlon family. It was strange that the tenants would be looking to put in a garden. Unless the Hanlon family decided an improved garden would encourage their tenants to stay long-term.

Returning to the photo, Luke studied the pair – the guy was tall, dark and good-looking, and the woman was a beauty. She looked really "Seventies" with her flowered-print loose pants and top, and the long dark hair. She came up to the man's shoulder, had her arms wrapped around him, and they looked in love.

Dad must have taken that shot of them pre-garden renos while he was there, Luke mused. *Wonder where the two of them are now? Geez, they'd have to be in their seventies or eighties. Probably dead.*

He went back to the garden plans and studied them. *Well,*

that's a good head start, anyway, if the new Findlater House tenant comes back, he thought. *Hope she's got a good-sized budget.*

∿

Holly poured them both a second cup of tea.

'I'd best tell you about the necklace first before I tell you how it came to be lost, shall I?' Esther said.

'Yes, please,' Holly said, 'and don't scrimp on detail!'

Esther smiled. 'No scrimping. My father was a jeweller and my mother assisted him in our family jewellery store. We lived a very comfortable life in Berlin. I was spoilt and adored, being the only child, but my memories are very sketchy now of what our life was like. I've spent many hours, many days, months and years, trying to remember the smallest details about my family, as you can imagine. But it all came to an end when I was seven. Holly, we were Jewish.'

'Oh,' Holly said.

'Yes. I am sure you know your history, you know of the Nazi Party and the genocide of the Jewish people?'

Holly nodded. 'Of course.'

'Good. Well, it started as early as 1933 – the Nazi propaganda to boycott Jewish businesses. My father had to close the shop front of our business and just take private jewellery commissions and bespoke orders. I imagine they were worried financially about the future and the business, but I don't know... I was only a baby then, I have no memory of it. I was seven when I was sent away in 1939 and I only have a window of memories prior to that as well.'

Esther stopped to sip her tea and then continued. 'I can't remember a time that there wasn't tension in our city, but I guess my parents screened me from it as best they could. But the year before I was sent away, 1938, was the worst. I had started school but then wasn't allowed to continue. I couldn't visit some of my friends or go to birthday parties if they lived in an "Aryan" zone and some of my relatives lost their jobs because they weren't allowed to serve German clients – and you know enough from your history lessons of what was to come.'

Holly nodded. She didn't speak; anything would have sounded hollow.

Esther continued. 'My mother and father were very frightened and they told me they were sending me to boarding school in England to help me study English. They said it would only be for a few years and then we'd all be reunited. I didn't want to go, I was terrified. So I sailed away from them thinking I was terribly hard done by – I'd never known any other life than with them – and if it hadn't been for all the other children around me, it would have been unbearable.'

'And did you come to this village then or in later years?' Holly asked. Occasionally, she thought she caught movement from the corner of her eye and subtly glanced around, but the room was empty; the Sergeant was in his frame.

'I was very, very lucky to be taken in by a lovely family in London and I never returned to Germany. Both of my parents perished and my English family has long since passed away, but I came to this village when I married. My husband, who has passed as well, was born here. So, to the job...' Esther got back on track.

'Esther, I'm so very sorry for your generations of loss,' Holly said. 'There are no words.'

'No,' Esther said, 'but thank you, my dear.' She took a deep breath and continued. 'My parents had some valuable paint-ings and as you can imagine, as jewellers, some beautiful jewellery. It was all stolen by the Nazis, and retrieving it has been... well, a life-long battle.'

'But shouldn't it be legally returned to you?' Holly said, with a dismayed look.

'In an ideal world, yes,' Esther said, 'but there was so much stolen... I found out in my searching that auctions were held for months on end in 1941 to sell items looted from Jewish homes.'

Holly groaned.

'Yes, some days I wondered if it was worth it... for my health,' Esther said. 'It's a complex area and I won't get into the detail of it with you this visit, but in a nutshell, there has been considerable support from organisations worldwide to assist Jewish family to recuperate their possessions. Here, in Britain, since the late Nineties, museums across the country have undertaken detailed research of their collections to identify objects which may fall into this category. There are working groups that look into what they call the spoliation of art during the Holocaust and World War II period. There was also a large conference in Washington in 1998 to address Holocaust assets.'

Holly nodded, taking it all in. She made a mental note to research this for herself; she had never heard of it prior to now.

'That's a good thing though, isn't it?'

'It is my dear, absolutely. But in many cases and in my case, these items are not in museums, but rather, in personal collections.'

'In German households?' Holly asked.

'Sometimes, or sold to collectors around the world,' Esther said, 'so you can see how futile it can become unless someone puts the piece up for sale and it is identified. Several decades ago, I joined a class action of Jewish descendants trying to retrieve stolen goods. As part of this, I was able to reclaim several of the original paintings that were taken by Nazis and were hanging in German homes. I've since donated them to the

British Art Gallery,' she said, and stopped. 'You see, Holly, I don't want the objects returned for money... I don't need it. It's the principle of the matter and I would rather have these works enjoyed by many, or sold with the proceeds going to charity, than sitting in a private home where they have no right to be in the first place. Does that make sense?'

Holly nodded. 'Perfect sense, and I couldn't agree more. But do the current owners always know the history of the artwork in their possession?'

'Not the descendants... to them, it was a gift handed down from their relatives and they are often quite shocked, as you can imagine.' Esther looked down at the folder in front of her, opened it and pulled out a photo. She slid it in front of Holly.

'Oh, wow,' Holly said, admiring the piece of jewellery – a row of perfectly round creamy pink pearls with a clasp featuring a large diamond. Even from the faded photo she could see its beauty. It was a rare colour photo, it looked painted. 'Is that a pink diamond?'

'Yes,' Esther said, looking at the photo fondly. 'A rare pink diamond. My father made this for my mother as a wedding present. It was such a rare design and rare stone that it symbolised one of a kind for my father; for me, it epitomises my feminine mother and how my father truly treasured her. It holds a lot of sentimental value for me. It's also so rare that I couldn't put a price on it.'

'Wow,' Holly said, again. 'I've never seen anything like it.'

'Unfortunately, I have,' Esther said. 'I think it was around the neck of a socialite at the Parisian wedding of a fashion designer about a year ago.'

'No! It's been sold, or is in a private collection? Could the investigator for the class action not track it down?' Holly asked.

Esther sat back and sighed. 'I've used a number of investigators over the years, my dear, and without a passion or a purpose, it is just a job for them... for some of them it went on for months and months. I decided to stop looking, but I never gave up hope of seeing it again. My mother would wear it on their wedding anniversary every year. They would dress formally and go to dinner. They looked so beautiful, both of them.' She sighed.

'And you want me to try and find it?' Holly said, a little daunted by the task at hand.

'I have a genuine claim so, if you can locate it, I can get the lawyers to manage its retrieval.'

Holly nodded. 'I don't want to look a gift horse in the mouth, but I'm just curious as to why you would be trusting me to do this and now?'

Esther smiled. 'It's unfinished business for me, and I can't tell you why, exactly, but when I heard there was a tenant here and then I saw your sign, I had a good feeling. Now, let's talk payment.' Esther mentioned a fee and a travel allowance and Holly gasped.

'You're very generous, but that's way too much,' Holly said, instinctively.

Esther laughed. 'My dear, you'll never run a business like that. I don't think anyone has ever turned down a good rate.'

Holly blushed. 'I'd feel terrible taking that much. What do you think about an hourly rate, a fortnightly report and set hours so we know what the budget is each week?'

Esther held out her hand. 'Done, shall we shake on it?'

Holly smiled and reciprocated. 'I hope I can find it for you, to give you that peace, and I'd love to see it... the real thing.'

'So would I, my dear, so would I. And I suspect with all the new technology these days,' she said, with a nod to Holly's laptop on the desk in the corner, 'it might be easier to track down than ever before.'

Late that afternoon, the day's last light was glorious as it painted the white horses of the waves a pink and orange hue. After seeing Esther out, Holly had made notes on their discussion, read through the file and started her research journey.

Now, she changed into her track gear, runners and, grabbing her keys, went to clear her head with a beach walk. She hadn't expected it to be so busy, but the evening beach promenade was clearly a village activity. For a new girl in town, she was already able to give a nod and a wave to the grocer and librarian. *Not bad*, she mused.

What a day, she thought as she looked back on it. *A ghost, a client and now, hopefully, a good night's sleep since I've established boundaries and won't be waiting for a ghost to spook me.* She carried her shoes and let the saltwater rush in over her feet; the water was freezing, but the salt air was wonderfully cleansing.

I could get used to this, she thought, and smiled.

As she returned home, she found a beautiful white cat sitting on her doormat.

'Well hello, are you lost or just visiting?' she asked. The cat rubbed against her and then leapt the small fence and ran off.

'Just visiting then. See you again,' Holly said. She heard a tinkling sound and thought it was a small bell on the cat's collar, but no. The white cat had knocked the doormat askew and a set of house keys tumbled to the step below. Found – Aunty Kate's spare house keys! Plus a visiting white cat is a good omen, she thought, happily pocketing the keys. Perhaps coming to *Findlater House* was the right decision after all.

MISSING MEGHAN

The Sergeant watched her leave. Sometimes, depending on the angle of her head, or the way she walked, Holly looked like his Meg. *Weird.* He remembered the last time he saw Meg in this very cottage. The day he walked away from her. She had looked up at him, trying to be brave as she prepared to bid him farewell as he went off on another mission.

'Now, remember the three rules,' Meghan Austen had told her husband, as she stood in his embrace at the front door of *Findlater House.*

'Remind me again?' he teased, looking down on her.

'Number one, be careful; number two, come back to me; and number three, be careful!' she said again and leaned up to kiss him.

'Got it, consider it done.'

Sergeant Alexander Austen hated departures and he did his best to keep them light and positive. His mission to Northern Island was not one he or Meghan felt good about. Meg had family there, and Alexander, while he didn't have any strong views on Ireland one way or the other, was forced to develop some when he found out he was heading to Belfast.

He'd never given any thought to whether the Irish nationalists or republicans should get an independent Ireland, or whether the unionists or loyalists were right in wanting to stay part of his United Kingdom. He'd never had a leaning towards religion, nor had his parents, so he didn't feel swayed by the Catholic side or Protestant argument – he was Switzerland... neutral. He learnt quick-smart not to have that discussion with Meg, who wasn't short on opinion. And he knew from his own military experience that in nearly every location where different people attempted to co-exist, invariably, the shit would hit the fan.

But he was a professional soldier and his regiment was part of Operation Banner. He recalled what a weird power trip their last tour was; people were either cowering in fear or attacking him. Sometimes he could smell the fear as he passed residents on the street; they'd avert their eyes, go deadly quiet and quicken their pace. Some of the lads in his regiment got off on it and used it to terrorise the locals even more. The residents that weren't frightened would stare and even challenge him. The Sergeant never really knew which reaction he was going to get, and the cops were spent, so he and the boys were pretty much on their own.

He sometimes wondered if he was cut out for this life... there seemed something fundamentally wrong about "lifting" people, taking sides, doing your best to protect whatever the mission of the day was, only to be balled out for it, not to mention the searches that they did on the homes of war-weary people with glazed eyes. He would never mention it to Meg, but the bombing and the shootings were getting worse. He found himself subconsciously listening for the low whistle of ammunition or flinching at the sound of a bang, be it a car backfiring or a door slamming. Maybe it was time he hung up his uniform and thought about his next career move... especially if he and Meg wanted to have kids.

A smile from Meg brought him back to the now.

'You look so gorgeous in your uniform,' she sighed.

'It's true,' Alexander agreed, and she laughed, hitting his arm.

'Now, you remember *my* three rules,' he said, pulling her far enough away to look in her blue eyes.

Meghan frowned at him. 'I don't think I've heard these before, have I?'

He rolled his eyes with added dramatics. 'Of course you have. Don't open the door to anyone handsome, don't walk on the beach after dusk unless you have Benson with you...' Benson the Setter's tail thumped at the mention of his name, '... and lastly, don't forget me.'

He knew he'd just blown it with the last line and sure enough, tears rolled down her face.

'I'll be back before you know it,' he promised.

'You better be, Alexander Austen, or I'll never forgive you,' she said, and held him like it was the last time, like she did every time he went away.

The Sergeant came back to the now with a thud... Meg – no, Holly – was walking up the path towards the house; it was in darkness. He turned a lamp on for her and disappeared into the frame of his portrait.

Holly came home from her dusk beach walk feeling lighter. She saw from outside that a lamp was on in the living room.

I didn't leave that on, did I? Maybe it automatically comes on... like on a timer. Hmm. Maybe the Sergeant was being thoughtful. She felt grateful and a little scared at the same time.

Holly unlocked the door and glanced inside; the Sergeant was in his portrait. She glanced around, and he was nowhere else in sight. She wasn't sure if he could manifest in a few places as yet. Holly didn't call out for him; she didn't really want to see him at night... *I wonder if he is visible during the day?*

Anyway, what's the hurry? We're going to be living together for at least six months so no need to be immediately acquainted, she thought. It reminded her of something one of her best friends, Simone, used to say – 'beware of instant intimacy'. She didn't know why, but clearly Simone had some experience in that area.

She whispered the words, 'Thank you' because she couldn't help herself. It was thoughtful if he did it. But if the lamp came on at the same time tomorrow, she would know it was a timer system.

Tonight felt so very different from the night before, she thought. She was settled, felt a little safer in the house – she had got through one night without him appearing and she had set down ground rules – and she had things to look forward to, like an interesting job and client in Esther.

Who was she kidding? She was still frightened the Sergeant would appear at night; nobody wants to wake up to a man standing in their room. She shuddered at the thought. 'Please don't scare me at night, Sergeant,' she whispered, and hoped he could hear her.

He could.

She took a deep breath and headed to the kitchen to see what she could whip up for dinner. Tomorrow, she would head down to the garden centre and have a chat with them about the front garden. It would be a nice way to say thank you to Aunty

Kate for the massive rent reduction and to make the house looked just that little bit more charming.

The Sergeant heard her plea. She was frightened, and he didn't want to do that to her... he might have in the past, but she was so like his Meg.

Just as quickly as he had this thought, he felt cranky at himself. *Step up, man, you're a ghost,* he scolded himself. *For the love of God, scare her off and get it over with. Soon, she'll be having friends and boyfriends over and that will be a chronic pain in the butt.*

True, he had to do it, but he didn't have to scare her to do so.

I'll send her packing tomorrow, he told himself with resolve and felt much better for it.

HOW DOES YOUR GARDEN GROW?

*H*olly could get used to not waking to an alarm clock. For the last five years at her London home it woke her every morning at 6.15 am – in the light of summer, in the dark of winter – always too early, but necessary. She had a husband to get to work and she opened her own home office from 8 am, so there was a run to be had, followed by showers, lunches packed, breakfast eaten, and more.

But now she was up not much later than that, anyway, because the day was hers and she was an early riser. After washing her face and changing into leisure gear for her run, Holly raced down the stairs and stopped with a gasp. She looked around, frightened. This was too much.

In front of the door sat her two suitcases.

They were there, waiting... waiting to leave. She walked towards them, picked one up and tested its weight. It was heavy.

'No way!' Holly gasped. She laid the suitcase down flat and unzipped it. It was full of her clothes. She looked at the portrait; he was in the frame in the same position as usual.

Holly took the stairs two at a time and raced back upstairs. The wardrobe and drawers were empty. Somehow during the night, someone – the ghost – had been in her room as she slept and packed her bags. He had touched everything and then left the bags at the door. She turned again and looked around the room; no-one appeared. She was frightened now, genuinely frightened.

Holly quickly went back downstairs and moved the suitcases away from the door. She grabbed the key, left the house, locking the door after her and headed to the beach for a jog.

'What will I do now?' she said, aloud. Her heartbeat was accelerated long before she hit her stride. This had thoroughly unnerved her.

Holly reached the hard sand and breathed out. 'Okay, stay calm.' She talked it through. 'It's a clear sign that he's in the house and he wants me out of it. But it's not angry or brutal... yet. If I go now, where will I go? I could rent something else but I don't want to. If I stay in the village, I want to live in *Findlater House*. It's my family's place. I'm meant to be in *Findlater House*... I'm the girl who finds things! If I don't leave, how bad might it get? Will the Sergeant get worse?'

She ran her usual route, not seeing it or feeling the run as her mind raced over the scenario. By the end of the run, she had made a decision.

I'm going to go one more round with him, she thought. *I'm not sure I'll sleep tonight, but I'll never die wondering. I just need to harden up. I can do this.*

Holly slowed her pace as she came back to the starting point of her run and eventually stopped. She looked out across the ocean to the far horizon and drew in deep breaths. After a while, she removed her running shoes and socks, pushed her leggings above her knee and, leaving her gear on the beach, walked into the shallows of the ocean, dipping her feet in the chilly saltwater.

'Freezing!' She soon got used to the cold temperature and enjoyed it. There were a few people on the beach – runners, dog walkers and several people doing yoga or something similar. The dusk parade was much larger than this morning's turnout.

She thought over the situation with the Sergeant again. Grandma Lily wouldn't run from the challenge. 'You can do this,' she said aloud again, and as if on cue, she felt something grab around her toe.

Holly jumped back onto dry sand, worried she would get stung by whatever it was, and found a tiny seahorse wrapped around her toe. She had never seen a seahorse before, let alone one that was alive and clinging to her!

'Hello little one, where's your partner?' Holly knew very little about seahorses but enough to know they pair for life and they usually like deep water... well, so said the documentary she once watched. 'You're in a bit shallow. Come then.'

Using her hands, she cupped the little creature in the water and, bracing herself for the cold, waded out to waist depth before releasing him out of the pull of the tide. He was gone within seconds.

'Travel safe,' she called to him and waded back to shore, cold and wet.

As she arrived, a tall man who didn't look much older than her was walking towards her. A big brown Labrador bounced around nearby.

'Are you okay?' he asked. 'It's just that we don't get that many swimmers this time of year, especially entering the water dressed!' He smiled.

'I'm fine, just an idiot,' Holly said, and made him laugh.

'I doubt that.'

'I found a seahorse... first one I've ever seen and he appeared to be struggling to get back out, so I was giving him a hand.'

'Ah, there'll be good karma for that,' he said. 'I'm Matt, this is Buddy... or that *was* Buddy,' he said watching his dog take off up the beach. He whistled him back.

'I'm Holly.'

'You know a seahorse is considered to be a symbol of strength and power. Or is that just a horse?' he mused and Holly laughed.

'Are you making this up as you go?' she asked.

'Maybe.' He grinned. 'No, my ex-girlfriend was into symbols, astrology, signs from the universe, all that stuff,' he said, waving a hand around as though the idea was ridiculous. 'So if you're signing any deals today or doing business, strength and power to you!' he teased.

'As a matter of fact, I fully intend to negotiate one. Thanks, Matt, you've made my day.'

The Sergeant felt bad for frightening her; he hated that he felt bad even more... it really bugged him that he was going soft. But he had freaked her out and now, he admitted, he felt like a cruel bastard.

He got the two suitcases and returned them upstairs. He unpacked her things quickly, as best he could... *She'll just have to suffer the socks in the wrong drawer if I've stuffed it up*, he thought.

God, I'm pathetic.

THE BATTLEGROUND

*H*olly returned all fired up. It was going to come to a head today with the Sergeant, she decided, empowered by a sign from the seahorse and Matt!

'I am strong, and I am staying,' she said, putting her key in the front door. 'The battle lines have been drawn... whatever that means. And I'm freezing.' She shivered and, leaving her shoes and socks at the front door, she had no choice but to enter in rather a wet state. She made a mental note to leave a towel near the front door in future, just in case she had to perform any future rescues or a swim was in order.

Full of bravado, she swung the front door open, and again stopped short.

What the...? The suitcases were gone. This scared her as well. *I hope he hasn't thrown my things out.* Now she was angry.

Holly raced up the stairs and into her room. The suitcases were back on the top shelf of the closet and all her gear was hanging up, her shoes back where they belonged and... she pulled open a drawer... everything was back inside as before.

'You're doing my head in,' she muttered. Holly wasn't sure if this was even more creepy, or a peace offering. Was she going to come downstairs tomorrow morning and find the bags there again, waiting for her?

She sighed and, stripping off her wet jogging gear, she hit the shower, relaxing in the warm water. It was then that she decided she would engage with the Sergeant as if he was there with her, whether he chose to show himself or not; *two can play at this game!*

From his well-placed position hanging on the wall, the Sergeant watched her. Dressed warmly now and with her hands cupped around a half-filled mug of tea, Holly sipped the contents and looked around. Then she placed it on the garden wall and began to pace from one end of the front cottage garden and back again. She looked up, and then went the opposite way, taking huge steps. It wasn't a very big front yard, more of a square near the steps, but it was a great spot to have tea or wine and to watch the ocean and parade of people. That's what he and Meg did often.

What the hell is she doing now? He saw her scribble down some notes, then retrieve a tape measure from her pocket and do measurements. She placed a small garden gnome on one end and did parallel measurements first.

The Sergeant moved from his frame to the doorway, leaning against the door, confident in the knowledge she couldn't see him.

'Good morning, Sergeant,' she said, with a casual salute and grin.

His mouth dropped open and he instinctively stepped back inside. Then he realised she was bluffing; she couldn't see him at all. She was good, this girl, very good, he thought. Just to be sure, he moved, but her eyes didn't follow him. *Phew.* But was now a good time to appear? It was daytime, they were outside and she was expecting him, sort of?

But he couldn't bring himself to do it yet. He didn't know why, he just sensed she really didn't want him to appear; she was frightened and besides, he was intrigued by this new play.

'Ms Hanlon, you are going to be the end of me,' he said, but not so she could hear. 'I should have sent you packing the first night with a bloody good scare... I've been too subtle. So, may I enquire... what the bloody hell you are doing?'

He watched her, wishing he could help as she balanced objects on one end of the tape measure, then the other.

'You may wonder what I'm up to,' she said.

Uncanny, he thought, enjoying her banter. He moved out of the doorway and sat on the small garden wall and watched her.

Holly continued talking to herself, and the Sergeant. 'I'm going to fix up the garden. Since I'm going to be staying for a while – lucky you! – I thought it would be lovely to have a burst of green and a scattering of flowers here. We can sit out here and enjoy tea or something heavier if we like and watch the ocean.' She turned to look at the waves hitting the rocks on the nearby horizon. 'I don't think I'll ever tire of it.'

The Sergeant nodded. 'That's what my wife used to say,' he said, contributing to the one-way conversation. *Definitely the weirdest conversation I've ever had,* he thought.

Holly continued, assuming he might be listening. 'It's a shame you can't help me here... I wonder if ghosts can put any real weight on things? Hmm. I'd get you to stand over there with the tape measure,' she said, with a sigh.

He came and stood beside her, observing the area.

'Damn shame, wish I could help,' he said, with an insincere smirk.

He thought back to the time when he and Meg were going to do this garden up, too. They had big plans for their little love nest as she used to call it... *funny girl.* He smiled at the memory. Meg had spoken with their landlady, Lily, and she was happy for them to get some quotes. Money wasn't really an object for Lily and she had long wanted to make the garden a highlight of the house. He remembered them seeing the landscaper, and getting the plans drawn up. The Sergeant realised how long ago that was now... Holly wasn't even born then... it must have the late Sixties or maybe it had just tipped into the Seventies.

I was alive after all so it must have been before 1972. Meg didn't go ahead with it after she heard of my death, she just got out of here. The Sergeant pulled himself back to the now, but there was something about Holly that always took him back to Meg. He was surprised that he felt emotional about it; it had been so long ago.

Holly cut into his thoughts, chattering away.

'Anyway, I'm going to see about getting the garden done professionally, Sergeant.' She lowered herself onto the small brick wall in the front garden, almost on his lap and he hustled along further to observe her.

She continued. 'I'm going to go to that large nursery just past the main street. That's where I got the flowers on the table inside from, that afternoon I moved in. I'm sure you liked them,' she said, and smiled. Her eyes scanned over him and kept moving. 'I spoke with an older guy, Alfred, but I don't know if he's the designer or the manager... we'll soon find out, no doubt.'

'Alfred!' The Sergeant sputtered. 'Can't believe he's still alive. He was working at that place when Meg and I lived here in the Sixties. He would have been in his twenties then, I'm guessing. Ha, that's amazing. He must be ancient!' He turned to her for a reaction, but forgot she couldn't hear him; he hadn't appeared to her.

Holly shrugged. 'Regardless of his role...' she continued, 'Alfred is most charming. He must be in his mid-seventies, I guess, maybe older. Anyway, he doesn't want to retire and probably doesn't have to if he runs the business.'

The Sergeant scoffed. 'I bet he's charming, the old devil. I vaguely remember Meg saying the same of him when he was a young bloke. Must be a lady's man. And no, he's not the owner, or he wasn't then, anyway. The owner was a young bloke back then, too, I think he and his wife moved here from the city to start the business.' The Sergeant shrugged. 'Long time ago. Fancy that, Alfred's still going, hey? Give him my best... on second thoughts, better not. What am I saying? You haven't heard a word I said.'

Holly got up and began to collect her measuring instruments. She smiled and waved at the doctor as he went past. Nice old fellow.

'Lovely morning,' she said.

'Indeed, young lady and good morning, Sergeant,' he said, doffing his hat and continuing on. The Sergeant raised his arm in a casual salute.

Holly's eyes widened and she turned, looking for him, but there was no-one there.

'He can see you?' she said. 'You've been here the whole time.'

The Sergeant didn't respond. Not yet. Clearly, she wasn't going anywhere fast, Alexander thought. But that's okay... he had a new plan. After hearing her discussion with the elderly woman about finding the family jewel, he had made a decision. He was going to hire Holly, too; hire her to find his wife, Meg, and find out why she had never come back to feel his presence and remember his happy years.

He wanted to know, was Meg angry at him? After all these years, had she still not been able to forgive him for going to Northern Ireland? Was it too painful for her, or did she resent him for it? After almost four decades, the pain must be replaced by melancholy... surely? Did she know what really happened to him? More importantly, did she know the truth of why he never returned home to her?

Yep, he had some cash hidden away in the cottage and he'd introduce himself to Holly and insist on a professional contract with her so she would take it seriously. He felt a strange mixture of relief and anxiety that soon he might actually hear some news about Meg at last. He felt even more out of sorts that he felt relieved and anxious; he was a ghost, after all.

Now that he needed Holly, he just had to work out when he was going to appear to his new tenant, and how best to do it without sending her running. He knew enough about people to know her bravado was only because it was daylight and she was outside – he could sense it and feel her heartbeat. He needed her to want to see him inside the house and not only during the day, but when the sun set.

And then, before he realised what was happening she rushed for the door and stopped dead in the doorway. His framed portrait was empty.

AN UNWANTED GUEST… NO, NOT THE SERGEANT!

'*S*he's here,' Alfred said, giving Luke a nudge.

Luke looked up, a sense of foreboding passing his face at the thought of one of his regulars calling in with a date on their mind. He wiped his arm over his forehead, where he smeared a streak of the dirt he was transferring from the packet to a pot. 'Which one?'

'No, not one of your harem,' Alfred said, lowering his voice, 'Holly – the lovely young lady who has rented *Findlater House*.'

'Oh,' Luke said, looking towards the nursery's entrance, his eyes wide with interest. Then he saw her; she was cute – petite, her hair tied up in a ponytail and wearing a long-sleeved cotton t-shirt and jeans.

Alfred thought it was nice to see someone not in fitted Lycra; the young ones today left nothing to the imagination and in many cases, the imagination did not want to go there! As Luke was still staring, Alfred looked away.

Luke cleared his throat. 'Do you want to deal with her? I

found the plans, meant to tell you, so if she does want to talk landscaping...'

'Great! I'll be sure to bring her over,' Alfred said, aware of Luke's discomfort and interest. His nervousness was a good sign, Alfred thought; he wasn't at all nervous around the ladies in his harem that he didn't connect with. This was good, very good. Alfred wiped his hands on a nearby towel and walked towards Holly, straightening a few items along the way.

'Hello again, Holly,' he said, with a nod of his head.

Holly smiled. 'Good morning, Alfred, what a beautiful day.'

'A wonderful day to be alive,' he agreed. 'Did the flowers grace your home as they were meant to?

'Absolutely, thank you. I'm back to talk about some serious gardening,' Holly said, threateningly and Alfred laughed.

'Now I'm guessing you mean for *Findlater House* then?' Alfred said.

'Yes. I don't have a huge budget... doesn't everyone say that?' she asked, with a smile, and continued without waiting for an answer. 'But the front yard is bereft, for want of a better word, and I'd love to have some greenery and flowers there.'

Alfred nodded. 'Best you speak to the owner and our landscaper then, they're one and the same. Come, I'll introduce you to Luke Mayer.'

And so it begins, Alfred thought, happy to be part of what he believed would be history in the making... well, at least a potential wedding invitation. But then again, it was Luke after all. Best not to rent the suit just yet.

Holly left *How Does Your Garden Grow?* and its owner, Luke Mayer, very satisfied. An appointment was set up for Luke to visit *Findlater House* on Friday for a personal inspection of the garden and there were existing garden plans. How exciting, Holly thought.

It was not long after midday, so Holly decided today would be a good day to explore more of her new home village. She parked the car at the end of the main street and, on foot, weaved her way along it, intending to do a loop and window-shop on both sides of the street, or maybe go in and explore if the right premise called her in. She hadn't got more than three stores along before she found a delightful café called *The Cup and Saucer*. She entered and a little bell chimed over the door. Most of the tables were for two or four, and whatever wasn't covered in lace wore a doily. Adorable, she thought, like a trip back to grandma's time.

Two ladies behind the counter greeted her and invited her to sit anywhere. They were obviously mother and daughter; so much alike. Holly chose a small table for one on the edge of the front windows where she could watch the street traffic and not take up a larger table should a late lunch crowd surge in. There was a buzz of conversation from the other tables and several other people dining alone... well, with their phones, as they stayed glued to the screens, occasionally flicking or messaging. Holly perused the menu, selected some homemade fruit toast and a pot of tea and after ordering from the most senior of the two women, who was charming, stopped and relaxed to enjoy the pace. She vowed not to look at her phone, as tempting as it was.

She sat back in her chair and leapt forward in pain. *Ouch!* Holly looked around but no-one had noticed she had jumped a foot off the chair. She subtly rose and lifted the chair cushion ever so slightly.

'Aha, there's the culprit,' she said, pulling out a bow-shaped marquise brooch with pretty blue stones and little diamonds, the pin unclipped. 'You're pretty, but there are more subtle ways to tell me you are here!' she scolded it.

Not long after, her morning tea was delivered by the younger woman wearing a name tag that read *Doris*. A very old-fashioned name. Holly wondered whether she swapped name tags with her mother just for fun; if only she could see it and confirm her suspicions! The teapot was huge, enough for at least three cups of tea and the fruit toast was a generous serve.

'Ooh, wonderful, thank you,' Holly gushed. She offered the brooch. 'It just found me,' she said, with a smile. 'It was wedged between the cushion and the frame under the seat.'

Doris gasped. 'Betty's bow! Oh, you have no idea how long and hard we have searched for that,' she said and carefully took it from Holly's hand as though it might disappear again.

'Betty?'

'Mum,' she said. 'I call her Betty during shop hours.'

Well, that blew that theory, Holly thought. Doris and Betty!

'Thank you, she will be thrilled,' Doris said, still smiling at the brooch. 'We vacuum under these cushions every day, it must have been clinging on for dear life. It's a good thing we didn't vacuum it up.' Doris looked around and lowered her voice. 'Mum thought it might have been stolen – we're a bit careless with leaving our possessions out.'

'I can't take all the credit,' Holly said, 'the bow found me... gave me a little jab to tell me where she was.'

Doris laughed. 'Morning tea is on us, please.'

Holly began to protest.

'Oh no, I absolutely insist. Mum will be so happy. This was my grandmother's. Not worth much, but sentimental none-theless.'

Forty minutes later, with one empty teapot, a very clean butter plate and a kiss on the cheek from Betty, she declared

The Cup and Saucer one of her new favourites. Holly resumed her walk down the village street. She noted the hardware store, gift store, book store, another gift store and a takeaway which seemed to have attracted every tradesman in the village. There was a chemist – good to know; a small grocery and liquor store – even better; and a fabric store – wow, that was unique! Were people still making their clothes? And yet another gift store. Seriously, she thought; the weekend tourist trade must justify it.

Holly crossed the road and made her way down the other side. Another café, but a very modern one that was doing very well and had the best display of cakes... hmm, dangerous; a newsagent; a bike hire store – nice idea for the tourists. There was the real estate agency where Holly rented *Findlater House*. She glanced in but there was no sign of Damien Flat, so she waved to a young office girl who gave her a reciprocal wave. Holly had a quick look at the properties for sale and couldn't believe *Findlater House* would be worth so much by comparison. Good grief!

Onward she went, her car now coming back in sight and then she spotted it... the library. Without hesitation, Holly went in, organised a library card and immersed herself in the smell of books.

Seriously, who the hell is this now? The Sergeant saw a sporty, black, two-door BMW pull up outside *Findlater House* and a well-dressed man, groomed to within an inch of his life, got out and made his way to the front door. He rapped on it, sharp and loud.

'Yeah, at your service, buddy,' the Sergeant said from behind the door.

He watched the man glance at his watch and then knock again, before stepping back to look at the upstairs windows.

'No-one's here. Who the hell are you?' the Sergeant growled, taking an immediate dislike to the impatient intruder.

The BMW man pressed his face to the glass windows and looked in. He looked at his watch again and then returned to his car, lowered himself in and made a call. And there he stayed.

It was close to thirty minutes later, as the afternoon light began to wane, when Holly's car came into view. The Sergeant saw her reaction; she knew this guy and she wasn't happy to see him. He guessed she wasn't expecting to see him, either.

She parked and got out of the car; BMW driver got out and locked up. He gave her a grin and waved some papers at her.

'Miss me, babe?' he asked, leaning in to kiss her on the cheek. 'How's village life?'

'James,' Holly said, her voice icy. 'What are you doing here? How did you find me?'

'Going to ask me in? I've got the papers, the divorce papers,' he said, as if that would guarantee him entry.

Holly turned and walked towards the front door, her face pale and he followed in pursuit.

'Well, this is nice, great view. Must be worth a fortune,' James said, as he looked around.

'What are you doing here, James?' Holly asked.

'Yeah, great to see you, too,' her soon-to-be ex-husband said. He strode around, checking out the place and checking out his reflection in the windows where possible. 'Love a cup of tea,' he said.

Holly studied him. He looked good, he always did, she

hated that. She put her bag down and moved to the kitchen area. 'How did you find me?'

'That was easy,' he said, joining her. 'I knew your family owned a place here so I checked out the local real estate agencies' websites and only two had recent "rented" or "under lease" notes on properties, so I found them both and dropped in. He pointed to her business sign in the window. 'That was the giveaway. Got some mail for you,' he said, reaching into his coat pocket and dumping four letters on the counter. 'I'll get your stuff redirected to here now that I have your address.' He slipped his jacket off.

'You could have just mailed the divorce papers to Mum.'

'Yeah,' he shrugged, 'but I wanted to see how you were doing, and check you were really serious about this... that you haven't, you know, thought we were worth a second chance.'

She liked him better when he was a bit vulnerable and real.

'That would be our tenth chance at least,' Holly reminded him. 'Besides, what happened to the girl from the office?'

'Long gone.'

'And the girl from the gym?'

'Whatever,' he said, pulling out the papers and giving them to her. He had already signed them. Holly pushed a tea in front of him as he lowered himself onto a kitchen bench stool; she remained on the other side of the kitchen bench.

She took a deep breath and, pulling the papers closer, began to read through them. This made it official; she was going to be divorced.

Holly accepted the pen he pulled from his coat pocket, signed where required and gave him back the papers. James slid them back into the envelope. She was a divorcee; her marriage had failed, her vows were a lie, her commitment in the church just a joke... her love, still real.

'Well, that's that then,' she said, her voice laced with

sadness. 'Five years and we're over.' She couldn't see the Sergeant standing by her, offering her his silent support.

James nodded. 'When it was good, it was great.' He smiled.

Holly teared up, and nodded. 'We had our moments.' She smiled weakly.

'But when we were bad, you were really bad,' James said, and as Holly went to snap at him, he gave her a grin and a wink.

'Yeah, you'll keep,' she said, with another faint smile. 'Are you driving back tonight?'

'I thought I'd stay here,' he said.

You've got to be kidding, the Sergeant snarled, and moved through James.

'It's bloody cold in here, isn't it?' James asked, looking around and shivering.

Holly shrugged. 'I didn't notice. James, I really don't want you staying here. I'm trying to move on and I want this house to be full of new memories. If you stay... well, it won't be. I'll see you in the rooms and feel you here. This place will be... well, tainted.'

He held up his hand to stop her from talking. 'Relax, I get it.' James finished his tea. 'I've got a date, anyway. Had to kill a few hours before I got here so I went to the local pub. Met a nice lady. I'm having dinner at her place, so I'll probably crash there and head back tomorrow.'

The knife went into her heart, just when she thought he couldn't cause her any more pain. Holly couldn't believe it. 'Good-oh, don't waste any time. A date... or a one-night stand? Whatever, don't answer.'

'Yeah, just a one-night stand, I'm not planning on coming back,' he scoffed.

She frowned and shook her head. 'When did you become this person? Or maybe you were always like this and I didn't see it.'

'Maybe you bring out the worst in me.' He put it back on her.

Holly began to tear up.

'I'm just kidding. For the love of God, lighten up,' he said, and rolled his eyes. 'I'm heading straight back to London. Don't take me so seriously all the time!'

She nodded. 'Right. Lighten up. I'll get onto that.' She moved to the table and straightened the flowers in the vase.

'Who gave you those?' he asked.

'C'mon. New girl in a small town... the grapevine works well here,' she said, and inhaled them.

'You are kidding me? You've been here two days and some guy has sent you flowers? The bloody eagles are circling!'

Holly smiled. 'I bought them. Lighten up, James.'

'Oh, ha-ha,' he said.

Holly rolled her eyes. 'I'm as pathetic as you. Anyway, thanks for dropping in.'

'Right, I'd better go. A kiss for old time's sake then?' He gave her a smile that was part teasing, part charming and all brash.

'As enticing as the offer is, I'll have to refrain,' she said, and started to move towards the front door to encourage his departure.

'Always so sensible,' he said, reaching for his jacket and putting it back on.

'That's me, although I did make a couple of reckless decisions along the way.'

James grinned. 'You know what they say, opposites attract. Or they did once.' He grabbed her in a hug, placing his chin on her head and he held her for just a moment. He lowered his voice. 'I know I was a shit husband, Hols, but if you ever need me, you can still call on me.' He pulled away from her. 'Yeah?'

Holly couldn't speak. She blinked back tears, gave him a nod and a smile.

And with an air of enthusiasm for the future which she didn't have yet, James strode to the door, gave her a wave and departed.

She stood in the doorway and watched as he spun his car around and headed down the street. She watched until he was out of sight and she was alone.

Holly didn't know what to do. It was dusk, getting dark quickly and she was empty, and here. She couldn't see the Sergeant striding nearby her, debating what to do and how to help.

She slipped off her shoes and put on her joggers that were near the front door – she hadn't brushed the sand off them from this morning – and, grabbing the key, she closed the front door and headed to the beach for a walk to clear her head and heart.

MS HANLON MEETS THE SERGEANT

'It's too late to be heading out alone,' the Sergeant said, knowing she couldn't hear him until he chose to officially reveal himself. 'For chrissake,' he swore and leaving the house, he caught up with Holly. They walked alongside each other, Holly oblivious to his company.

'You might not be in the city, but you've still got to take some care,' he told her. He didn't like to leave the house; she was ruining his desire to stay in and be grumpy.

'Really, did I ask for this?' he said, continuing to moan. 'I should just go home and let you walk it off.' But he couldn't. It was almost dark and she shouldn't be walking along the beach by herself at this hour.

He had to admit, though, the beach was beautiful in the last moments of daylight; cool and quiet with only the occasional person on the beach now. Holly greeted a couple as they passed.

'Forget him, love. He's an ass, I wouldn't waste any time moaning after him,' the Sergeant advised her, even though she couldn't hear or see him. 'Don't know what you saw in him in the first place. Hardly your type.'

A woman and her little white dog approached them and the dog began to circle around the Sergeant, barking furiously. The dog's owner laughed and shrugged.

'He's always been a bit eccentric,' she said to Holly. 'Have a good night.'

'You too,' Holly said, with a smile. She gave the dog a quick pat and watched it follow its owner, with the occasional look back. She glanced around her to make sure she was alone, looking right through the Sergeant. Then, a man about her own age with a large brown Labrador soon came into sight and his dog repeated the performance.

'Hi, Buddy,' she said, patting the excited dog who kept circling the Sergeant.

'You know this guy?' the Sergeant asked. 'Nice doggy, for the love of God! Now, buzz off.'

The dog cocked its head to the side, licked the Sergeant's leg and ran off.

The guy laughed and greeted Holly. 'Yeah, he gets excited by the sand,' he explained.

Holly laughed. 'Don't we all!'

'So, staying out of the water this time? No seahorses to rescue?' he asked.

'Not so far, but can't promise I won't dive back in any second. Once a hero...'

The Sergeant stood with his arms crossed, watching the interchange between the two. *Who is this bozo? She's been here a minute and I've got an ex-husband and some guy with his dog already on the scene. Keep walking, mate,* the Sergeant thought, willing the guy along.

He watched as the pair exchanged a few more pleasantries and then continued on their way. Holly turned back to glance at him and he did the same. He gave her a wave and called for his dog, Buddy.

Holly drew in a deep breath; the small bit of contact with the real world was helping to distract her. He could feel her pain, hear her heart and her thoughts. He remembered what farewells were like. He'd blown it with Meg once and she'd left him, but he'd won her back. Worst week of his life until he talked her around. *Yep,* he thought. *Love sucks.*

Holly kept moving forward, one foot in front of the other. She greeted the nightfall walkers and their dogs and wished she had a dog to walk with – a trusted, loyal and loving companion; someone faithful. Seeing James had bounced her back to the past. She had regressed to where she'd been six months ago... to a place she'd crawled out of and left behind.

She buried her hands into her sweatshirt pockets and breathed deeply. The cool air on her face and the salty air was so good, a great distraction.

'I need to purge him from my heart and head... and home,' she said, muttering to herself.

The Sergeant nodded. 'That you do,' he agreed, not that she could hear him.

She placed her hand on her heart as if the warm contact would help with the overwhelming pain in her chest.

Why couldn't I just take what James was prepared to give me? Love, fun, a life together? she asked herself. *Because I wanted to be the only woman in his life,* she reminded herself, *and not just accept some part of him and have to continually hold back my love to protect my own heart. What's the point?*

'I'm here to escape him. There's no reminder of James here... he was here for a minute. Let it go, move on, carry on,' she said, coaching herself. She put her head back and straightened her shoulders. 'An exciting new start. Yep, that's what this is.'

'That's the spirit,' the Sergeant agreed.

She turned around and began the walk back.

'Good idea, let's head home,' he said.

As they neared the cottage, Holly stopped to make small talk with the neighbour who was watering his pot plants. The Sergeant pondered whether returning to a dark and empty house was worse than returning to a lit, warm house even if a ghost had set the scene. So, while Holly and the neighbour introduced themselves, the Sergeant took the opportunity to unlock the front door and make the house feel not quite so deserted.

Whatever, he thought, *I need to declare myself, anyway. I've got plans, I need her to work for me.*

He slipped in through the front door, turned on the kitchen light and lounge room lamp, and then, he had just the thing. He knew what would pep her up; he knew just what she needed to hear. The Sergeant went to the collection of vinyl records... 1960s... nope... 1970s... he thumbed through the vinyl albums. *Here it is,* he thought, and pulled the record from its sleeve. He slipped it onto the turntable and hovered the needle. As he heard the front door open, he put the track on.

She entered and saw the lights were on. Again, she stopped but it was different this time, he sensed it. Her heart rate wasn't thundering, she wasn't afraid. She was in need of kindness, some small show of solidarity. He watched as she looked around, looking for him. And then she heard the song and smiled, then laughed. Helen Reddy pumped out *I am Woman.*

Holly said the words aloud... 'Hear me roar!' She laughed again, then cried, then the phone rang. She wiped her face on her sleeve and reached for the mobile phone. It was her mother. 'Ah, a lecture... why not?' she said, and sighed. She answered, putting her mother on speaker phone as she went to turn Helen Reddy down.

'Oh good, you're still alive,' her mother said.

'I am. You'll be the first to hear when I'm not, I suspect. Everything okay?' Holly asked.

'Of course. I'm not the one who has deserted her job, family and friends to start a new life in a small village in a haunted house. I'm just living in suburbia with your father!'

Holly laughed and her mother relaxed and chuckled along. They spoke for a few minutes and as Holly hung up, she heard a sharp knock at the front door.

'What now?' she muttered. 'Ghost busters?'

The Sergeant watched her as she headed towards the front door with a worried look on her face.

'Don't worry, love,' he muttered, 'it's not the ex-husband back again.'

She opened the door and froze.

There was a man in the doorway who looked very familiar. *This is ridiculous*, the Sergeant thought, as she studied him on the front doorstep of *Findlater House. I'm introducing myself to someone living in my house, technically. Still, it's better than just appearing and going 'Boo' like bloody Casper the friendly ghost.*

He brushed off his annoyance as he watched her process him. She was a looker; cute. *Focus*, he told himself.

She smiled politely but he could tell she was desperately trying to work out where she knew him from.

The Sergeant cleared his throat. 'Uh, hello, you must be Holly,' he said.

'Yes,' she said, 'Hi.' Her eyes ran over his jeans and black collared shirt.

'I thought I should introduce myself,' he said, with a casual shrug, 'given we're going to be –'

'– Ah, you're a neighbour?' Holly cut him off.

'In a manner of speaking,' the Sergeant said.

Holly's eyes widened with sudden recognition.

'Um yes, that's me,' he said, with a glance to his portrait on the wall opposite that was currently empty. She turned her head and gasped, then turned back to look at him.

'I'm Alexander Austen, Sergeant Alexander Austen,' he said, with a nod to the empty portrait frame.

He watched as she backed away until she hit the bottom stair of the staircase and lowered herself down to sit on it before she fell down.

THE SERGEANT GETS A HOUSEMATE

'*S*ergeant Austen...' she mumbled, 'Alexander...'

'Yes, call me that, good idea, let's not stand on formality given we, uh, live together. Can I come in?' he asked, stepping over the threshold. 'Well technically, I'm already in. Living here, actually.'

Holly still stared at him. Her eyes were huge.

'No need to panic, truly, I'm a nice guy, handsome even.' He smiled. That usually worked, but Alexander noticed she didn't even register his charm factor. Only a matter of time, he thought.

'Perhaps I should make some tea,' he said.

'You drink tea?' Holly asked, snapping out of her state of reverie.

'I'm British.'

'Right, of course,' Holly said, 'I mean, you can make tea?'

Alexander shrugged. 'Sure, any ghost can push stuff around.'

'Right, yes,' she said, again, as if everyone should know that. Alexander watched as she gingerly pulled herself up from the bottom stair. 'I'm Holly Hanlon.' She offered him her hand, then pulled it back. 'Sorry, do ghosts shake... I mean, can they shake...?'

'Why not?' he said and took her small hand in his. Her hand was warm, he felt the blood and skin and all things lifelike about it. His hand, on the other hand, was chilly. She pulled her hand away quickly, still looking at him with a shocked expression. Eventually, she registered the chill of his cold hand and casually rubbed her hand against her jeans.

'Sorry, occupational hazard,' he said, and turned to the kitchen to put the kettle on. She watched as he looked at the water level on the kettle, flicked the switch down to start it heating up and nudged two cups into the centre of the counter. He knew where everything was.

'Well, kettle's on,' Alexander said, and turned to face her.

'Right, noted,' she said.

They stared at each other. Alexander wondered should he say something or let her get her wits about her.

Holly stepped up. 'So, you're not transparent then?' she said.

'No, apparently not.'

'You look very solid,' she agreed. Holly glanced again into the living room, at the portrait frame which was empty, then back to the Sergeant.

'Yep, still here,' he said.

'You're here and drinking tea. You are real, and I can see you and touch you. I am awake,' she said, convincing herself.

'Yes.' He nodded, slightly amused by her study of him. 'Are you thinking of writing down this sort of detail?' he asked, one eyebrow raised and a smile on his face.

'No, yes, I don't know. Do you think I should? No, that's silly, who would believe me? A ghost manual,' she said, and stopped, realising she was raving. 'Why don't you sit down?' Holly pulled out a chair for him.

'Yes, probably best,' he said, and sat on the chair at the kitchen table.

'Will you sit, too?' he asked.

'Oh, yes, sure,' she said, lowering herself into a chair opposite. 'So, you've been here all along. How come you didn't show yourself sooner?'

'It's only been two days,' he said.

'Wow, so it has. It feels like longer,' she said. Alexander noticed that she was trying not to stare at him, but her eyes ran over his face, hands and features. 'Were you just walking beside me on the beach?' she asked.

'Yes. You shouldn't go out by yourself when it's getting dark. It's not always safe, even here in this village,' he said, watching her. 'Even though you don't care if you live or die at the moment.'

She looked away, embarrassed and moved to pour the water from the boiling kettle into the teapot.

'I don't usually make a pot,' she said, as though she had to fill the silence until the situation became real or she woke from a dream. 'If it's just me, I stick a teabag into a mug, but this is nice, I think,' she said. 'I don't what I'm saying... for the love of God, I'm making tea for a ghost!' Holly shook her head. She turned to place the teapot on the coaster in the middle of the table, and the Sergeant was still there.

'Yep, not a dream,' he said, reading her expression.

She gave a wary smile, put a warmer over the teapot and put out two cups and saucers. 'I've got milk, and some biscuits,' she said. 'Do ghosts eat... never mind.'

Alexander nodded as she offered the milk, and added some to his cup and hers. She moved some of her library books off the table to reach the sugar pot and offered it to the Sergeant but he declined.

'Crime... crime... romance,' he said, looking at the three books and interpreting their genre.

Holly looked embarrassed. 'I like a good whodunnit, and as for the romance...' she looked away as she spoke, 'escapism is good.' She gave a false laugh.

For a few moments they both sat in uncomfortable silence, as Holly let the tea draw. She looked directly at him, again.

'You look so real,' she said.

Alexander smiled. 'You were expecting me to be in watercolour?'

She laughed again, a nervous laugh, but stopped suddenly. 'Maybe a bit faded,' she agreed. 'Did you put that record on? That particular song?'

'Yes, it was a big hit the year before I died,' he said, matter-of-factly. 'Not one of my favourites, I assure you, but I thought you could do with some boosting up.'

'Thank you. So you... um... met my husband, ex-husband?'

'Hard not to.'

'And you were in my room the first night when I was upset? The night you put the other song on for me with the hope message as well... the "bright, bright, beautiful day" song?'

Alexander rolled his eyes. 'I didn't see anything, I'm an officer and a gentleman,' he said, with a smirk, throwing her words back at her.

'Ah,' she waved a finger at him, 'you were in the room that day. I thought I heard you but you wouldn't reveal yourself.'

'Didn't want to send you screaming... actually I did and the sooner the better, but... doesn't matter,' he said. 'And I honestly didn't see anything I shouldn't have seen. I'm an honourable ghost,' he said.

She softened and could help but return his smile, some-what unwillingly.

'I did hear you crying,' he said. 'I felt your pain tonight.'

Holly flushed with embarrassment and, reaching for the pot, declared it drawn.

'I don't know what that means, but my grandma used to say the tea is drawn.' She poured the tea into their two cups, started speaking, then stopped, and started again. 'I know we're over, but it's still hard thinking of him with someone else, and right here in my new world.'

'He's not, he left,' Alexander said.

'He said that, but I don't believe him. It's just like him to pick up someone for a one-night stand.'

'He's driving back to London,' Alexander assured her. He hoped they didn't have to keep talking about bloody James.

'How do you know?' she said, her face brightening.

Alexander tapped his nose. 'There are things we ghost know and see.'

'Really? Like what?' Holly asked.

'Well, I can't tell you that. There'll be nothing to find out when you get to the other side – my side, that is.'

She studied him and he smiled. 'Do you know when I will die?' Holly asked.

'I could find out, but I won't. I do know who killed JFK and if Elvis is really alive or dead,' he said, 'but I can't tell you.'

Holly scoffed. 'That's so last century.' She cleared her throat. 'But seriously, you could watch me at night if you wanted to?'

'Sure, but why would I want to? Not saying you are not interesting, but you know, I've got things to do, too,' he said. He saw her unconvinced expression. 'Haven't we had the bound-aries talk? Even if it was a bit one-way!'

'Are you staying?' she asked.

Alexander's mouth fell open.

'Here, in this house?' she asked again.

'Of course! Where do you think I'm going to go?' What a cheek, he thought. 'I was here first! Are *you* staying?'

'Yes, for six months at least,' she said, putting her chin up with defiance.

'Me, too and for longer than that!'

Holly took a deep breath. 'Why? I heard you had some unhappiness in your life. Is that why you are still here?'

This time, Alexander looked away, tempted to disappear. For a moment, neither of them spoke.

'You're very direct, aren't you?' he said, frowning.

Holly raised an eyebrow. 'My husband... ex-husband, used to say that.'

'Poor sod,' Alexander said.

She narrowed her eyes at him. 'Trust a man to stick up for another man. And don't think I haven't noticed your evasion technique.' She also noticed Alexander lifted the teacup to his lips and drank, twice, but the cup remained full.

'Well, I guess we're housemates then,' she said.

'Hmm. I'll be sure to let you know *my* house rules then,' he said. Alexander disappeared before Holly had a chance to challenge him.

She narrowed her eyes in frustration, then couldn't help but smile. She looked to his portrait where he stared nobly out over the room. The ghost in her haunted house wasn't so bad, after all.

GHOST INCOMING

*L*uke arrived at the nursery's office early and after turning the lights on and turning off the security and answering service, he opened the file on the garden plans for *Findlater House* – his father's work. He printed two large copies and spread them on the desk to show Alfred. No sooner had he done so, Alfred arrived and Luke called him in.

'Hello, son,' Alfred addressed him as he often did. Luke was his godson, after all. 'Ah, you've printed them out. Let's have a look.' He stood beside him, taking his glasses out of his top pocket and took in the plans.

'Your father was good... really good, wasn't he?'

'Yeah. Better than I'll ever be,' Luke said, sentimentally.

'Ah, I wouldn't say that,' Alfred said, 'you both have very different skills. But wow, these are brilliant. Can you do it on a limited budget?'

'Sure,' Luke said. 'I can substitute some of the plants for cheaper varieties and if she wants to pitch in or hire some cheap labour to help, it'll cut the costs.' Luke's eyes roamed around the illustration.

'You've given this some thought then?' Alfred teased him. 'Can't believe you made the onsite appointment for Friday, though. She's single. What if she gets snapped up before then?'

Luke rolled his eyes. 'Then she wasn't meant for me. Not saying she is, anyway. Besides, how do you know she's single?'

Alfred took off his jacket, hung it on a hook beside Luke's jacket and put on one of the company's bottle-green and white striped garden aprons. 'I have my sources,' he said, tapping his nose.

Luke crossed his arms across his chest and Alfred held up his hands in surrender. 'Okay, ease up on the pressure! I play bridge with a lady who happens to be one of Holly's first business clients. She was told firsthand by the young lady herself that she was single. So, play your cards right...'

'Well, let's just try and get the garden job first,' Luke said, rolling up the plans, but Alfred knew him well enough to recognise there was a lightness in the young man's demeanour; he was definitely interested in young Holly Hanlon!

Holly jumped. 'Seriously, do you think you could announce yourself?' she said, glaring at Alexander and holding her hand over her heart.

Alexander cupped his hands around his mouth and announced: 'Ghost incoming'.

Holly laughed and shook her head; she wanted to be cranky at him but it was impossible. 'A cough would suffice. I was deep in concentration looking for a missing jewel,' she said, with a nod to her laptop screen.

It was Tuesday, mid-morning and Holly sat in her office, officially for work purposes; her laptop opened on the desk, a diet cola in front of her and view of the ocean through the window. She felt happy and strangely at peace for the first time in a long while.

Alexander stood beside her. 'So how does this thing work?' he asked, nodding at the screen.

'It's the internet. You can look up anything in the world,' she said.

Alexander scoffed. Then, seeing her serious face, he leaned over further. 'You're not kidding?'

'Nope, not kidding. I'm not saying what you will find is always correct, but you learn to sift the crap out.'

'Oh, so eloquently put,' he said.

Holly crossed her arms across her chest. 'What? Ladies didn't say crap in your day?'

Alexander conceded. 'It was the Sixties. They said and did a lot worse than that! But you're so...'

Holly narrowed her eyes. 'So?'

He rolled his eyes. 'Feminine and sweet,' he said.

Holly grinned. 'Well, thank you, Sergeant. Be careful, I might think you like me.'

'Yeah well, don't get carried away.' He walked around, or more accurately, suddenly appeared behind her and pointed at the screen. 'Back to this device. So, could you look up a person on it?'

'Sure. There's also a social site called Facebook where a lot of people are registered and connect.'

'Really?' he said, and looked confused. 'Why?'

'Because... well, I don't know what it was like in the Sixties and Seventies, but now, it's a little harder to connect. No one writes letters anymore or goes to dances. Instead, they spend most of their time online.' She stopped. 'How did people meet and connect in your day?'

'We met at school, and at work, at sport, in pubs and

through friends, and at dinner parties, concerts… how did you meet your ex-husband?'

'On an online dating site,' she confessed.

'No! You mean you found his picture on this machine and married him?' Alexander looked appalled.

'No, yes… well, no… it's more complex than that. We dated for two years before we married! It's not like I picked him out in a photo line-up… although I guess there was that original photo attraction,' she said, and shrugged.

'Sounds awful,' Alexander said.

'I guess so,' she agreed. Holly turned back to the screen, took a sip of Diet Coke and, realising Alexander was very quiet, turned to see if he was there. He was, and still looked appalled. He sat down beside her.

'Open up this Face site.'

'I was working, but aye, aye, Sergeant,' she said, and saluted. He gave her a smirk. He had quite a good repertoire of them, Holly realised.

She logged into the page and her feed came up. Alexander laughed. 'Well, look at that… it's you and there are pictures of this house and your aunty.' He leaned in to see the selfie of Kate and her aunt. 'Who took that photo?'

'I did.'

'But you're in it!'

'It's called a selfie,' Holly explained. 'You can hold the camera so you both get in the shot. If I took a photo of us, would you appear in it?'

'No.'

'Ah, so that one is true. So much to learn,' she said. 'Anyway, is there anyone you want to look up?'

'What do you mean? Like just put a name in and their photos will come up?' Alexander asked. 'Will I be there.'

Holly smiled. 'No, you have to create the page. But if I

searched for your name, it might come up if you were ever in the news or something like that.'

'Don't do that,' he said, quickly.

'Okay.' She studied him.

He cleared his throat. 'There's something I want to talk about with you first before you start researching me.'

'Right,' she said, still watching him.

'So don't.'

'I won't.'

'It's nothing sinister,' Alexander assured her. 'I'm not an axe murderer or anything.'

'That's fine, no problem. So, who do you want to look up?' Holly knew exactly who Alexander wanted to look up but she didn't think he'd go straight there... he'd have to process that thought.

He stood again, paced for a few moments and then sure enough, he picked a random name.

'Tommy Lionel. We served together. Think he'd be on there?' Alexander asked.

'Is he still alive?'

'Yeah. Well, I haven't seen him on the other side,' Alexander said.

'He wouldn't be down below?' she said, with a quick glance to the floor. 'Like in hell?'

'Ah, the old heaven and hell theory,' he smiled. 'Yeah, might be. You better be good then.'

'Don't tease me,' Holly said, and smiled at him. 'How do I know what's beyond the white light.' She turned back to the laptop with a petulant look on her face.

'Ooh, white light. That's good, too. Well, go on then, Tommy Lionel.'

She turned to face the screen, feeling self-conscious with a man-ghost standing behind her. Holly typed Tommy's name into the search and found half a dozen Tommy Lionels but Alexander discounted them all.

'It happens. Anyone else?' she asked.

'Hmm... how about Andy Davies? Better make it Andrew,' Alexander said.

Holly put the name in and Alexander corrected her spelling. Over a dozen men with the same name appeared in the search function. She clicked on several until opting for the eldest one and his Facebook photo took up the screen.

'For the love of God, that's Andy!' Alexander said, and laughed. 'Jesus, he's got ugly! He was never much to look at when he was young but age hasn't done him any favours. What's he saying?'

Holly laughed. 'He doesn't say anything. Sit!' she pulled out a chair. 'I'll show you how it works, even though you're interrupting me and I'm very busy and important.'

'Sure you are.' He smiled and sat beside her. 'It's cool, isn't it?'

'Yeah, I guess it is. It's good for when you are away, because you can stay connected. And it is free.'

'Yeah?' Alexander looked confused. 'How would you pay on this thing, anyway?' He pointed to the laptop.

'With an electronic bank transfer,' Holly said. She saw his blank look. 'Wow, you've got a hell of a lot of catching up to do, haven't you? About four decades!'

'Yeah, well, we've got six months, haven't we? I'm sure you'll have me up to speed by then.'

'Depends on whether I last the distance with you,' she said, and narrowed her eyes at him.

'Are you kidding? It'll be me that's packing up and leaving before you. But I'll do my best to endure flatting together,' he said.

Holly turned side-on to face him. 'We're not flatting

together. I'm paying rent and legally staying here, you're a free-loader... a trespasser, like a homeless dude.'

'Ha!' he scoffed. 'I'll have you know I was here long before you so, if you want to get technical, as a squatter I've probably got legal rights to claim the house as my own!'

Holly studied him. 'That's only a pretty recent law, how do you know about that?'

'I listen to the radio,' he said.

She grinned. 'You'd have a hard time winning that one, though, wouldn't you, ghost guy?'

'Don't push me, blondie.'

They stared at each other, ready for combat, but neither took the next move.

Holly softened. 'So what do you want to talk to me about before I'm allowed to research you?'

Alexander's expression became very serious. 'I've got a job I was hoping I could hire you to do. I can pay you... I've just got to get my head around what I have to tell you and how much you'll need to know. So give me a bit of time, and no sneaky research behind my back.'

She looked to the laptop screen and then back to Alexander. *This will be interesting,* she thought. 'Okay, I understand. No pressure and no hurry. Besides, you don't have to pay me.'

'I have to pay you,' he insisted, 'and I can pay you. If I don't, you won't take it seriously and it will always be on the back burner for when you get time,' he said. 'It has to be formal, I want to hire you.'

She nodded. 'I understand. And, when you are ready to look for Meghan's name, we can do that, too.'

She caught him by surprise, and his breath hitched. He nodded and when she turned back, he was gone.

∼

For the rest of the afternoon Holly focussed on her research. Alexander hadn't reappeared since he disappeared earlier in the day, which suited her just fine; she had some paying work to do and she didn't want to overwhelm him with technology on his first encounter with her laptop. Plus, truth be known, she had never had the patience for teaching. She'd have to be on her best behaviour.

Now she needed to focus on finding Esther's piece of jewellery; the pink heart. That was the name she had given the pale pink pearl necklace with its pink diamond centrepiece. Holly had opened her diary and logged her start time for billing purposes, and was narrowing down the options that had come up in her online search. Last night, she had waded through the file that Esther left her and read the earlier proof of sale and ownership documents, but the trail had faded out decades ago.

It had been confiscated by a Nazi who conveniently went underground post-war. There was a sale document about a decade later which showed it had been sold to a jewellery broker. He again had sold it to a private collector in Amsterdam. From there, it was left in a will to the buyer's daughter in the late 1970s, who sold it to a buyer that seems to have disappeared off the face of the earth. Their last address was in Paris. That was the mid-eighties, and now the necklace could be anywhere.

Holly hadn't expected to find anything when she typed in Esther's parents' names, but Freida and Uri Hirschel came up in several searches. Adrenaline surged through her; Holly loved the chase. She clicked on the first link, but it was a list of survivors and victims from the Bergen-Belsen concentration camp and Freida's name was on the victims' list.

Holly sighed. There was something terribly sad about seeing Esther's mother's name there... number 2345 of 50,598. All those names, but she now had a connection to one of them;

this name, Freida Hirschel, was a real person and loved. She closed the page and clicked on the next link. It was a list of businesses in Germany pre-war and there was the name Uri Hirschel and the business, Hirschel's Fine Jewellery and Collectables. Holly could just imagine the creative hands of Esther's father designing and producing delicate pieces like the pink heart necklace.

And then she saw the photo. *Oh my*, Holly whispered, *I wonder if Esther has seen this?* It was a photo of a very attractive, stylish couple standing in front of the window of the jewellery store. The name of the business was behind them on the glass, and the man had his arm affectionately around the woman, who was smiling happily at the camera. The caption read: *Mr and Mrs Uri Hirschel outside their store premises.* It was obvious from the photo that Freida was pregnant... it had to be Esther, she was an only child. It was 1932, and the Hirschels had no idea what was to come, or how many years they had left as a family.

Holly closed the office – or rather her laptop – at 4 pm on the dot and called it a day. She stood up, stretched, and saw the beach beckoning her for an afternoon walk.

'Coming for a walk, Alexander?' she asked, but his portrait image didn't move. 'Does that mean you are ignoring me, or are you somewhere else and that is just a shop front?'

Again, no reaction. Holly shrugged, got changed and left, locking the house behind her.

QUESTIONS ABOUT THE AFTERLIFE

*B*ack from her late afternoon beach walk, her lungs full of fresh air and the salt spray on her skin, Holly poured herself a glass of white wine and sat on her front porch, watching the sun light the waves and reflect off the rocks as it slowly made its descent.

She loved this new routine, it made her happy. But she couldn't help but be a little melancholy; imagine how wonderful it would be to have a man, a true love, sitting beside her. Just as she thought it, Alexander appeared on the chair at her side, in his customary dark jeans and long-sleeve grey T-shirt. He was ruggedly handsome, she had to admit, for a dead guy.

'Hey you,' she said, and smiled.

'And hey you,' he said, copying her. 'Can I join you?'

'Sure. Want a drink?' she asked, and he gave her a dry look. 'I would, but you know that would only make you look strange... the locals passing would see two glasses and just you sitting here. They'd be thinking that you're either stockpiling wine to work through, or you've lost it,' he said, with a smirk. 'Wouldn't be the first time, I'm guessing.'

She laughed. 'You're a funny ghost.'

'And you're okay,' he said, with a smile.

'Really?' She grinned. 'So, you think you might get used to me... might let me stay long-term?'

'Yeah, don't get carried away,' he said, putting up his hand. 'But you're better than some of the weirdos I've had here.' He turned to look out to sea, and sighed.

'Oh. Well, thanks.'

Another couple walked by with one of those trendy designer dogs that used to be called mutts – a cavoodle or similar – and Holly exchanged pleasantries with them. They couldn't see the Sergeant, but the cavoodle gave him a rousing reception.

'What is it with you and dogs?' she asked. 'Do you give off an I-don't-like-dogs vibe?'

'I love dogs,' he said defensively. 'They're just showing off that they can see me.'

'So, speaking of seeing you,' Holly began, 'I'd love to know more about what ghost life is like.'

'Yeah, it's not really the done thing to share the details with the living. Although you do get those clairvoyant types who have some skills and reveal stuff. But, it's not my scene.'

'Right,' she said, and made a note to work on him.

They sat in comfortable silence for a while – Holly trying not to feel self-conscious of the good-looking ghost on her left; Alexander conscious of the fact he had company he desired for the first time in what might be decades.

She smiled and waved at an elderly gentleman who was walking on the path past their home. She then recognised him; it was the doctor who had gone past the previous day. Would he see the Sergeant was with her again?

'Lovely evening,' Holly greeted him.

'Indeed, young lady. Good evening, Sergeant,' he said again, doffing his hat and continuing on. Alexander raised his arm in a casual salute. 'Doctor.'

Holly's eyes widened and she turned to face Alexander. 'I thought he was fluking the first time. So how come he can see you?'

Alexander shrugged. 'Some people can. Doctor Ron's always been able to see me.'

'Is he dead?'

It was Alexander's turn to laugh. 'No, he's very much alive, but he's seen his share of the dead. I suspect that might be why he can see me.'

'And that doesn't freak you out?' she asked.

'Why? What's he going to do? What are you going to do? Run around town telling people that there's a ghost in the house? Yeah, tell them something they don't know. Anyway, it's good for tourists and keeps the kids on their toes.'

Holly shook her head. 'Positively weird, the lot of you.'

The sun was dipping just on the water's edge and the view in front of them was lit orange.

'Spectacular,' Holly said. 'You know, my mum always tries to pick when the sunset or sunrise is at its peak – that moment when it is as intense as it is going to be before it begins to fade into day or night. It makes you appreciate the power of it.'

'Very poetic of your mum,' Alexander said. 'I think it is now... no, hold on, now... or wait up... now it seems even deeper...'

'Now,' Holly said, getting into the game. They watched for the next minute as the sunset began to fade. 'I win.'

'Not that you're competitive,' he said.

'And you're not?'

'Maybe, if the person is worth beating.' They slowly turned to look at each other.

'Play cards?' he asked.

'Only to win.'

Alexander laughed. 'Those are fighting words. Maybe we can invite Doctor Ron around for a game and find someone else who can see me. I haven't played a hand of cards for decades.'

'You'll be crap then. I'm bound to win. Great plan!' she sparred with him.

'Yeah, dream on. So, when do I get my next online lesson?' he asked. 'That was amazing today. A whole new world.'

'Mmm... about that next lesson,' Holly said.

Alexander crossed his arms and turned to look at her. 'I'll get there... with Meg, I will.'

'I know, that's okay,' she said, assuring him. 'I didn't mean that.'

'Oh,' he unfolded his arms. 'What then?'

'I thought we could have a trade. I get to ask two questions about heaven for every session where I train you or give you information, and you have to answer honestly,' she suggested.

'Ah, you are good,' he said, and wagged his finger at her. He realised she was going to get her way about insights from the other side whether he liked it or not. 'Didn't take you long to come up with that, did it?'

'So, what do you say?' she said, lifting her wine glass for a sip.

Alexander counter-offered. 'One question and I'll answer anything I can.'

'Honestly? You'll answer it properly... not flippantly?'

'Do I look like the flippant type?' Alexander asked gruffly. 'If I'm allowed to answer it...' he said, with a look above, 'I'll answer it. You've got a deal.'

'Really?' Holly almost squealed. 'I never thought you'd agree to that. Well, what do you know?'

Alexander faked hitting his ear to get his hearing back and Holly slapped his arm before remembering she would pass through. She subtly tried to wipe her cold and damp hand on her jeans.

'It's okay, I know I'm chilly,' he said, with a smirk.

'More like wet,' she said and returned his smirk – a much better version than his. 'I'm not worried if you are chilly,' she said and to prove it, she extended her hand. 'Let's shake on our new deal then?' She felt his cold, soft grip on her own skin; a most unusual sensation.

'So, my first question...' she began.

'Hold up!' he said, 'No one said anything about it being backdated. That contract starts now.'

'Well, if you're already backing out on our agreement on a technicality... then I think I'm pretty busy for the next week. I've got Esther's necklace to find, and Luke the gardener is coming over tomorrow.' She picked up her glass, took another sip and waited for his reaction.

He rolled his eyes. 'Fine. Ask your question,' he said, then her words hit him. 'Luke the gardener?'

Holly put her wine glass down. 'Yes! *From How Does Your Garden Grow?* nursery. He's found some original garden plans and he's bringing them around and measuring up!'

'So, he's still got them. Wow!' Alexander exhaled, surprised.

'They're yours?' Holly asked, surprised.

'Yeah. Lilly wanted the garden done and gave us a budget so Meg and I had the plans drawn up by that nursery. The owner did them, I'm guessing that's Luke's father. But we didn't get a chance to run with them.' He looked out to sea as he thought about the day they walked the small area, planning their future cottage garden.

'Well, that's cool. I'll be able to see what you and Meg came up with, and you can see how the plans stood the test of time. It has been over forty years – they might be totally unhip!' Holly said, sensing his mood and trying to lighten the conversation.

'Ha,' he scoffed, 'I'm the coolest cat out, they won't be unhip.'

'Coolest cat?'

'Yeah, whatever.' He shrugged. 'Ask your question.'

Holly grinned and clapped her hands together. 'Goody. Okay.' She cleared her throat, narrowed her eyes and looked at him as if she was thinking of it, when she knew what she wanted to ask all along.

'Why are you here and not on the other side?'

Alexander groaned. It wasn't a simple answer but it was an obvious question. He took a deep breath.

Holly studied him; he was so completely in the flesh, so real, you would never guess he was a ghost except for the coolness around him.

'You know how I said I had a job I wanted to hire you to do?' he asked.

'Yes. I was wondering when you'd get back to that or if I should raise it again in about a week's time, given that you disappeared last time we were talking about it,' she said. 'But I'm guessing I know what you want me to do...'

He raised an eyebrow and nodded at her to continue.

'You want me to find Meghan,' she said, confidently. 'So, is that related to my question... why you stuck around? Are you hoping she'd come back or you could find her to – what? Say goodbye, or make sure she is okay?'

'No, wrong on both accounts. I didn't stick around just to wait for her to come back, although that would have been great. And no, I don't want you to find Meghan, but that would be a bonus,' he said, staring straight ahead and not meeting Holly's eyes.

Holly reached for her wine glass and finished her last sip. It was chilly now; the warmth of the evening had gone, the sun had dipped and the street lights were warming up – time to go in, but she wanted to finish this discussion first. She never knew when the Sergeant might next appear or talk about this subject.

'I'm still here because I have other unfinished business,' he said.

'I guess that's the short answer to why you are still here,' she said, unsatisfied. 'So why do you want to hire me then?'

Alexander met her eyes. 'I want you to find out who killed me, and then tell Meghan the truth.'

THE SERGEANT'S LAST MEMORY

1972, NORTHERN IRELAND

$\mathcal{S}$ ergeant Alexander Austen grumbled along with the rest of his company. January weather was shit in Belfast, but the weather wasn't much better at home at the moment, so it wasn't as if they were missing out on anything. It was freezing during the day, bloody freezing at night, and as a bonus, raining. Add to that, the sun rose after 9 am and set by 4 pm... yep, enjoy that window of the day.

But Alexander didn't really care... it was a deployment, like all other deployments. Do the job, do it well, or get out. He never could understand people who stayed in jobs they didn't like. His father was one. Hated what he did all his life, then died. Alexander... well, he liked the military life, except for leaving Meghan, but coming home was so sweet.

If he were honest, though, he'd have to agree the current operation was his least favourite of all his deployments to date, and it was putting a strain on his marriage. It started in 1969, the "request" to deploy to Northern Ireland after the riots and they were still there now in 1972. Not that Alexander had been there that long himself; he arrived in 1971 so it was a fairly new gig for him compared to some of his mates.

It was a hairy mission... men died. There were paramilitary attacks and public attacks; there were areas where the locals loved them and areas where they were despised. To make it worse, Meghan had relatives on both sides of the argument, and being present to assert the authority of the British government in Northern Ireland wasn't making for a happy marriage. He'd be glad when the gig was up. It was the first time in his career that he'd thought of getting out and doing something else with his life.

It was Friday afternoon. Not that it mattered much to Alexander given he was working the weekend, but there was a Friday feeling in the air and he was hoping to have a few drinks in a couple of hours when he was off the clock. He and his team had been sent to a suburban location in Belfast; specials forces had received a warning of two bombs being planted and that they were going to be set off in under an hour. It wasn't the first warning they'd received, or even the fiftieth, for that matter. Warnings came in all the time – some for real, some hoaxes which were traps in their own right.

Geez, he hated bombs, it just wasn't a fair fight. An armed fight was different – all fair in love and war. The fight took some skill, some stealth, some luck even, but bombings were just a lottery – a draw in the lucky or unlucky dip and they took out innocents.

Following his Staff-Sergeant, Andy Davies – he who had to 'do something or he'd die of boredom' – Alexander stopped suddenly, nearly ramming into the back of him. He'd been right on his back all afternoon. It'd be nice to have a view that didn't include Andy's arse!

He felt the rumble.

Then the noise of an explosion engulfed the area.

The signal came to drop, and Alexander followed suit. Another bang... somewhere a street or so away... screams, choking smoke and then another.

'Fuck, fuck, fuck!' his mind screamed as he rose and, squatting, stumbled behind Andy, following him straight into the risk zone.

This one was no hoax!

His adrenalin was pumping. Fear was overridden by alertness and his training kicked in. The noises around him couldn't be described – it was as if the city had come alive and was immobilised.

Another two explosions shook the area, one to his left, one straight ahead. His group broke up, smoke, flying debris... and in moments, Alexander and Andy, who was running beside him, were surrounded by civilians. Some were running the opposite way, screaming, eyes huge, hysterical mothers pulling children along, men in suits... everyone was on the move. Traffic was backing up in the streets, with many trying to turn around and go back, most of them sitting on their horns like that would miraculously clear the road.

More bombs went off.

He couldn't hear the commands being yelled around him; all he could do was act on instinct and head in the direction of the action with the intention of shutting it down.

For a split second, his mind went to Meg as he ran towards the danger.

He'd counted five explosions now but nothing was directly in sight except for smoke, panicked crowds and traffic. Alexander tried to edge along the wall and increase his speed, but panicked people ran into him, barging in their hurry to get past. One guy literally bounced off him.

Alexander put his hand down to help the guy off the ground before he trod on him.

Shit, he knew the face. He knew this guy.

Ronan – Meghan's cousin. Alexander had met him half a dozen times, and he'd come over to attend their wedding and led the stag night astray! He was a top young bloke.

'Bloody hell, Ronan, it's you!' he said. He didn't know if he was talking loudly as his ears were ringing.

Ronan laughed. 'Ha, well lad, here ya are! That's grand!' He took Alexander's offered hand and, rising, pulled Alexander to him and they hugged and slapped each other's backs.

Then Alexander felt the pain. He gasped, pulled away from Ronan to look in his face.

Ronan's eyes were huge in shock.

And that was Sergeant Alexander Austen's last living memory.

Holly could feel the chill in the night air setting in but she couldn't move after hearing his story. They both sat in silence for a while until he eventually stirred.

'I'd give you my jacket, but maybe we should just go in,' he said, and rose.

Holly stood and followed him inside.

A BEST FRIEND COMES TO VISIT

*J*uliette Holmes – no relation to Sherlock, despite her love of crime books – sometimes marvelled at the fact that she and Holly had remained best friends for so long. They were polar opposites by nature and looks, but if opposites attract, then they were suited. In true form, Juliette had given Holly exactly two hours' notice that she was arriving for a long weekend visit to check up on her best friend. Juliette liked impromptu. "Surprise" was her middle name. It wasn't technically a long weekend, but Juliette had taken Friday off from her antique buyers' job in London and skipped out midday Thursday, so ta-da, call it a long weekend! She was arriving late afternoon on Thursday.

Holly on the other hand liked to plan. For years, she had drummed into Juliette that she didn't like surprise parties, or spur of the moment changes of plan. Holly couldn't accept an immediate invitation; in most cases she would attend, but being put on the spot panicked her. Advance notice of a week or two was ideal. Not that Juliette wanted to panic her best friend, but she also didn't want her running around for days prior to Juliette's arrival, cleaning, preparing, preening and worrying when after all, they were as good as family. They had started and finished school together, had met each other's boyfriends and lovers, travelled together and lived together while at university. Now, Juliette was going to crash at Holly's new abode and give it the tick of approval... whether she liked it or not. That's what friends did, after all.

She glanced into the car mirror and checked she looked "together". Her auburn hair was a little out of control, as it always was where salt and sea air were involved, her make-up was wearing off, showing the small array of freckles on her nose and cheeks, but her green eyes were alert... she was looking forward to this weekend. Besides, Holly wouldn't care if she arrived with a potato sack on and a cucumber face mask on her skin.

Juliette's GPS device told her to turn left and announced, 'destination'.

'Thank you, sexy voice,' Juliette said. She'd often wished the GPS guide was a real guy sitting beside her, saying 'At the next turn... take the third exit... then kiss me'. She sighed; Juliette had a good imagination.

'Wow!' she said, taking in the glorious ocean view as she reached the top of the lane. She recognised Holly's car in front of a large white cottage and turned to park on the kerb. Juliette leapt out of the car – she had been driving for over three hours – and breathed in the salt air.

The front door opened and Holly burst from the house, rushing to embrace her best friend. They held each other tightly, then Juliette pulled away to look at Holly.

'You look fine.'

'I am fine.'

'Are you?' Juliette asked.

'Sure,' Holly said.

Juliette's expression begged the truth. She held Holly at arm's length. Holly gave a slight shrug.

'Some days are easy, others take a little more work to get out of bed... but I'm definitely on the improve,' Holly said. 'In fact, I've got my first client, I know some people from the village already, I've found the library and four lost items since I've been here and... I'm raving. I'm fine!'

'Of course you are,' Juliette said, and squeezed Holly's arms. 'Of course you are. I know it has only been a few weeks, but I miss you.'

Holly pulled away from Juliette. Open emotions weren't her strong suit, unlike Juliette, who wore her heart on her sleeve.

'Then we'll need a system,' Holly suggested. 'I'll come and see you once a month and you'll need to come here regularly. It will be good for you to unplug from the connected world and breathe in the salt air.'

Juliette looked slightly panicked.

'I have WiFi, you only need unplug for an hour or so a day,' Holly teased.

'Phew,' Juliette said, removing her hand from her heart, 'you had me going then.'

Holly grinned and shook her head. 'So, welcome to *Findlater House* in Findlater Lane.'

'I can't believe you of all people are living in Findlater Lane,' Juliette said, shaking her head.

'I know, right. Weird!' Holly opened the back door of Juliette's car and grabbed one of the three bags. 'How long are you staying?'

'Just the weekend,' Juliette said.

'Really?' Holly asked, her eyes narrowed.

'I didn't know if we'd be staying in or going out, if it was a casual place or smart casual, if I needed beachwear or café society wear...'

'I get it,' Holly said and grabbed all three bags, closing the door with her hip. She passed one to Juliette. 'Let me give you the tour of *Findlater House*.'

~

Holly glanced around. Where was Alexander and would he behave now that she had a guest staying? She knew only too well that he wasn't keen on her being there, let alone anyone else having a sleepover, but he would just have to suck it up, she thought.

Holly turned and caught a glimpse of him at the door. *This will be interesting*, she thought, and returned her attention to Juliette, who was still in her work gear and high heels and wrestling with her bag up the few steps to the front door. She followed Holly inside.

Juliette couldn't see the Sergeant, and Holly was selfishly relieved, and surprised that she was possessive of him already. But, truth be told, she wanted to keep him to herself, at least for a while. Juliette had the power to charm and captivate everyone immediately, and Holly was the type who grew on people once they got to know her. She was cautious with her connections, but once made, fiercely loyal. And, she just wanted to have Alexander's attention on her for a little while.

'Well, this is lovely. I could live here, especially with that view,' Juliette said, standing inside the doorway and doing a complete circle.

'Great! Move here then, that would be brilliant!' Holly exclaimed.

Juliette grimaced. 'I'd miss the city.' She glanced to the wall where the three paintings hung. 'Nice landscapes,' she said, looking outside and back to the one that matched the view. 'That's clever. And who is this serious and handsome-looking man?'

Holly smiled. 'Meet the Sergeant!'

'Sir,' Juliette said, and saluted the portrait. 'Most dashing.'

Holly cocked her head to the side.

'I guess he's not bad looking,' she said, knowing he'd have a go at her later for that. But right now he couldn't even flinch. It was too easy, Holly thought.

Juliette tore her eyes away from the Sergeant and turned back to Holly. 'So, have you seen him?'

'Who?' Holly asked, knowing perfectly well who Juliette was asking after.

'The ghost!'

'You know that was Grandma's fantasy... it wasn't real,' Holly said.

'How disappointing,' Juliette sighed. 'I was hoping Loopy Lily's ghost relationship was real. I was thinking, you could ask that reality TV show to come here and see what they can find... you know, *Ghost Hunters!*'

'No way! All those people and cameras traipsing around trying to get a reaction in the dead of night.' Holly grimaced. 'It's bad enough that most of the town is curious about me moving into the ghost house, without making it a tourist attraction.'

'Well, that's no fun,' Juliette pouted. 'But it would be kind of cool to be in love with a ghost. I bet Lily loved the Sergeant ... I wonder if you could, you know, do it with a ghost?'

Holly nodded. 'I've given that some thought myself.'

The two best friends giggled like schoolgirls as they walked away from the Sergeant's portrait. Holly felt her face reddening and she hoped Alexander had left just his imprint in the frame and gone elsewhere well before this conversation started. *I wonder if he can do that?* she thought.

'Did I say thank you for having me?' Juliette asked.

'I think it is me who should be saying thank you for coming. I'll show you your room, come on,' Holly said, taking to the stairs. 'Then, I planned a dusk walk on the beach, a cocktail hour here, dinner at this lovely little restaurant in town, and I've got your favourite coffee capsules in!'

'All that and you had barely any notice!' Juliette said. 'Can't wait.' She raced up the stairs behind Holly, declaring everything quaint or marvellous.

Holly didn't see Alexander relax in his portrait and roll his eyes. If she had, she would have noticed his displeasure at the interruption to his household, and his time with Holly. They had things to do and this invasion was not welcome.

It was just after 11 pm when Holly bid Juliette good night, entered her bedroom and closed the door. She turned around and jumped in fright. Alexander was lying on his back in the middle of her bed.

'For the love of God, you scared me,' Holly said, placing her hand over her heart.

'Really?' he asked, rising and pushing himself over to the edge of the bed. 'You must be the safest person in this town, truth be known.'

She crossed her arms across her chest and studied him. 'Oh? How do you figure that?'

'You've got a ghost for a bodyguard. That's enough to freak most people out. So, you're not going to consider the reality TV idea, are you?'

Holly smirked. 'No, of course not. Why, do you want to?'

'Hell no. They're bizarre... one of the tenants that stayed here watched the show a few times. They walk around asking the ghost, "is there something you want to tell us? Can you give us a sign you're here?" What the bloody hell for? Like I'm hanging around waiting for them to arrive.'

Holly laughed. 'But you were hanging around listening...'

'Of course, I live here. Where am I supposed to go?'

'Shh,' she said, indicating Juliette was in the room next door. 'I don't want to explain why I'm talking to myself.'

Alexander rolled his eyes. 'She can't hear. She's got the French doors open and the ocean's louder than we are. And I heard the question about whether ghosts make good lovers! Hmph!' he said, not addressing it.

Holly walked towards her French doors and lowered herself into an olive green chaise chair beside them.

'So, do they?' she asked.

He shrugged. 'You know that agreement we had about answering your questions?'

'Yes.'

'Does this count as one of them?'

Holly sighed. 'Mm, I can see that plan is not going to work... I'd be better to catch you unawares with random questions. Okay, yes, it counts as one of them.'

Alexander grinned. 'Well, since you asked, I'm a brilliant lover whether I'm flesh and blood or in spirit form, but I can't give you references.'

Holly laughed. 'Sure you are. So, is this how will it work if I get a boyfriend? You'll hear everything we're up to then?'

'I bloody well hope not.' Alexander grimaced. 'Just do whatever funky thing you need to do upstairs and I'll stay downstairs. Easy.'

'Funky?' she teased. He smiled and looked away.

'Can you leave the frame and still be in it?' she asked. 'Sort of like leaving an impression of yourself?'

'No.'

'Mm, interesting, thanks for the detailed answer.'

Alexander smiled again. 'Okay, no, I have to be there or not there. It's the same answer but hopefully that makes you happier.'

Holly smiled. 'Ah, the fine art of conversation. Clearly you didn't get that skill.'

'And there have been so many people to converse with since I died over forty years ago.'

She grimaced. 'See, now I feel bad, but I'll get over it.' She noticed they were becoming very good at sparring, and she had to admit she was actually enjoying having the ghost around. Who would have thought?

Holly broached the subject she was most concerned about. 'Are you going to show yourself to Juliette?'

'No, she's bolshie. When is she leaving?'

'Bolshie? What do you mean?' Holly asked. 'A communist?'

'No. She does what she wants, steamrolls you, a bit full of herself...'

'Don't be crazy, she's nothing like that. She's just comfortable with me and she knows that I'm a bit of an introvert, so she likes to give me a hurry along, I guess.'

'Hmm,' Alexander said, unconvinced. 'We've got work to do.'

'She'll be gone late Sunday,' Holly said.

'Expecting anyone else after that?' he asked. 'You're not running a B-and-B here, you know.'

'No one else at this stage, Sergeant Grumpy,' Holly said. 'Oh, except for Luke, the gardener – he's coming tomorrow morning with the plans.'

'It's like bloody central railway station around here.'

'I promise that by Sunday night, you'll have your house back... well, except for me, I'll still be here. But we'll focus on you and only you.'

'If you say so,' he grumbled. 'I'll do my best to stay out of your hair until then, but after that, you're on my job. Yes?'

'Aye, aye, Sergeant,' she said, and saluted him. 'Now go away so I can go to bed.'

Alexander rose and, with a smirk in Holly's direction, slunk through the bedroom door without opening it, and disappeared from sight.

She sighed. *I really must get better at smirking,* she thought. *I hate being out-smirked.*

PLANS AND PLANTS

*A*lfred could smell Luke before he saw him. Luke had applied some cologne which Alfred couldn't remember him doing before... well, not since he had the crush on the young lady who used to deliver seedlings to the nursery every Friday. Luke had asked her out but she had just broken up with someone and wasn't ready. Next time he saw her, she was back with her ex-boyfriend, engaged, and that was that. No seeds to sow there.

Alfred hoped this time it might work in Luke's favour, if he got motivated. Alfred knew from experience nothing was perfect when it came to relationships... somewhere down the line comprises had to be made. Not that he was advocating Luke should settle, but rather step to it!

'What?' Luke asked, seeing Alfred staring at him.

'Good morning. You look and smell very presentable for your on-site visit this morning,' Alfred teased.

Luke reddened. 'Too much?'

'Not for a moment. Have you got the plans?' Alfred asked.

Luke nodded. 'Plans, tape measures, soil sample bags, pen, and pad.'

'Flowers?' Alfred asked.

Luke shuffled. 'Bit too much too soon, don't you think? I mean, how many people go to quote on a job and take the owner flowers? She'll think I'm hitting on her.'

'Yeah, we don't want that,' Alfred said, and rolled his eyes. 'Just take a fresh bunch of daffodils and say they are from me – they're cheery. Say it's a housewarming present to refresh the last bunch.'

'Yeah, that's good. Thanks. Do you want to give me an earpiece and feed me some smooth lines I can use as well?' Luke teased him.

'Oh, if I could, I would,' Alfred said, with a smile. 'Good luck, son.' He saw Luke's exasperated look and added, 'I mean, with getting the job!'

'Right,' Luke said, 'I'll be back with her order.' He grinned and walked out.

Alfred watched him walking away. As Luke passed the freshly cut flowers, he grabbed a bunch of the sunny daffodils and handed them to one of his team on the counter to wrap the stems.

Luke might not top the class in charm, but he knew gardens and that was the main focus of the visit, after all, Alfred mused. He might just make an impression.

Juliette jogged in from the beach just in time to see Holly removing her business sign from the front window of the house. She burst through the door.

'What's happening? Are you packing it in already?' she asked, panting, hands on her hip.

Holly looked confused. 'Packing it in?'

'The sign'.

'Oh, this,' Holly said. 'No, I never take on more than two jobs at once, so I take it down in between gigs.'

Juliette took her shoes off and shook them just outside the door, wiping the sand clear.

'You've been here five minutes and you've got two jobs already. That's impressive.' She sank down on a chair at the kitchen bench.

'I could use your help with one of my clients,' Holly said, thinking about Esther's necklace. She opened the fridge and waved a bottle of cold water at Juliette, who nodded.

'Do tell,' Juliette said.

Holly told her about the pink diamond and pearl necklace that went missing during World War II. She went to her desk in the open plan area nearby, grabbed the photo and placed it in front of Juliette.

'Oh my God, I so want to help you with this,' Juliette exclaimed.

'I knew you would, it's right up your alley,' Holly said. 'So, you've never seen it come up for auction?'

'No, I wouldn't forget a necklace made of pink pearls and a pink diamond, or a design like this... so unique. But if Esther thinks she saw it in Paris, then I'll do my research and maybe we should head there... if we can find a likely source.'

Holly grinned. 'That would be fun and Esther has paid me generously, so I can afford to cover our expenses.'

'Don't be ridiculous, you don't have to do that,' Juliette said, 'I'll cover my own. I've got clients to visit in the city, anyway. How exciting!'

'Except it's tragic,' Holly said, sobering and feeling a little guilty for her enthusiasm.

'Except for that,' Juliette agreed. 'Who is the other client?'

'Ah, that's a local village person who wants me to help with a missing relative... a descendant, not a recent case,' Holly explained.

'Family tree stuff. I'll leave that with you,' Juliette said, her disinterest obvious.

Holly glanced around to see if Alexander was in view, but she couldn't see him or his portrait from where she was standing. The next minute, she felt something brush her arm and she knew he was nearby. *Don't worry,* she thought, *I wouldn't betray your confidence.*

'Can't believe you've been here so little time and you already have two clients. You're amazing,' Juliette said, rising to go and shower after her jog.

Holly smiled. 'They're a supportive lot here, probably trying to give the new girl a break.'

They both turned to the window as a white work Ute pulled up out the front.

'Ah, that's Lucas, the landscaper,' Holly said, 'come and meet him before you shower.'

'I guess I can... I'm not too smelly,' Juliette said, with a quick sniff under each armpit. She glanced out of the window as Luke alighted. 'Oh wow, he's brought flowers. That's sweet.'

Holly went to open the front door. *The poor Sergeant,* she mused. *To think he once lived here happily alone and now he's got a houseful. Still, this energy might be good for him,* she decided.

Holly was always trying to fix something.

A TENDER HEART

*A*strid Bellerose placed the necklace back in its red velvet box. She lined the pink diamond in the centre and gently brushed her finger over the pale pink pearls. At twenty-one years of age, she wasn't really sentimental, yet. It was fair to say she hadn't even looked through the boxes of photos or antique pieces that sat in the attic. They reminded her of better times, when her mother was alive, before the accident. She had been raised by a workaholic absent father and a procession of aunts. Like her father, when she came of age she had thrown herself into the family business – work was her life and her father was happy for the publicity and exposure she brought the business, with her glamour and increasing social media following. They had got closer now they had a non-emotional connection, something they both understood.

But the necklace wasn't about her father or her mother – it was a love story. As a child, every time her grandmother had put the stunning necklace on her elegant neck, Astrid had asked her to tell the story again... how her great-grandfather had presented it to his bride-to-be with love. Her grandmother only wore it on very special occasions, when she accompanied Astrid's grandfather to balls and ceremonies. He always looked so handsome in black tie, a formidable figurehead for their family empire. Her grandmother called the necklace The Tender Heart and she promised that one day, it would be Astrid's to mind for the next generation. It was her birthright. Handed down by her great grandmother, to her grandmother – it skipped her mother, who died before it could be handed down – and now, it was Astrid's. All the women in her family had worn it at least once, even her Mum wore it on her wedding day and one day Astrid would pass it on to her own daughter.

It was breathtaking, and she didn't mind admitting that she looked gorgeous with it around her neck. Set off by her olive skin, raven shiny bob and pale green eyes, the necklace never failed to draw attention in person and on social media. And that was just how Astrid liked it.

'These plans are wonderful,' Holly exclaimed, as they pored over the designs. 'I love it, I love this garden!' She wished Alexander could be there to share his thoughts. She glanced around but could not see him, and then she felt a familiar cold brush against her arm and moved slightly to allow him a better view. He appeared before her eyes.

Holly glanced towards Juliette and Luke but they couldn't see him. She returned her gaze to Alexander as he studied the plans, and raised her eyebrow for his consent.

'I'd forgotten these,' he said, and smiled. 'They're great, let's do it.'

Holly smiled and nodded, then turned to see if anyone had noticed. *Phew, no.*

'Your father had so much talent,' Juliette was saying to Lucas.

'True, although it's been said I have more,' he said.

'Really?' Juliette grinned, 'And who says that?'

'Me mostly,' he replied, and Juliette and Holly laughed. He quickly added, 'I'm just kidding, he was much more talented.'

'I suspect talent runs in the family,' Juliette said, looking up at him as he towered at least a head over her in height.

Holly stood back, took in the garden and then returned her attention to Luke.

'I want to do this, Luke, it would be wonderful... but it all comes down to budget.' She sat down on the stone wall as he delved into his satchel.

'I've brought three quotes. One is for Dad's design as it is. The second is for a version of this design but with fewer established plants, which makes it a little cheaper but it takes longer for the garden to mature, and the third is a version of the second quote, plus you and your friends doing a little bit of the work as well to cut your costs.' He handed them over. 'Might be able to talk your resident ghost into doing some digging,' he teased.

Holly smiled. 'I'm sure he'd be happy to get his hands dirty.'

'Have you seen or heard anything?' Luke asked, curious. He looked from one woman to the next as he asked the question.

'No, but I've been on the alert,' Juliette said.

'I'm always open to company,' Holly said, and grinned. Again, she had got out of answering without being forced to lie. 'The three quotes are really thoughtful of you, Luke. Thank you. Can I have a few days to go over them and come back to you?'

'Have as much time as you need, you know where to find me and Alfred,' Luke said. 'Those are a copy so keep them on you.' He rolled up his own set of plans. 'Oh, I forgot, I've got something for you.' He pulled out an envelope and handed it to Holly.

'What's this?' she asked, opening it.

'The original photos my father took on his first visit here,' Luke said. 'I've copied them, so I thought you might like the originals back. There's a great shot of the couple that used to live here... the couple that commissioned the garden.'

Holly glanced at Alexander who was sitting on the opposite wall, visible to her only. He froze – anticipation, sorrow, she couldn't read him.

'Wow, thank you, Luke, I'd love to have them,' Holly said. Alexander was by her side in a heartbeat. She pulled the shots out and began to thumb through them.

Juliette moved to look over her shoulder, pushing the Sergeant out of the way. He moved to Holly's other side.

'These are great, the cottage hasn't changed much at all,' Juliette said, taking one of the shots from Holly.

Then Holly came to the shot of Alexander and Meghan. The Sergeant looked pretty much the same. He gasped beside her.

'Cute couple,' Juliette said, glancing over.

'It's Alexander – the Sergeant – and his wife, Meghan,' Holly said. 'They lived here once. She's beautiful.'

'He's pretty hot, too,' Juliette said. 'Where are they today?'

Luke glanced over Juliette's shoulder. 'They'd be pretty old now... in their seventies, eighties maybe, if they're still alive.'

Holly answered. 'I'm not sure what happened to Meghan, but the Sergeant has passed away... his portrait is inside.'

'Oh, that's him! I thought he looked familiar,' Juliette said.

Alexander faded away beside her. It was just the three of them now.

'Thank you, Luke,' Holly said, again.

'My pleasure.'

'So, if you've lived here all your life, you must know the best places to go,' Juliette said. 'I'm only here for the weekend and Holly is new in town, too.'

Holly gave her a slightly panicked look. Was she trying to set her and Luke up?

'I qualify for that,' he said, 'but I don't do nightclubs. I do know the best bar, pub and I'm not bad on the restaurant reviews, either. Looking for a tour guide?'

'Thought you'd never ask. It is Friday after all!' Juliette said, shooting Holly a grin.

'Right then... how about...' Luke began to make plans.

Holly faded out of the conversation as she slipped the photos back in the envelope. She had to find Meghan, for Alexander's sake and, more importantly, she had to find out how he died... so maybe then he could move on.

FINDERS' KEEPERS

lfred saw Lucas arrive back at the nursery looking pretty pleased with himself. He placed the last of the potted palms in Mrs Higginbottom's station wagon and, with a wave, saw her off. Alfred, too, wasn't without his admirers.

He fell into step with Lucas as he re-entered the nursery.

'So, did you get the order?' Alfred asked.

'No, but I will. I gave Holly three quotes and she made it perfectly clear that she was keen to accept one of them.' He nudged Alfred as they walked. 'You would have been very proud of me, Alfred. I was bordering on charming.'

Alfred laughed. 'Ah, I knew hanging around me would pay off.'

Lucas smiled and rolled his eyes as they entered the office.

'She's lovely, isn't she?' Alfred said, with a smile.

'She's great,' Lucas agreed. Alfred noticed he tried to hide a smile as he thought of her.

'I knew the first moment that I saw Holly, that you two would hit it off,' Alfred said, congratulating himself.

Lucas stopped and turned to Alfred.

'Holly?'

Alfred looked confused. 'Yes. Weren't you out quoting on Holly's garden?'

'Oh, sure. Yeah, Holly's nice, but Juliette, she's great. I'm taking both of them out on a tour of the town tonight. I'll have to leave early to get prepared,' he said, and wandered off towards the garden supplies.

Alfred stared after him. 'Juliette? Who's Juliette?'

Holly had the house to herself for a few hours at lunchtime on Friday while Juliette explored a few local antique stores and introduced herself to the owners and potential clients. She had been commissioned to find and buy articles for many antique dealers and it didn't hurt to network and press the flesh in person. Plus, despite the amount of luggage that she'd arrived with, Juliette was keeping an eye out for a new outfit for their night on the town.

'What do you want me to do first?' Holly asked, pulling a mug down from the rack. 'Want a cup of tea?'

'No, I'm good, thanks,' Alexander answered, leaning against the kitchen counter in his solid form.

Holly frowned. She wasn't sure why she asked the ghost in her house if he wanted a cup of tea but it seemed normal.

She continued. 'Do you want me to find Meghan first or find out how you died? What happens if I can't do either?'

Alexander shrugged. 'Then you're not much good at your job, are you? How have you been making a living?'

Holly's jaw dropped open and before she could snap back a retort, he grinned at her.

'Hmm, you'll keep,' she said, narrowing her eyes at him. 'What if I find out things you don't want to know?'

Alexander sighed. 'Well it's got to be better than what I'm going through now, hasn't it? Knowing nothing.'

Holly sighed. 'Okay.' She finished making her mug of tea and took it the table, lowering herself behind the laptop. 'You know, I thought that once you got to the other side, all would be revealed,' she said, fishing for a response.

'Did you now?'

'I'm guessing since Meghan's not with you, she's still here,' Holly continued.

'I can confirm that.'

'What happens if you tell me about the afterlife? Do you get thrown out? Oh, you have already been thrown out. Or are you here by choice?' Holly asked.

'Is that thing warmed up yet?' Alexander said, looking at her laptop.

'Fine then, don't answer,' Holly said, unimpressed.

'Is that your official question that I'm allowing you to ask, or are you just throwing random questions at me?'

'That's definitely not my official question.'

'Good, I won't answer then.'

She ignored him for a few minutes while she opened web pages and checked her email. Alexander paced in front of the table like a duck at a shooting gallery.

Holly took a sip of tea and started. Normally, she would begin with official records, but she was worried that the results might be too quick and direct with Alexander lingering. She wanted to break any news to him slowly. So, she began with Facebook profiles... a basic search to see if Meghan Austen was on social media. She didn't really expect her to be... but if she was anything like Holly's mother, the "old girls" had a good, strong network going!

Ten people with the name Meghan Austen came up, and of

course there was always the possibility that Meghan had remarried or gone back to her maiden name.

Alexander came around to look over her shoulder. Six of the Meghans could be eliminated immediately as they were clearly in the wrong age-group and one of them was alarmingly in-your-face with her assets.

'Bloody hell, I can't believe they put all that stuff up there for everyone to see!' he said. 'In my day, you'd buy the magazine and take it home in a paper bag.'

Holly laughed. 'Everything that was in that magazine is on here, if you want to go into the right... or wrong areas.'

He shook his head. 'Should be illegal.'

Holly opened up another Meghan profile.

'Is that her?' Alexander asked, stopping his pacing as the profile of an attractive older woman with Meghan's name appeared. 'That doesn't look like her. I suppose it could be her... no, can't be.'

Holly couldn't see much due to the protections this Meghan had put in place; you had to be a friend to see more.

'Do you know any of the friends in her list?' Holly asked.

Alexander lowered himself into the seat next to her. 'Nope. Show me the photo again.'

Holly blew it up, and they both agreed it wasn't an older Meghan. Holly did that for three more women, but none of them was Meg.

'How long will this take?' he asked.

'I don't know... however long it takes. I've spent weeks on some cases, while others, I've sorted out in half a day.'

'What if she's not on there?' Alexander asked.

'Then we search for other records.'

'What if...'

Holly raised her hand and stopped him mid-sentence. 'You know, you are going to get very tiresome, very fast. If you want me to continue, I think you should sit over there and chill out. I'll call you if I find something.'

'Fine,' he grumbled and appeared at a chair at the opposite end of the table.

'I'm going to go back to basics. The Birth, Death and Marriages records,' Holly said. 'Clearly we won't be needing the deaths, or you would have run into her.'

Alexander made a sound that resembled a *hmph*.

'So, marriage,' she continued.

Alexander almost flinched at the thought, and it wasn't lost on Holly. She stopped and looked at him with more sympathy.

'I can do this at the library if it upsets you.'

He shrugged, feigning indifference. 'It's fine, it's been decades. Of course she married... probably has grown-up kids and grandkids all over the country,' he said, his voice growing louder towards the end of the sentence. He threw his hands up in despair, and then disappeared.

Holly exhaled. *The poor Sergeant. All those years, and now he might find out the truth.*

'Right then, I'll keep you posted,' she said in a quiet voice, and returned her gaze to the screen.

Running through her normal procedures, Holly identified that Meg was still alive and was now seventy-five years of age. She did marry, but kept the name of Austen... interesting. Meghan's husband had died almost twenty years ago when Meghan was in her fifties. She had one child, also deceased. Holly would need to look into why, and who the father of the child might be. Was it Alexander, or her second husband, or someone else again? It obviously hadn't been an easy life for Meg. *Does she want to be approached or reminded of a painful time in her life?* Holly wondered. She pulled the photo of Alexander and Meg out of the folder and looked at it again;

they both looked so happy then. They had no idea what lay ahead.

Holly went to the newspaper archives, her subscription giving her full access – it was a necessity for her job. She looked up death and funeral notices and found the notice for Meghan's second husband. She now had a starting point of where she lived... she was in Salcombe then, when she was married... not that far away from *Findlater House.*

Holly ploughed on, returning to the basics – the phone directory. It always amazed her how many people didn't try the obvious first, but Meg was not listed there. She put Meg's name into the search engine and found some relevant local entries. It was coming together ... there was a Meghan Austen that played Bridge in that area, and was in a painting group – she was the coordinator of the painting group so she must have been into it. Her name was also listed for completing a two-day walk for charity with an all-female walking group.

And then, her eyes widened and she held her breath – she found a group photo of Meg's painting group at their Christmas party. She looked around but Alexander was nowhere to be seen, and she knew he wasn't hovering nearby, she could sense that. Enlarging the photos, she didn't have to search for Meg... there she was. Beautiful. Still slim and petite, silver hair cut to shoulder length, her little face and pointy chin... her sparkling eyes. She looked happy, and Holly was not sure she wanted to change that.

WOULD THAT BE JEALOUSY?

*A*lexander stood invisible, listening to the excited banter of Holly and Juliette as they prepared for their night out. Juliette turned to the left then to the right as she sized up her new dress in front of the mirror.

'I thought...' Holly teased, '... given that you came for two nights and brought three bags, that you had an outfit for every occasion.'

Juliette laughed. 'I didn't really have a night on the town outfit. I had a pub dinner outfit, an off to lunch on Sunday ensemble, walk along the beach clothes, a "tennis, anyone?" outfit, a "meet the gallery owners" dress and...'

'I get the picture,' Holly said, holding up her hand. 'Well, the sexy-night-out outfit looks fantastic.'

Juliette twirled around. 'There's nothing like a new dress to make you feel great, and this little boutique I found is brilliant... I could spend a fortune there,' she agreed, admiring her new blue fitted dress with a kick skirt that moved with her. Her heels were a little high for a seaside village, but Juliette insisted they made the outfit. Holly looked perfect in a crisp white dress complimenting her pale blonde hair. Finished off with gold jewellery, it said smart night-time beachwear.

Alexander studied Holly. He realised with some annoyance that the niggling feeling overcoming him was jealousy!

Pffft! How ridiculous, he thought, watching her.

I'm dead, she's not.

I'm happily married, she's single.

There's a decent enough bloke hanging around who might be interested in her, with a good gardening business... good riddance to them both. And she might get an even bigger discount on the garden if they get together – brillo!

He crossed his arms across his chest.

As long as he doesn't start having sleepovers. I'm prepared to let her live here, but I'm drawing the line at extras.

He saw the lights of a car pull up out the front.

'The taxi is here, let's go,' Juliette said, grabbing her handbag.

'I'll just lock up and leave a few lights on,' Holly said. 'Why don't you let him know we're on our way?'

Holly lingered behind as she waited for Juliette to get down the stairs and head out.

Alexander appeared.

'Are you okay?' she asked.

'Sure, why wouldn't I be?'

'Did you look over my shoulder this afternoon?'

'I thought about it,' Alexander admitted. 'But no. Not that I'm worried. I just thought I should leave you to do your thing.'

'Right.' Holly nodded.

'Did you find anything?' he asked, then shook his head. 'Forget it, tell me later.'

She nodded again. 'I'd better go, I'll see you later'.

'You look good,' he said, with a casual shrug.

'Thanks,' she smiled. 'Don't wait up'.

'Yeah, not likely.' He descended behind her down the stairs and watched as she closed the door, locked it from the outside and, with one last look at the window in his direction, set off happily and disappeared into the warmth of the taxi. It drove off and he was home alone. Again.

Alexander returned to Holly's desk, sat and flipped open a cream manilla folder that sat beside her laptop. He saw her scribblings... there was no hint to what she had found out about his own death or Meg. He moved on and saw the photograph of the necklace... that'd be worth a pretty penny, he thought. He read the story.

Then, deciding he'd do something good for Holly, just because, he faded from sight and left to make "enquiries". One hour or so later he reappeared and wrote on the edge of the file: *Check the family line –Bellerose of Paris.*

He put the pen down, closed the file and called it a night; or he would have, if ghosts slept.

LOVE AND SEA SPRAY IS IN THE AIR

*H*olly was just about to pour pineapple juice into her glass when she felt a chill near her arm, and a voice behind her said in a whisper: 'Incoming ghost alert.'

She chuckled, poured the juice and turned to face him. He looked so solid, even with the sun streaming into the kitchen through the window behind him; you'd never pick him for a ghost, she thought.

'Morning, Sergeant,' she raised her glass to him. 'Juice?'

'Good morning to you and no thanks, I'm not a pineapple guy. So that was a piss-weak party effort, wasn't it?' he said. 'Home at 12.30 pm? I know there was never a lot to do when we lived here... but in the last forty years I've been dead, haven't they opened anything after midnight?'

He leant on the edge of the table, folded his arms across his chest, and observed her.

'We could have partied on, but we had a good night and it was a good time to put an end to it. Besides, Juliette and I are driving to Salcombe for the day. We're going to check out the

village and the antique stores, do brunch, a bit of clothes shopping, and then head home mid-afternoon, so, we didn't want to
be wasted.' She studied his face as she mentioned Salcombe,
but Alexander showed no reaction; perhaps he didn't know that
Meghan lived there.

'Lord, so sensible,' he said, with a shake of his head.

'Yeah, sorry not to live up to your party standards. I feel like
a failure,' she joked.

He made a scoffing sound. 'Sure you do. So, did you have a
good night?'

'We did, thanks, it was great.'

'And this guy, Luke?'

'He's lovely.'

'What's lovely?' Juliette asked barging into the kitchen. She
looked around. 'Who are you talking to?'

Holly flushed. Alexander disappeared – not that Juliette
could see him yet.

'Myself. I do that a bit, talk to myself... I was just saying this
juice is lovely,' she said, holding up her glass. 'Just what I
needed. It will be fun exploring a new village today for a spot of
shopping, sightseeing and coffee!' she exclaimed, trying to
divert the conversation with excitement.

'I know. I haven't been there since I was a kid on a road trip
with Mum and Dad,' Juliette agreed. 'Last night was brilliant,
thank you. He's dreamy, isn't he?' she sighed.

Holly grinned. 'I think he thought the same of you,' she
said, waving the pineapple juice and when Juliette nodded,
filling a glass and passing it to her.

'Do you think he is interested?' Juliette asked. 'I couldn't
get a read on him.'

'Trust me, he was watching you every chance he got. You
should go out with him tonight, just the two of you,' Holly said.

Juliette sat at the table. 'No! I've come to visit you. That would be bad form.'

Holly could tell Juliette would love a date night out with Luke. She continued. 'And you've visited me... seen me Thursday night, all day Friday and last night, and all day today,' Holly said, generously. 'Luke hinted he'd like to see us Saturday night, meaning you, so let me have a night's recovery – you know I'm not as social as you are – and we can have breakfast out somewhere together Sunday morning before you return.'

'Really? I feel bad about that. Are you sure?' Juliette asked.

'Positive. Want some breakfast, or shall we do brunch at Salcombe?' Holly asked.

'Definitely the latter.' Juliette sighed. 'What are the stats on long-distance relationships surviving?'

'I'm not sure a three-hour drive from London could be classified as long-distance.'

'True. And I've always wanted to start my own antique buyer business. I could make this my base and travel everywhere and anywhere I need to,' she said.

Holly grinned at her. 'Um, you've given this some thought since you met Luke yesterday, haven't you?'

Juliette looked sheepish. 'You know me... plunge straight in. Life's short, or so they say. Although most of my relatives have lived to a ripe old age. Oh well, I'm off to the shower. Leaving in twenty minutes?'

'I'll be ready!' Holly said. She watched as Juliette drained the pineapple juice from her glass, placed it in the sink, and headed up the stairs to the shower.

Holly exhaled. Alexander didn't reappear.

Then Holly realised something. 'Oh great, I've become Loopy Lily!'

It was a quieter than usual morning at *How Does Your Garden Grow?*, but Alfred didn't mind a slow start on a Saturday. Luke was of the same mind – he hadn't got to bed until 1 am and even then, he didn't sleep much after that; he was happy for a quiet day at work.

'... so it went really well,' Luke said, giving him a summary in under a minute. 'I'm hoping to see them tonight, or just Juliette if I'm lucky.'

'Praise the Lord,' Alfred said, looking skyward. 'As long as she moves here when you settle down and you don't move to London.'

'Yeah, well hold that thought... we haven't had an official one-on-one date yet. I've got plenty of time to put her off,' Luke teased Alfred.

'Don't even joke about it. Seriously though, I am really happy for you, son,' Alfred said. 'I hope it will be wonderful.' He sighed, looked around and shook his head.

'What?' Luke said, concern sweeping his face as he glanced around to find out what was going wrong in the business.

'Well, it's quiet already... I knew it would be bad for business.'

Luke grinned. 'C'mon, not everyone saw me out with the two of them last night.'

'Just most of our single female clients,' Alfred said. 'Oh well, leave it to me, I can step up when the company needs me. I'd better increase my wooing of the old girls.'

Luke laughed and hit Alfred on the shoulder. 'Thought you'd be glad to see me showing an interest in something other than the plants,' he said, and lifted a bag of soil onto his shoulders.

'Oh, trust me, I am. Neither of us is getting any younger

and we need to start grooming someone to take over the business. How soon until you have kids, do you think?' Alfred winked at him, and went to serve a customer who was looking confused near the hydrangeas.

Luke was surprised by how much he liked the idea – that was a novelty.

ALONE TO BEGIN AGAIN

Juliette left later than she had planned – after 2 pm – to head back to London and to psyche herself for work on Monday. At last Holly found herself alone. Well, not really, as Alexander was there, but she was officially on her own now to begin her new life.

She realised since she had arrived last week, that her Aunty Kate, her ex-husband and Juliette had all arrived almost back-to-back, but she had run out of immediate visitors – she was alone, starting again. She really had to do it. Holly waved goodbye to Juliette until she was out of sight and then she stood there, not knowing what to do. There was no work to go to tomorrow, although she had work to do for clients; there was no-one to meet and no-one local she could call and say, 'Hey, want to meet for a drink?' She was alone for the first time in years, and she couldn't move.

She didn't want to go back into the house, which would feel empty now, so she headed to the beach, determined to go for a long walk from one end of the cliffs to the other. She needed a few hours to think through life, and get back in the good space she was in when she first rented *Findlater House* and was excited about the change. Perhaps the visitors were too soon – it would have been better if she had established herself in her new zone first.

It was a beautiful afternoon; the sun was out, the air was fresh, and the beach was dotted with families, walkers, and the occasional optimistic sunbaker. She took off her shoes and walked along the waterline. Holly had only been walking for about fifteen minutes when she stood on something cold. She jumped away from the object, expecting to see a jellyfish, but it was something shiny and metallic. Holly reached for it and picked up a gold pocket watch. She looked around to see if anyone had recently walked that way, thinking they might have dropped it, but there was no-one nearby.

Hmm, she mused... yet again a lost item had found her. They always did. It was why she started *Lost, Found and Broken* – she was the human magnet for all things missing or broken. The watch was old, perhaps even an antique, with a slim chain full of sand and, surprisingly, not rusty. Holly kept walking slowly ahead as she pried open the clasp. She gasped; it was beautiful. Inside, it was decorated with small moon and sun engravings and had distinct Roman numerals. It was not working, but she expected that when it had been lying in sand and saltwater.

'Where have you come from, my friend?' she asked. 'You're very special.'

Holly looked out to sea and imagined it falling off an old sailing ship, hopefully not with its owner attached; or being washed ashore from buried pirate's treasures; she had a good imagination. Suddenly, the watch had made her feel better; it had reminded her of her usefulness.

'Well, we'd better find your family and get you home,' she

told it. 'We've got a pearl and diamond necklace, and a wife to find, too, not to mention a mystery to solve!'

And with renewed energy in her step, she hastened her walk, shoulders back, inhaling salt air and everything looked better.

Alexander had *Findlater House* to himself for the first time in days. Holly had headed for the beach, her best friend was gone, the ex-husband had vanished back to London, along with the Aunty, and hopefully the gardener was watering his own plants!

He sat on the couch with a glass of the finest port and the Stones on the record player. His foot tapped away to the tune and he contemplated having a cigar. He didn't really care if the "tenants" didn't like the smell and complained to the real estate agency. But he begrudgingly cared if Holly didn't like it, not that he was really prepared to admit that. He rarely had a cigar, but every now and then, with a good port, there was nothing better.

Then the door burst open. Holly slipped off her shoes, banged them together to get the sand off and, leaving them outside, came in with a show of energy. She heard the music and her eyes scanned the room, spotting Alexander relaxing in the lounge area.

'You're back,' he said.

'You sound surprised. Did you think I had left, too?' she asked. 'Or were you hoping?'

'No way, young lady, I've got plans for you,' he said, rising from the couch.

'A pocket watch found me!' she exclaimed excitedly. He

was relieved. He'd expected her to be morose and was contemplating ways to lift the mood, but now he could just chill out.

'Yeah, a hat, a key, a dog collar and one of those modern CD-things found you as well. I picked them up from the front yard,' he said, indicating the items on the kitchen table.

'Oh well,' she shrugged, 'we'll find their families.' She looked up at him. 'And yours, too.'

He smiled and nodded. 'I believe you will.'

THE RESEARCH BEGINS

*T*he next morning, armed with her laptop, Holly arrived at the library right on opening time. It was in a large building that appeared to be a former church and church hall. She intended to go through the microfiche and seek any relevant local news stories on Alexander's death – she could have looked up the news clippings at home but she didn't want him hovering behind her. Not that Holly could stop him coming to the library and hovering there, but she figured he wouldn't leave the house unless he had to; he sure as hell grumbled enough about accompanying her to the beach when he thought he had to protect her. Kind of sweet really, she thought.

Hmm, I must find out if that's a choice or necessity, she mused. He might have a radar whereby he can only travel so far, or maybe he's not strong enough to be too far from his base. So many questions, so little time...

'Wow,' Holly said, entering and taking in the beautiful surroundings. There were bookshelves on every available inch of floor space and climbing up the walls as well, accessible by stepladders and staircases. Long, dark timber tables ran down the middle of the room for anyone wanting to study, read or work, and tasteful black and silver chairs were pushed in, waiting to be used. There had been some money spent on this library. Add to this, beautiful stained-glass windows featured saints, not books and the occasional original church pew was placed around the library for those who wanted to sit and ponder or read.

She was the first to arrive, admitted by the librarian – a woman in her thirties who looked like she had just stepped out of a gothic fancy dress store. Her name tag read *Abby*.

'Yeah, it's pretty special, isn't it?' Abby smiled. 'Newbies always react like that. You're the lady that just rented the ghost cottage, aren't you?'

Holly grinned. 'That's me! Word travels fast. I was hoping to use the microfiche to research the ghost's history.'

'Sure, that's doable,' Abby said, indicating Holly should follow. 'So, seen the ghost yet?'

'I made tea for him just this morning,' Holly answered, and it was Abby's turn to laugh. She knew the truth would do... who would believe that? 'This place is amazing. I never thought a small town... well...'

'Would have a library like this?' Abby finished. 'We were lucky, a benefactor provided it. One of our elderly citizens who loved to read and spent a lot of time at our previous dinky library, bequeathed his fortune to build our village a landmark library. Fortunately, one of our old churches and its hall became available so it was converted. That's our dedication area over there,' she said, nodding to the pew under the stained-glass window.

'How good of him. Shame he never got to see it,' Holly said. 'Have you been working here for long?'

'Feels like it,' Abby said, dramatically. 'Just kidding. I love it here. I've been here for ten years and two months now.'

'No way! You don't look old to be working here for that long,' Holly said, narrowing her eyes suspiciously.

Abby switched on the microfiche reader to let it warm up, and leaned on the edge of the large, dark timber table where it sat. Holly placed her bag and laptop down on the table and pulled out a chair.

Abby continued. 'My grandmother was the village librarian for a hundred years... well, maybe forty years, and I came here to do work experience with her after doing my library qualification. Thought it'd be fun, you know... small town, stick around for a few months and leave.'

'And you stayed? Seems to be catching,' Holly said.

'I stayed for three months, then six months, then a year, then two years, then Grandma passed away and I just kept going.'

'Oh, I'm sorry about your grandma,' Holly said.

Abby shook her head. 'She died doing what she loved. Literally had a heart attack while reading a romance novel in her lunch break in the A to F section. All over in a second,' Abby said, clicking her fingers. 'Worse ways to go.'

'For sure,' Holly agreed.

'Although I wouldn't be caught dead in the romance aisle,' Abby said. 'If you find me dead there, promise me you'll drag me to fantasy?'

'Consider it done,' Holly promised, with a grin.

Abby turned to the door as a couple of customers entered. 'Righto, you're all set.' She returned her attention to the screen. 'On the left is the date column. Click through to what year and month you want and keep clicking until you find it. Use this button to blow things up bigger, this one to reduce the size.'

'Got it, thanks,' Holly said, keen to start.

'If you need a hand, just yell. I'll just be over there getting my checkout stamp ready,' she teased, and with a flurry of black skirt and flick of long black hair, left Holly to it.

Holly went straight to the year of Alexander's death – 1972. If only she knew the month. She grabbed her phone, went to the deceased search function at the cemetery he was buried in, and searched for him. She found him, and a photo of his headstone. Holly felt a weird stabbing pain, a sense of heartache. The rational part of her brain knew that he was dead, but seeing this meant he really *was* dead!

She looked up, took a deep breath and chastised herself for being stupid. 'He's a ghost, a ghost who needs your help... get on with it,' she told herself. She checked for the date on his headstone and jotted it down. *Righto.* Holly returned her attention to the microfiche, scrolling to that month, and the date.

She expected the story to be on the front page, or early general news as it was called, and she was right. Two days after his death, it was a large headline on the front page – *LOCAL SOLDIER DIES IN BELFAST* – followed by a few paragraphs and a page number to direct readers to the rest of the story.

Holly felt her heart quicken; she was becoming far too emotionally attached to Alexander, it was insane. She'd end up being Loopy Lily at this rate, she mused. But then again, Alexander was looking for his wife, not Holly, so probably no fear of the two of them forming a life-long bond; well, her life, anyway given Alexander's life was technically spent!

Before she increased the file size to read it, Holly looked around. She knew it was crazy, but she wanted privacy and didn't want anyone asking what she was doing, or an unexpected ghost glancing over her shoulder. To her relief, she found that the coast was clear.

This was it, the article on the death of Sergeant Alexander Austen. She widened it to full screen and read:

Local soldier dies in Belfast

*Well-known resident Sergeant Alexander Austen who
resides in Findlater House on Findlater Lane was
fatally injured on duty in Belfast yesterday.*

*The Austen name is long associated with the village,
and Sergeant Austen and his wife, Meghan, moved into
Findlater House two years ago with a view to following
in their ancestor's footsteps, contributing to the village
and raising a family.*

*The Sergeant's death is being investigated but it appears
he died from a single stab wound to the heart, delivered
from the front.*

*Mrs Austen was unavailable for comment but relatives
of the Sergeant thanked the public and the Royal
Victoria Hospital staff who came to his aid and did their
best to save him.*

*A spokesperson from the military said Sergeant Austen's
death occurred during an incident in Belfast where
several bombs caused panic and confusion in the streets.
Sergeant Austen died just after admission to the hospital. A military enquiry is underway. Funeral arrange-
ments will be advised.*

'Wow,' Holly said, quietly. It was surreal to read about his
death. Now, she just needed to find an article about the official
cause, get her hands on the coroner's report and find out why
Meg left the village. Simple, she thought, and sighed.

LOVE IT WHEN A PLAN COMES TOGETHER

*H*olly packed up for the day. Not because she had been at the library that long, maybe two hours at the most, but because the drama of what she was reading had to be absorbed incrementally.

She had a plan. She needed to do her research and thoroughly, so she could tell Alexander how he died accurately and sensitively. Then, and only then, would she have a reason to contact Meghan on the basis that she had historic information to share. If Meghan chose not to see her, well, that was her prerogative but at least she had a reason to put her foot in the door, Meghan's door. Right this minute, though, she wanted to go to *The Cup and Saucer* and have tea and cake; she felt that she had earned it.

'Find what you need?' Abby asked her, as Holly came up to the front desk. Abby didn't look quite so out of place with half of her black attire and boots hidden behind the counter.

'I did, thank you. But there's a lot more I need so I'll be back. I'm just pacing myself,' Holly said.

'Well, we're open every day. If I'm not here, Sebastian Cartwright the Third is in,' Abby said.

Holly's mouth dropped and then she laughed. 'Really? Is that a person or a cat?'

Abby grinned. 'Sebastian Cartwright the Third – Seb – is great, but he's seventy-nine years of age and is very formal. So, I always call him by his full official title, he likes that.'

'Formal? Do I have to curtesy to the gentry?' Holly teased. She had a floral dress on which looked rather ridiculous next to Abby's gothic fashion, but she dropped a quick curtsy, extending her skirt nevertheless, to show it could be done.

'Oh, you've got it down,' Abby said. 'I suspect he'd appreciate it, but no, Seb is very laid back and he has a wicked sense of humour. I once found a paranormal zombie book shelved in the women's self-help section!'

Holly laughed. 'Cheeky.'

'He can be,' Abby agreed. 'Seb had a very distinguished library career in London but he retired here, and likes to keep his hand in. Besides, he can't bear a library to be closed, so it works out well for me, him and the community,' Abby said. She had an idea, snapped her fingers and her eyebrows shot up. 'Come to think of it, he's an expert on history and he's lived here now for a couple of decades, so he might be able to give you some first-hand insight to anything you are looking for. Just a thought. He's in on Wednesday.'

'That's a great idea,' Holly said. 'Thanks, Abby, I'll come back then and pick his brains!'

A woman with three young children came to the checkout desk; all of them had their arms full of books. She saw Holly's surprised expression and explained, 'We read a couple of books a night and if we run out, I have to make the stories up!' She rolled her eyes.

'Good Lord, no!' Holly played along.

'My thoughts exactly,' the exhausted mum said. 'This is a week's worth!'

'How wonderful! Well, I'll leave you to the books. See you soon', she said, with a nod to Abby. 'By the way, you didn't lose a quill, did you?' Holly held up a replica of an old fashion pen, made with a long white feather.

'Oh wow, that went missing months ago!' Abby exclaimed. 'Where did you find it?'

'It found me, I think,' Holly said, handing it over, pleased to have found its owner. 'It was wedged down the side of the chair at the microfiche.'

'How did you get there?' Abby asked the quill, then returned her attention to Holly. 'I do my book signings with this quill, it's very special,' she said, and smiled, grateful to have it returned. 'I thought I'd left it at my last talk. Thank you.'

'You're an author? How exciting!' Holly said. 'Are your books in the library?'

'They are. But they are all about vampires, ghosts, zombies, guardian angels and girls that kick butt... I like the fantasy genre,' she said. 'Let me know if you want to read one.'

Holly grinned. 'Sounds like real life to me,' she said, and this time Abby laughed at the thought.

'Yep, you and Seb will get on very well.' Abby nodded.

Holly left her stamping the children's books; after all, tea and cake were calling Holly's name.

The house was quiet when Holly entered after her café break. There was no sign of Alexander – no music playing, nothing left underfoot or evidence that he had been around.

She changed into more casual wear and fired up her laptop

THE HOUSE ON FINDLATER LANE

again. This afternoon, she was working on Esther's beautiful missing necklace. She could almost feel those pearls around her own neck, they were so creamy and beautiful. Instinctively, her hand went to her throat where the necklace would rest; it was often how she found things... visualising them in their natural state.

Holly opened Esther's folder and saw the handwritten scribbles on the first page – handwriting that wasn't her own! It read: *Check the family line – Bellerose of Paris.*

She froze. Who wrote that? Alexander? Juliette when she was visiting?

She didn't have time to call Juliette. She preferred to do that on her afternoon walk on the beach so she could dedicate a good twenty minutes or more to agreeing that yes, Lucas was lovely. No, Juliette wouldn't have had a chance to do her research and write this clue, it had to be Alexander. And when did he write this?

She made another cup of tea – she was quite the camel and could drink copious amounts of the amber fluid – and with her laptop warmed up, began to investigate the Bellerose family of Paris.

Alexander appeared, seated opposite her at the table and she jumped in fright.

He cleared his throat. 'Sorry, incoming.'

'A little late now, isn't it?' Holly said, drawing a deep breath. 'Where have you been?'

'Where have *you* been?' he countered.

'To the library, to do some research,' Holly said. 'I met Abby, the librarian.'

Alexander sat back in his chair and crossed his arms against his chest. 'Abby... nope, can't say I know her. When Meg and I lived here, the librarian was an old duck.'

'Ah, that would have been Abby's grandmother. She had a

heart attack one day at work – clearly after your time – and Abby, who is a librarian as well, stayed on!'

'Are you sure it was a heart attack and not a bloodless coup?' Alexander asked, narrowing his eyes.

Holly grinned. 'That's a fairly drastic way to get a job, don't you think? But you tell me, was there foul play?' she asked, raising her eyebrows theatrically.

'No, I'm just winding you up. She was a hundred when we lived here, so it was only natural that she'd drop over soon enough,' he said.

Holly shook her head and returned her attention to her laptop.

'What?' he asked.

'So sensitive.'

Alexander shrugged. 'I'm dead, too, I can get away with it. What were you researching at the library?'

'You,' Holly said.

He brightened. 'An interesting morning for you then!'

'Indeed!' Holly smiled. It was impossible to pretend to be affronted by Alexander, he just cut through her mood. She studied him without being too obvious. He really was very handsome but she'd be the last to tell him that. Imagine how big his head would get, she thought.

'Yes, a fascinating morning,' she continued, 'but I'm not telling you anything until I know everything. Then I'll share and then we will work out a strategy for Meg.'

'Well, bollocks to that! How long will that take?' he groaned.

'Why? Are you worried you'll get old waiting? That you'll kick the bucket before I get results?' she asked. 'You are one of my few, make that my only client, who doesn't have a *dead*line.' She laughed at her own play on words.

'Oh, ha-ha. Technically, that's not quite true, I could be

recalled,' he said, looking skyward.

'Can that happen?' Holly asked, wide-eyed.

'You never know,' he said.

Holly scoffed. 'You're making that up.' She sat back with her cup of tea. 'Isn't it beautiful in here? The light coming through the windows, the sun on the water, the froth rising as it hits the rocks.' She sighed.

Alexander turned to look. 'Yeah, lovely.' He turned back. 'So, did you find something?' he asked.

Holly rolled her eyes and sat forward again, putting down her cup.

'Yes, and I'm going back on Wednesday to do more research, and talk to a library historian who is in on that day,' she said, making up an appropriate title for Sebastian Cartwright the Third. 'What happens if you get recalled?'

'Back to that? Is this your allocated question for working on my file?'

She frowned. 'It's tough. I don't know if I want to waste my limited questions on that one. By the way, did you write this on Esther's file,' she pointed to the blue ink writing, 'the name Bellerose?'

He nodded. 'Thought I'd cut you a break.'

'Thank you, Alexander!' she said, pleased. 'So why can't you find out about your own death if you can find out snippets of history like this?'

'It doesn't work like that. We can't access... ah-ha, you just tricked me into an answer. Mm... I'm onto you.'

Holly grinned. 'Okay then. Well, who is the Bellerose family? What's the story?'

'I can't do your job for you, that's for you to find out, but my source is reliable,' he said, tapping his nose.

'Thanks again, that's great to have a head start.'

'Yeah, don't mention it. The quicker you finish that case,

the more time you have to spend on me. Anyway, got to go,' he said.

'Where?' Holly asked, but he had vanished before she had finished the question. She sat alone with the afternoon light pouring in and felt content. Outside, she could hear the waves crashing against the rocks. The tide was in, and the village was back to its normal, peaceful state with the weekend tourists gone.

I wonder where he goes and what he does when he's not here? she mused. *Maybe that's my next allowed question.*

Holly glanced at the clock; it was just after 2 pm. She liked a structured day, so she planned to keep working until 4 pm and then take her afternoon walk along the beach. 'Right, two hours on Esther's file,' she said to herself, and marked the hours on the front of Esther's file for billing.

'To work!' she declared.

Just before her 4 pm walk, her phone pinged with a message.

She smiled as she read Juliette's note. *Coming this weekend to see you and Luke.* She had inserted a smiley face. *Can I stay Friday night? Might not need to stay Saturday night if I get lucky!* and another smiley face.

Holly messaged straight back. *Absolutely! Looking forward to it. Bet Luke is too* and inserted her own smiley face and a kiss or two.

A GREEN DELIVERY

*H*olly was a morning person, usually up and jogging before 7 am – most days before 6.30 am – but the sound of a van pulling up out the front at 6 am had her jumping out of bed. The side of the van featured the logo *How Does Your Garden Grow?* and Luke slid out of the driver's seat accompanied by two other staff members, who were squeezed on the front bench seat with him.

'They're here!' Holly exclaimed and quickly pulled on her running gear and a sweatshirt. She raced down the stairs, and Alexander appeared just before she opened the front door.

'What's going on? Everything okay?' He looked around, alarmed.

'Yes, good morning! The plants are here,' she said, excited and clapped her hands.

'Christ, I thought we were being raided and I'd have to hide my stash,' he said, and rolled his eyes.

Holly stopped dead in her tracks and looked at him, confused. He opened the front door for her and she stepped out – with a quick backward glance to Alexander. She greeted the delivery guys and Luke. He beamed at her; after all. Holly was the source of introduction to his new romance and current happiness.

'I come bearing greenery,' he said, 'and labour.'

'Fantastic!' Holly said. 'How exciting.'

Luke introduced his staff. 'This is James Johnson, call him J.J., and Michael Batton, he prefers Mick.'

Holly nodded. 'J.J., Mick... I'm Holly.'

'We know.' J.J. grinned at her. 'We've heard all about you and your best friend.' He rolled his eyes with exaggeration. Luke reddened and thumped J.J.'s arm.

'So, this delivery is for you, I believe,' Mick said, opening the back of the van with a flourish. Holly moved around the back of the van and looked in.

'It's a forest!' she declared and they laughed. She felt a cold rush of air beside her and turned to see Alexander; no one else could see him. He nodded, impressed.

J.J. and Mick started unloading, while Luke grabbed his clipboard and got Holly to sign to say the delivery had arrived.

'You know everyone around here complains about the sandy soil, but the best thing about this delivery,' Luke said, watching as it was being hauled out of the van, 'is that by the time we leave in a couple of hours, you've got an instantly beautiful garden. Pots are great for that.'

'It's going to make such a difference, Luke. Thanks!' Holly agreed.

Luke threw the clipboard and pen back on the front seat, and rejoined her.

'So, Juliette's back this weekend. What do you say about a double date on Friday night? You know, just a chilled-out group of four friends, having a drink and dinner?' he asked, clarifying the double date comment when he read her reluctance.

'Um, I don't have a partner,' she said, her eyes wide with

alarm. She felt Alexander disappear beside her. Surely Luke couldn't see him?

Luke continued. 'I know, Juliette told me. But J.J. is free Friday night and wouldn't mind a quiet drink or two. No pressure, but what do you think?'

Holly glanced over at the guy of about her own age who was carrying huge potted plants out of the back of the truck. His muscles were flexed, his legs strong, he was fit and handsome. A baseball cap hid his hair and he wasn't as tall as Holly would have liked, but hey, they weren't getting married, just making up a group for a night out.

'Sure, sounds great,' she said with a small shrug, and turned back to Luke. 'But I'm up for a quiet night on Saturday night, so if you and Juliette wanted to do your own thing... no pressure to have her home,' she said, raising her eyebrows suggestively.

'I'm hearing you, thanks,' Luke said, with a grin.

'I'm off for a run. I'm guessing you'll be here when I come back?'

'For sure. We'll be here for about three or four hours. We should be done by then,' Luke said, taking photos for his before and after album at the nursery. 'Run hard,' he said.

'Always,' she agreed. 'Okay, well, most times...'

He laughed again. She saw J.J. and Mick look her way as she started off running. It was good for her ego.

She felt happy. It was all coming together. She had a cottage she loved for the next six months; good company at home, even if it was a ghost; work already and she hadn't counted on getting any assignments at least for a few months; a happy best friend; and a new garden. And something to do Friday night. Yep, *Findlater House* was showing her a good time.

∾

Holly came through the front door after her run feeling super-charged, not to mention excited by one-third of the new garden being completed already. But that's when she hit a brick wall – or rather an ice wall: Alexander.

He stood, arms folded, just inside the door, waiting for her. He looked handsome for a dead guy; tall, domineering, dark and brooding.

'You can't go out with him,' he said.

Holly breathed out, looked around and frowned. 'Sorry, what?'

'The double date... you can't go out with that delivery guy-cum-gardener,' Alexander said, again with a nod towards J.J. in the front yard.

Holly looked out as well.

'Why not? He seems like a nice guy, he clearly looks after himself,' she said, watching the muscles flex in his arms and legs as he squatted to move a very large pot plant, 'and if Luke can speak for him, that's a good enough character reference for me.' She moved away from the window and into the kitchen to get a glass of water.

Alexander made a *hmph* sound.

Holly returned with her glass of water and looked through the window again. 'So exciting, seeing it come together, isn't it? It's going to look great.'

She noticed Alexander hadn't said a word about the garden despite staring out at it. His gaze was exclusively reserved for the workers, J.J. in particular.

'So what don't you like about J.J.? Do you know some-thing?' Holly asked, her attention still focussed on the front garden activity.

Alexander shook his head. 'How could I know something? I just met him, too, and he's alive.'

'Well, you knew something about the history of that necklace and whoever has it now is alive.' Holly finished her glass of water in several long gulps, and spent much longer looking at J.J. than she normally would, partly to stir up Alexander.

She turned to him. 'If you don't know anything about J.J., then one might think you were jealous.'

'Ha!' he scoffed. 'That's ridiculous. I'm married, and dead.'

'Exactly,' Holly said and, giving him a smile, she returned her glass to the kitchen, took the stairs two at a time to the shower, and turned back in time to see Alexander still looking out the window with a distinct frown on his brow as the new garden evolved.

THE SERGEANT DIES... AGAIN

*S*ebastian Cartwright the Third was charming. If she didn't know better, Holly might have thought he was a stand-in for Santa Claus at Christmas. He was portly, well-groomed, dressed in a tweed suit and had white hair with a matching white beard. Abby, the librarian, must have briefed him and before Holly could finish introducing herself, he was shaking her hand vigorously.

'If only we had more young people interested in exploring history, my dear,' he said. 'You are most welcome. The microfiche is expecting you!'

Holly thanked him with equal enthusiasm.

'I'll just finishing opening up and help a few customers, but let me know when and if you want my help or want to reminisce,' he said, with a wink. 'Well, I'll reminisce. You, of course, weren't born before the nineties, I imagine.'

'Correct, Mr Cartwright!'

'Please call me Sebastian, everyone does... except for Abby who likes to use my full name. But I secretly think she wants me to reciprocate and call her Lady Abby of the Village by the Sea.'

Holly laughed. 'That does suit her.'

'It does indeed,' Sebastian agreed.

'Thank you, Sebastian, I would like to pick your brains, but no hurry,' Holly said, as several people came through the door and an elderly lady made her way to the reception desk. With a wave, Holly ventured to the same microfiche reader she had used during her last visit; she was a creature of habit.

As she waited for it to warm up, her phone beeped with a message. For a moment, she expected it to be Alexander, forgetting that he hadn't conquered that technology yet. It was from Juliette. Holly saw the first line and held her breath.

Got an update on your necklace. I think your source is onto something. The Bellerose family of Paris have a pearl and diamond necklace insured. They got it valued a few years back, that's how I found the record. Tell you more at the weekend. Fancy a trip to Paris? Jx

She typed back: *Wow, this is big! Can't wait to see you and hear more. Thanks, J. Hx*

The timing was perfect. Holly was due to give her first report to Esther on Monday of next week, and she was going to have to throw herself heavily into the research for the next few days to have something to present. Juliette's first visit, the social weekend, Alexander's research and now the garden had put her slightly behind... not to mention her ex-husband's visit and the day required to get back on her feet.

She opened her notes and found the date and article she was up to last Monday when researching Alexander's story. She started searching for it again on the microfiche.

'Let's get to work,' she said, coaching herself. 'Lots to be done.'

~

Alfred would be pleased to have Luke back at the nursery. It was always the way. Traditionally, mid-week at *How Does Your Garden Grow?* was quiet, but of course today, when Luke and the boys were on a job, it seems the whole village needed plant supplies. It was nearing 11 am, so he expected him back at any moment.

As Alfred saw off another customer, and left the two young ladies at the checkout to finish the orders, he saw a classic old car – a Riley – turning into the nursery car park. He knew the driver and this was one customer he was pleased to see. Alfred waited and raised a hand in a wave. Esther looked equally pleased to see him as she returned his wave and rolled up her car window. He'd always been a bit sweet on Esther, and he suspected she felt the same, but they had both lost the loves of their lives and felt too eminently sensible to tempt fate by seeking out another.

He was also a great admirer of her choice in vehicles – a classic 1959 Riley Two-Point-Six, 4-door saloon. The car wasn't a great success in its day, but it looked like a mighty classic now in its green duotone colouring of Shannon green over leaf green, its bodywork preserved to perfection.

Alfred moved towards the vehicle and opened the car door for the handsome woman inside, who was but a few years younger than him.

'She's looking grand, the old girl,' he said, admiring her car.

'And I'm feeling it!' Esther joked, taking the compliment for herself.

Alfred laughed. 'The car looks good, too,' he teased. He offered his hand to assist her out of the car, and Ester accepted, grabbing her basket from the floor opposite as she exited.

'One owner, and it only gets driven here, to the shops, and to church on Sunday, so it should be in mint condition,' she agreed. 'Busy morning, clearly.' She noted the car park traffic. 'I'm after a few new herbs for my herb garden... the coriander doesn't seem to like me.'

'I wouldn't take it personally. Coriander is very temperamental. Care for a cup of tea first? I'm long overdue for a break,' Alfred said.

'Love one.'

Alfred led the way. The nursery had a lovely tea room for staff and their guests – a greenhouse with caffeine.

'I hear a romance has kindled between Holly, the young lady at *Findlater House,* and Luke,' Esther said, placing her bag at the foot of a chair. She took a seat as Alfred put the kettle on and found some cups.

'Ah, I wish it was that simple,' he said. 'Luke's fallen for Holly's best friend, Juliette. Might be a good thing. At least she doesn't live in the village yet, so he's not likely to send another lass running from here.'

Esther laughed. 'He's a good catch, that boy. You know that I've hired Holly to do some work for me?'

Alfred turned to face her. 'You did mention that, along with the fact she was single, which I dutifully passed on and will continue to spread the word. I'm glad you have Holly on the job. Your sentimental family pieces should not be lost to history.' He placed a milk jug and sugar bowl on the table.

'How do you know that's what I've hired her for? I might have hired her to type up my memoir.'

Alfred laughed. 'The memoir you keep threatening to write?'

Esther smiled. 'Yes, that memoir.'

'Sorry about the mug of tea, the teapot went missing. I

suspect Luke hid it to stop me lingering in here drinking the whole pot,' Alfred said.

Esther laughed and accepted the mug of tea from him with a nod of thanks.

Alfred continued: 'I'd like to get my hands on your memoir – a mighty fine read that would be, too. But Luke told me about Holly's business line so I guessed that the necklace would be a logical business proposition.'

Esther nodded. 'I thought it was worth one more go to try and retrieve it. I have a catch-up with her on Monday. I hope she won't be as disappointing as all the others... but I feel positive about this young lady.'

Alfred sat opposite her and was about to shake some biscuits out of a packet when Esther held up her hand.

'I've just baked. I was bringing you some of my shortbread,' she said, reaching into the basket.

'Ah, make my day!' he said, sitting back. Returning his thoughts to Holly, he said: 'She has been here a minute and already she's got Luke hitched to her girlfriend, scored a job from you, and hired us to landscape her yard. I think she might be a go-getter. Strange she's staying in *Findlater House* on her own, though. Did she mention the ghost to you?'

'No, but the strangest thing... She kept looking at the chair beside her as we spoke – as though it was occupied and she was including someone in the conversation. Do you believe the Sergeant is still there? In the house?'

'Well, if he is, she's tamed him, too,' Alfred said, and shook his head in wonder.

Holly's father would have called it a conspiracy; her mother would have said it was a mystery and the librarian, Sebastian, suggest it was a time in history best left buried. For Holly, it was a tragedy. That's what any untimely death was and the Sergeant's death was definitely premature.

Sebastian took a deep breath.

'You have to understand,' he said, 'it was a different time then. There have been a lot of battles that soldiers fought because it was their duty... they didn't question their orders, that's not their role. If your subject...' he stopped to look at the name on the top of Holly's page, '... Sergeant Alexander Austen was a soldier in Northern Ireland, then he had a job to do, like it or not.'

'I don't think he liked it,' Holly said. 'His wife Meghan certainly didn't, she had relations there. But he wants...' she stopped short, realising what she said, '*I* want to find out how he died. His descendants are caught up with mine and I was hoping to give some closure to his wife.'

'So, she's still alive?' Sebastian asked.

'Yes. Not living here, though.' Holly didn't mean to imply that Meghan was looking for answers but she didn't want to correct that, either.

Sebastian nodded and studied Holly. 'Well, those news clippings won't tell you much. When did you say the Sergeant died?'

'It was 1972... almost five decades ago,' Holly said.

'Mmm... Give me an hour or so. I know someone in military records,' Sebastian said, tapping his nose.

'Really?' Holly said, brightening. 'Thank you, Sebastian.'

He rose from the edge of the desk where he had been leaning. 'Don't thank me yet, lassie, I might be as useful as a hip pocket in a singlet. Let's wait and see if I can turn anything up.'

He wandered off with an air of purpose about him and Holly felt excited. She returned to the news clippings in front of her from the time when Alexander was killed. There wasn't much in national news, but the local papers ran a number of stories, given Alexander and Meghan were part of the community. She called up another story.

BELFAST, Northern Ireland, April 10 – *Two British soldiers were killed today in Belfast during an upsurge of Irish Republican Army violence. Lieutenant Robert McIntosh, 27, of Surrey and Sergeant Alexander Austen, 29, of Seafield, died in separate incidents.*

Lieutenant McIntosh was on patrol when struck down by bullets fired by a sniper believed to be hiding in a nearby warehouse. He was dragged away conscious and taken to hospital but lapsed and could not be revived.

Sergeant Austen was undertaking foot patrol when a series of random bombs went off in the vicinity. On his way to respond, Sergeant Austen came up against opposition in a tunnel and died from a stab wound inflicted at close range. The matter is under investigation.

The deaths bring the total of British Army dead to 58 since the current troubles began in Ulster in 1969. The overall death toll stands at 302.

The Official wing of the I.R.A. took responsibility for Lieutenant McIntosh's shooting.

Sergeant Austen resided at Findlater House with his wife of two years, Meghan. He will be laid to rest this Friday at 10am at St Joseph's.

Holly read back over the details: *A stab wound inflicted at close range.* Alexander must have seen who did it, surely? Why the mystery? Why not just admit that he was taken out by the opposition, the enemy?

Holly continued to scroll through the clippings until she came to the funeral story. There was a photo. Not a great photo, but clear enough to see that Alexander, or maybe Meghan, had drawn a crowd. Meghan was all in black, of course. But even from the dark photo, Holly could see how beautiful and frail she looked. She was being supported by an older couple on either side... her parents, by the look of it, although the photo caption only identified her as the bereaved widow. That was that. With one swift stabbing, Alexander was gone and her life had changed.

So why hadn't she been back? No reminiscing, or was it too painful? Or was she angry?

Holly continued to search for mentions of Alexander or the investigation outcome, but there were only a few small lines about three months later, advising that the investigation was closed. *Why?*

It didn't take Holly long to find that there were terrible deaths on both sides – innocent people killed in bombings, random attacks, and crossfire. And for everyone that was killed, retaliation was sought. She didn't know who was right or wrong... perhaps both, or neither. Holly sighed. It was complex and not something she could understand in one day, maybe not ever. But she did know one thing; she had to isolate Alexander's death and just concentrate on him in a vacuum; the questions being why did he die and how did he die?

She moved away from the microfiche to a working bench in the library and opened her laptop. Holly took a stab in the dark. She put into the search engine the date of Alexander's death and searched for other deaths in Belfast that same day. A few came up in her searches and she scanned the context, but there was nothing that seemed related, or was in the same area. She went to British records to find out what was now in the public domain... she had access! Declassified files that fell under the thirty-year rule were available.

She checked her notes: Alexander died in 1972 so information relating to his years of service should be online for this period. *Time to dig!*

HEARTS ABOUND

*A*strid Bellerose's boyfriend of one year, Timothée, called it the *Hitler Channel*, not the *History Channel*, because of the large volume of WW2 content, especially Hitler documentaries. To date, Astrid had shown very little interest in that era in history, but he was obsessed by it. They had met at the museum, at a touring exhibition of the Russian Fabergé Eggs. As Astrid's family and several other notable French families contributed financially to the museum, they were always on the patron guest lists for these events, so Astrid wasn't surprised that her own necklace's heritage would fascinate her boyfriend, who she called Timo.

Yes, her great-grandfather was a German soldier, but after the war he had married her great-grandmother, whom he had met during the German occupation of France. She knew little of the story except that he moved to France to be with her and it wasn't an easy life for them; they were not accepted for many decades. Her grandmother was born in Paris; her mother was born in Paris and married her father, Mathis Bellerose; and she was born in Paris, too. The German side of the family had no real bearing on her and, like many young people of her generation, she didn't share the collective guilt from their great-grandparent and grandparents' generation – be it French or German. Why should she? She wasn't even born then.

But her boyfriend had shown a great deal of curiosity in her Tender Heart necklace when she had worn it tonight to his debut; he was a violinist with the Orchestre de Paris. She knew it was risky to wear it – it was worth a fortune – but what was the point of keeping things hidden in a box with their beauty not seen or shared? She would only wear it on special occasions and his debut was certainly one. Sitting beside his parents and brother, and watching Timo debut on stage surrounded by France's best musicians, she was overwhelmed.

Later, after the concert and celebratory drinks with major orchestra sponsors (of which the Bellerose family was again present), Timo had asked her about the necklace and Astrid had shrugged off Timo's surprise when she mentioned her great-grandfather had presented it to his bride in Berlin after the war and before they settled in Paris. He knew enough about her history to know she had some German ancestors.

'So, it was created by a German designer?' he asked. 'Or is it stolen fortune... Nazi loot?' She remembered his eyes widening and the interest in his voice, as if it were a great mystery.

Astrid became defensive. 'It is no such thing. As if my great-grandfather would present his bride with a stolen necklace!'

'Well, the Nazis didn't consider their confiscated goods to be stolen,' Timo informed her.

'He wasn't a Nazi!' she snapped.

'I stand corrected,' Timo said. 'Not all German soldiers were Nazis.'

'Besides, the necklace has been in my family for generations... it's a love story,' Astrid said, brushing the pearls around her neck fondly.

'It will have papers,' he persisted, 'especially a piece of jewellery of that value – it's quite unique.'

Astrid became annoyed. 'So, are you interested in its history or its value?'

'Both,' he said, surprised. 'You know I'm a collector at heart – my double degree is in music and history so, if the orchestra sacked me, I can teach. Didn't your parents always harp on about having something to fall back on?' he said, with a roll of his eyes.

'My father was too busy working to lecture. He just wrote the cheques and expected me to be brilliant and step up in the business one day!'

Timo grinned. 'Well, he got what he wanted.'

She smiled coyly. 'Thank you.'

'Want to get out of here?' he asked, with a glance around. 'Let's grab a taxi out the front and head back to my place.'

They slipped through the cocktail crowd, with a few guests patting Timo on the back or shaking his hand to congratulate him on his debut. Outside, he opened the door of the first taxi on the rank for Astrid, gave the driver the address and slipped in beside her, settling his violin on the seat as she finished a social media post of a selfie from the cocktail party.

Astrid caught his expression. 'It's my work,' she said. 'Dad expects me to promote the family business and this is giving it profile. All this ribbon-cutting and being seen in the right places promotes our brand and leads to awareness of our pharmaceutical discoveries... ho-hum,' she said, in a mechanical fashion, as if she had to justify her profile.

'Fair enough. It is important, though... science,' Timo reminded her. There was only a five-year age difference between them, but sometimes she felt as if Timo was channelling her father with his maturity.

He continued. 'Science, history and the arts, they are the foundation blocks of our community. Take my violin, for example. It's Italian, a Giulio Cesare Gigli, dating back to around 1760. To think of where it has been, who has touched it, and what it has seen!' His eyes roamed the encased instrument beside him with affection. 'Dad remortgaged the house to buy it for me. I will pay him back one day.' He rested his hand on it as the taxi negotiated the evening traffic on the way to Astrid's home. Like most musicians, the instrument was his most prized procession and highly insured.

'Bet your brother was impressed by that,' Astrid said, pushing a strand of her dark hair behind her ear. 'What does he get?'

Timo looked surprised. 'Whatever he needs, I imagine.'

Astrid softened. Timo was a gentle soul, one of the few guys she had met who wasn't impressed by her name, fortune or social media following. And she loved him, for now. But the Tender Heart necklace was hers and it was staying that way, regardless of what history said.

Before she knew it, two hours had passed. Holly had had her nose buried online in the Public Record Office of Northern Ireland, reading every file she could from Alexander's last year of life and last few months of conflict – from the prime minister's speeches, future policy group notes, to proposals for political settlement.

She realised it was after 11 am and her garden should be completed. *Exciting!* Sitting back, she turned her gaze away from the screen and observed some of the library's comings and goings. While she knew a lot more now about the situation Alexander was involved in, she had no insights into Alexander's death. It was then that she saw Sebastian approaching with a sheet of paper in his hands.

'You've been busy,' he said. 'I didn't want to interrupt you until I saw you surface.'

'Oh, please interrupt me,' Holly said, and Sebastian laughed. He sank into the chair beside her.

'It took me a few hours, too, but I have a snippet of information for you from my colleague. Now, this never came from me and you must die with your source on your lips,' he said dramatically, looking to his left and right, and then giving Holly a smile and a wink.

Holly nodded and leaned forward. 'I swear an oath to you that this information will be kept watertight! I can swallow that piece of paper after you share it with me, if you like?' she teased.

He laughed. 'I'll get a message to you if that is required. So, it is only a snippet from the Coroner's report with the cause of death. It might be distressing...' Sebastian hesitated.

'Thank you, but that's okay. I accept the Sergeant is dead and that his death was brutal. I'm ready.'

Sebastian nodded and slipped the paper to her. 'I'll leave it to you then.'

'Thank you, I really appreciate what you did for me,' Holly said.

Sebastian smiled and, looking pleased with his contribution to the cause, returned to the desk.

Holly read the note in front of her: *Death was caused by one stab wound to the body resulting in haemorrhaging and death in minutes.*

Haemorrhaging, she mused; *that's blood loss*. So, Alexander bled out and very quickly, before he could be saved. She grimaced at the thought of him being so far from home and unable to be saved, dying on the street where he fell. She read on as the Coroner outlined the type of weapon – a double-edged knife with a blade length of 11 cm and a width of 1.5 cm. Holly drew a rough image of the knife. It could be concealed up a sleeve perhaps.

The report mentioned that Alexander's thick jacket absorbed a lot of the blood. Holly thought about this. Perhaps people around him didn't see how bad the wound was because of this. Did it just look like a dark stain on his uniform? Was it dark? Was he in a tunnel, or was all the noise creating havoc and no-one noticed he'd been stabbed? Finally, the report noted that by the angle of the wound, the knife had entered the skin at an oblique angle and was thrust upwards into the body at close range.

Oblique angle? What's that? She quickly looked it up on her phone and felt none the wiser. 'Acute or obtuse, not a right angle. Well, that helps... not!' Holly muttered. She looked around for Sebastian and, spotting him placing books on a shelf, she caught his eye. Holly began to rise but he motioned that he would be right there. She made a few quick notes before he dropped down in the chair beside her.

'Can you help me with two questions, please?'

'I'll do my very best,' he agreed.

'Oblique angle. If the knife entered the body at an oblique angle, what does that mean?' Holly asked.

Sebastian nodded. 'Hmm... the more important question might be whereabouts in the body did it enter at an oblique angle. I'll come back to that question. Your second one?'

'The knife – it's a double-edged knife. So the knives at home are single blade, I think.'

'Ah, good pick-up, young lady. Double-edged knives are often more ceremonial, like daggers, combat knives, push knives... so it is a knife chosen for its purpose, if you understand my meaning?' Sebastian said.

Holly nodded. 'So it is likely a soldier, a military person or someone serious about a fight might have been carrying it... it's not a knife that was grabbed from the kitchen drawer before the assailant left home.'

'You have it in one,' Sebastian said. 'Now, my contact did give me one more page of information which I didn't give you because he asked me not to print it out and I thought it might be distressing.'

'Not a photograph from the post-mortem?' Holly said, with trepidation.

'No, just a drawing illustrating the knife entry to the body... it's a common part of autopsies that marks are made on a body drawing. I'm prepared to show you if you feel you are up to it.'

'Yes please, that would be very helpful.'

'Come then,' he said, and headed to the desk. Holly followed and remained on the customer side.

Sebastian called up the email and the image and, with a quick look around to make sure they were alone, he turned the screen to face Holly. 'See, this drawing marks where the knife entered the body and its upward trajectory.'

Holly took it in, trying to capture the image in her mind so she could go back and quickly draw it. 'So that's the oblique angle and right near the heart.' She looked away. 'Thank you, Sebastian, this is really helpful information.'

'My pleasure. I'll just file this somewhere confidential, but if you need to see it again, it will be here.' He turned the screen back around and closed the email.

Holly returned to her desk and quickly sketched a human

body shape and marked the knife wound area and entry. She sat back and read the report again.

There was no denying the obvious – the last person that Alexander saw in front of him, or the person who was directly on his left, was most likely his killer – and Meghan's cousin, Ronan was the top contender.

A BREATH OF FRESH AIR

*J*uliette breezed into *Findlater House* like a gust of wind herself.

'Oh my God, it is great to be back, and the garden looks amazing. Are you delighted with it? Lucas is so talented.' Juliette didn't wait for a response as she finished embracing Holly and pulled away. 'I miss not having you to drop in on or call up for a drink, and I've missed the salt air.' She breathed in deeply.

Holly laughed. 'Hmm, it's more likely you missed breathing in the same salt air that Lucas is inhaling.'

Juliette grinned. 'Well yeah, there's that. Okay... let's get organised. We should go for a walk on the beach, and then we've got to come home and get ready. It's only two hours until we meet the guys.' As she spoke, she slipped off her heels and started unbuttoning her work jacket.

Holly agreed. 'I'll put my walking shoes on.'

Juliette grabbed her suitcase and headed up the stairs, calling back, 'So excited to be back.'

Holly watched her friend disappear up the stairs, admiring

how Juliette had the knack of fitting in wherever she landed as if she had always been there.

She grabbed her runners and as she sat on the sofa to pull them on, she felt a sudden cold rush beside her.

'Is she always so full-on?' Alexander asked.

'Yes. Great, isn't it?'

'Sure,' he said, sounding less impressed. 'So are you still going out with this J.J. guy tonight?'

'I am, but I wouldn't call it a date, I'm just making up numbers.' Holly looked up at him as she tied her shoelaces. 'I have some more questions for you, about your... end.'

'You've found out something,' he said, his eyes growing wider, 'or is this just one of your freebie questions?'

'No, it's for research purposes and I don't know yet if I've found out something until I have a bit more context. Just a few questions will help me sort things.'

'About what?' Juliette asked, coming down the stairs in her leisure gear and runners.

Holly quickly looked to the stairs. 'What... sorry?'

'You said you have a few questions.'

'Oh yes, a few questions... um, I'm dying to hear about the necklace, whatever you found out. I've got a few new insights, too and I'm meeting Esther on Monday to give her an update.'

'I'll tell you as we walk,' Juliette said, already at the door. 'It's so great to leave the office behind and get outside.'

Holly grabbed her house keys and glanced around, frowning. 'Try and stay out of trouble,' she whispered, pulling the door closed behind her.

~

'What a cheek, stay out of trouble! This is my house unless you've forgotten!' he called after her. *Women. Alive women!* He shook his head.

Alexander went to the record collection and selected one of his favourites.

'Time for a little Creedence,' he said, pulling the album from its sleeve and putting it on. He relaxed as the dulcet tones of John Fogerty asked him if he had ever seen the rain.

'I've seen more, so much more, John my man,' Alexander answered.

He knew what Holly was going to ask and it didn't take her long to get there. Yes, the last person he saw was Ronan and the wound that killed him was inflicted from where Ronan was standing. But they were good friends, and Ronan loved Meghan; he would never have done anything to have caused her pain.

Something else happened… there's got to be another explanation. Was it an accident? Were Ronan and his mates coming to defend their turf but Ronan hadn't counted on seeing me and had to follow through to save face, or to save himself? Did someone push Ronan forward onto me and it was an accident?

Did Meghan know the truth?

Juliette linked her arm through Holly's as they strolled along the firm sand of the beach, slowing down to village time.

'It truly is spectacular, isn't it?' Juliette said, taking in the sheer cliffs and the dramatic sea crashing against it.

'I don't think you could ever tire of it,' Holly agreed.

'So what do you think of J.J.?'

'Nothing,' Holly said, and looked at Juliette with surprise. 'I haven't thought about him at all.'

Juliette rolled her eyes. 'It could be a great fit, the two of you.'

'Nope, no spark but he's nice and he looks fit. But we're just there to prop up you two. I'm sure J.J. feels the same. He wouldn't be short of a date.'

'Thank you,' Juliette said, and squeezed Holly's arm.

'You're welcome. You've played wing-girl for me over the years, too,' Holly said, and they both smiled at the thought. 'So, tell me what you found out about the necklace.'

'Ah, the necklace,' Juliette said. 'Well, you were right about the Bellerose name. The necklace is currently in the possession of the Bellerose family of Paris and has been for three generations, judging from the trail of insurance paperwork. It is currently insured in the name of Astrid Bellerose. I checked her out and she's in her early twenties, young, rich, and a Paris society girl by the looks of it.'

'So, did they buy it originally... can you tell?' Holly asked.

'You can tell if the original purchase certificate is lodged with the insurance claim and many insurers insist on this, but given this necklace came into the family in the 1940s – well, that's the earliest registered date for it – there's no purchase information. There is a valuation, but that's at the time of being insured.' Juliette shivered and Holly suggested they turn and walk back. They said hello to an elderly couple walking past.

Juliette continued. 'This doesn't mean anything sinister. During those war years, a lot of original documentation was lost due to fire, bombings, deaths and transfers.'

'Hmm, so it could have been confiscated from a Jewish family by the Bellerose ancestors,' Holly said.

'It could have, but I'm not sure how you prove that.' Juliette smiled.

'What?' Holly asked, narrowing her eyes. 'You look like the cat that swallowed the cream.'

'Meow,' Juliette agreed and they laughed.

'Tell me, what do you know?' Holly asked excitedly.

Juliette drew a breath. 'Well, I did come across something that might help your investigation. I can't take credit for it, though. I have an aged buyer who has a bit of passion for rare and unusual pieces and he brought it to my attention.'

Holly held her breath.

'A lot of jewellers leave their mark on pieces they create – symbols or initials, something unique to them. There is a register of German jewellery makers' marks, some dating back as far as the late 1800s. Now, Esther's father was a German Jew and jeweller, and when I showed my colleague the photo of the necklace, he said he was likely to have registered his mark,' Juliette said, as they came to the end of the beach and turned for Holly's home. 'There's a website for the Antique Jewellery University which lists many of them.'

Holly felt her heartbeat racing. 'So, if he had a mark registered and it was registered with this university...'

'... then we need to find that mark and – this is the important part – you need to see if you can find that mark somewhere on the piece of jewellery. If it is there, then you know that Esther's father made it.'

'Wow, that's brilliant,' Holly said, processing the information. 'It doesn't prove it was stolen, but it proves that he created it and we definitely have the right piece of jewellery, not a replica.' She turned to Juliette. 'You are amazing! Thank you.'

'It's exciting,' Juliette said, as the end of the beach and their entry point came into sight.

Holly was thinking aloud: 'And if Esther had a photo of her parents with the necklace, maybe her mother wearing it, that will help to show that they owned it for a time... that they didn't make it for someone else and it was unlikely they sold it.'

'Especially if she's in her wedding dress!' Juliette agreed.

'No bride would sell that romantic necklace, surely, unless the family was destitute.'

They headed off the beach and up Findlater Lane towards Holly's house.

'When are you meeting with Esther?' Juliette asked.

'Monday morning.'

'If you like, I could stay an extra night and come to your meeting... if it would help?' Juliette offered.

'That would be brilliant and you could explain all this to her,' Holly said. 'Will your boss be okay with that?'

'Are you kidding?' Juliette asked. 'If I tell him I'm got an elderly client with some jewellery pieces for discussion, he'll be asking me to stay. We could have dinner Sunday night, just the two of us and –'

'C'mon... new love – I'm not standing in the way of all that passion!' Holly teased and rolled her eyes.

Juliette grinned and flushed with pleasure.

Holly continued: 'You and I both know that all you will do Sunday night is think of Lucas and you'll be totally distracted and I won't get one sensible thought out of you. So here's a plan – why don't you spend tonight with Lucas, then tomorrow afternoon with me, Sunday night with Lucas and come back here Monday morning before heading back to London?'

Juliette grinned. 'Are you sure? I feel like I'm jilting you.'

'Don't be crazy. I moved here on my own, remember? Besides, it's a bonus for me. I've gone from missing you to seeing you one night, two afternoons and a morning! Bargain.'

'Brilliant, how exciting. Unless...' she hesitated, '... Lucas and I don't hit it off again tonight, then I'll be crying on your shoulder for the rest of the weekend,' Juliette said, a little anxious.

'I've got wine and tissues,' Holly assured her, 'but that won't happen. He's crazy for you.'

'Do you think?'

'I can tell.' Holly felt Juliette relax beside her. She remembered only too well the anxiety of new love. She hoped to feel it again one day.

They arrived at *Findlater House* and stopped to admire Lucas's work in the front garden as they walked to the cottage door.

Juliette stopped. 'Someone's in your house. I can hear music!'

Holly froze. *For the love of God, Alexander!* She could hear the record playing as well.

She took a deep breath. 'It's fine, I put it on just as I was leaving – I like to come home to a house with the lights on and a bit of noise in the background.'

'Phew.' Juliette patted her heart. 'For a moment there, I thought we might have a home invader with dubious music taste.'

Holly laughed. *Oh, I've got a few of those,* she thought, *and one of them is two-legged.*

A COMFORTABLE PAIR OF SHOES

*S*aturday night was the first time that Holly had the opportunity to talk with Alexander alone since her library visit. She saw him watching and waiting for her return on Friday night, and then he disappeared once he saw her in safely and on her own, not with J.J. in tow. She couldn't work out if he was being paternal, a protective friend, or acting like a jealous boyfriend.

Tonight, they had the house to themselves after a full-on day; Juliette was out to dinner with Lucas and would not return until late the next morning.

Sitting outside on their small terrace surrounded by her new garden, Holly sipped her white wine. It was a beautiful sunset; the air was crisp, the sky was red, and she greeted the occasional passer-by. Alexander sat beside her looking chilled out and not cranky for a change. He, too, sipped his drink, which he hid from view when someone passed. The glass remained full.

'So peaceful,' Holly said.

'I know. I've always loved it here,' Alexander said, and sighed.

'Loved it enough not to leave?'

Alexander smirked. 'C'mon, you'd miss me. Look at us, we're like a comfortable pair of shoes.'

She grinned. 'Strangely, I think I might miss you. It's only been a short time but you've grown on me.'

She waved and greeted some walkers on the other side of her street. It was an admirable effort that some villagers walked up Findlater Lane to the top of the crescent, seeing as it was reasonably steep.

'It does worry me just a little, though,' she said.

'What? That you'd miss me? Luckily you don't have to,' he said.

'No, that I'm turning into my grandmother, Loopy Lily,' Holly said.

Alexander scoffed and sipped his wine. 'Becoming crazy? You've been there for a while, sweetheart, let me assure you. How many people have things find *them*! Not to mention seeing ghosts.'

She turned, frowning in his direction. 'Hmm, perhaps you are right. But on the upside, the author Lewis Carroll said all the best people were a bit bonkers... or something like that.'

'Speaking of finding things,' Alexander said, 'two of the items in your "found" basket were claimed this morning,' he said, with a nod towards the basket sitting beside the post box with the FOUND, PLEASE TAKE IF YOURS sign attached. 'I could tell they were the owners by the expression of complete surprise on their face when they saw their things in there.'

Holly brightened. 'Well, that's good news, I love things to find their home.' She sighed, pleased with herself.

Alexander became serious. 'So, given we've established

you're already nuts, are you worried you won't meet anyone while you're living here with me?'

She turned to look at him. 'I hadn't given it a lot of thought. But no, not really. Unless you're intending to scare off any prospective lovers I bring home.'

Alexander grimaced. 'It's crossed my mind, especially if I don't think they are suitable,' he said.

'Really?' Holly exclaimed. 'How does a ghost manage that?'

'I have my ways and if I fail to scare them off, I'll find some dirt on them. Like that *Fast Express* courier driver who's currently having an affair. His wife is pregnant and doesn't know. So many good lines there, but that's another day.'

'No! I've seen him around town. Now I'll never be able to look at him in the same way. What a rotter,' Holly said.

Alexander laughed.

'Well, he is. Men!'

Alexander continued to laugh.

'What's so funny?'

'*Rotter*. You read too many Victorian novels. I thought you'd say scumbag or asshole.'

'Well, that too,' Holly agreed.

He smiled and shook his head. They sat in silence for a while, enjoying the dusk light and the scent from the newly established garden.

Alexander turned to Holly. 'You know Meg and I loved Lily, your grandmother. When we first met her, she was only about a decade older than us, but because I died, I knew her right up until her death,' Alexander said.

'Thanks, that's kind of you to say,' Holly said. 'She was seventy-one when she died – a good innings for our clan.'

Alexander continued: 'She was good-looking. Even when she was an old girl, she still had her looks. When she was reunited with your grandfather on my side, it was very touching.'

Holly's hand went to her heart and her eyes filled with tears.

Alexander cleared his throat. 'Christ, didn't mean to say that, sorry.'

Holly looked out to sea and wiped her eyes. 'I'm so glad you did, thank you. Grandma Lily died about fifteen years after Grandpa. How romantic.'

'Yeah, guess it's nice to know that they rock on together in the afterlife,' Alexander said. 'But back to you. I'm more worried that because I'm such great company and so good-looking, you won't be seeking the real thing,' he teased.

Holly chuckled. 'Yes, that's keeping me up at night.'

He laughed... a deep baritone laugh which Holly found very attractive.

Out of the blue, Holly asked, 'Why didn't you scare me off?' She finished her wine and turned to face him.

He shrugged. 'I tried.'

'Not very hard.'

'That's true.' He sighed and looked into her eyes. 'You reminded me of Meghan, and I'd hate for her to be scared or worried,' he admitted, his voice lowered.

'Thank you.'

Alexander nodded. 'Should we talk about what you found out?'

'Lets,' Holly agreed.

'I know what you want to ask me... it's about the last person I saw, because of the proximity of my wound, isn't it?'

Holly nodded.

Alexander continued: 'I know it might have been Meg's cousin, Ronan, but he's still alive so I don't know for sure. I can't believe that, though. I don't believe it. Something else happened. Tell me what you found out.'

Holly took a deep breath and filled Alexander in on her findings, the coroner's report, the description of the weapon, its entry into his body and the inquiry after, which was shut down rather promptly.

Alexander listened without interrupting. When she finished, he thanked her.

'So what now?' he asked.

'I need you to think back and tell me who was on your left, in front of you, to your right and anyone you can recall who was in close proximity to you... from your squad and from the enemy camp. Then I'm going to track those people down and ask to talk with them, if they are still capable of remembering the past.'

'That sounds risky. I'll come with you. They won't see me but they'll bloody well feel me if they try anything on.'

'You can do that?' Holly asked.

'Of course. I just prefer not to leave the house unless I have to, but we're going together,' Alexander announced. He took a deep breath and closed his eyes as he spoke. 'You have to remember it was chaotic that night. There were bombings and people panicking, running and screaming past me. The emergency vehicle sirens were so loud and the whole time I was trying to keep my eyes on my squad so I didn't get separated from them, and also watching out for what was going on around me.' He opened his eyes and saw Holly studying him.

She shivered. 'It's getting cold, the sun is almost gone.'

'Want to go in?' Alexander asked.

'One more question first,' Holly said. 'Tell me who was around you at the time. Do you remember?'

'Yes. There were really only two people close to me. The

rest were a few feet away, or hurrying past. Ronan was directly in front of me. I pulled him up off the ground after we collided.'

Holly thought about the trajectory of the knife and if Ronan could have put it into Alexander as he rose up from the ground.

Alexander continued. 'Beside me was the Staff-Sergeant, my commanding officer Andy Davies. He's the guy I'd mentioned to you once before – my mate that we checked out on Facebook.'

'Do you think he –'

Alexander cut her off. 'Absolutely not! We went way back. He had my back.'

Holly nodded, not taking her eyes off him.

Alexander lowered his eyes and she heard him mumble the word, 'Maybe.'

IN PURSUIT OF THE TRUTH

$\mathcal{I}$t was a whirlwind weekend. Juliette was in love, Holly was delighted for her and happy with her new surrounds, Alexander was getting more relaxed with his new tenant-cum-housemate, and life was good. Then the night tipped over and it was Monday. Holly could see Esther walking up the path to *Findlater House*.

'She's here,' Holly said, going to open the door before Esther knocked; behind her, Juliette finished making tea. Alexander was waiting patiently in his portrait until Esther was shown into the kitchen and then he threatened Holly that he would join them in there.

Holly opened the door with gusto, enjoying the blast of salt air that rushed in. It could be a touch windy on Findlater Lane, hence the need to keep the door closed sometimes – Lord knows what might blow in for Holly to find.

'Esther, hello, it's lovely to see you again,' Holly said, moving aside. 'Please come in.'

Esther – looking smart in dark green and blue tweed pants, a matching navy jumper and sensible shoes – entered.

'It's good to see you again Holly, and I love what you have done with the front garden, well done,' she said, stopping on the doorstep to cast an eye over it.

'Thank you. Lucas from *How Does Your Garden Grow?* did it. I love it.'

Holly noticed that as Esther came in, she glanced at the portrait and gave the Sergeant a nod. Holly looked over in a panic. Phew, Alexander was framed in there, for now!

'We're just making tea,' Holly said, closing the front door and moving into the kitchen area. 'Let me introduce you. This is my best friend, Juliette Holmes.'

'Ms Bohmer.' Juliette extended her hand.

'Please call me Esther. Lovely to meet you, Juliette, and Holly tells me you've been subtly using your networks to help our case.'

Esther accepted a seat, placing her folder on the table and her handbag on the floor beside her. Juliette brought the teapot to the table and sat opposite Esther as Holly joined them with a plate of fruit cake. They made small talk about the weather and village life as Holly poured tea for the three ladies and passed each a cup when done.

She saw Alexander join them and made a mental note not to keep looking towards that part of the kitchen. Holly filled Esther in on Juliette's subtle involvement.

'I've been an antique dealer and jewellery buyer for some time now and there are several people I trust implicitly... they are always happy to share their knowledge. But I'll let Holly fill you in on what we know so far,' Juliette said.

'Right, down to business. It appears that you were right,' Holly started, 'we think the Tender Heart is in France – in Paris, to be exact. If we have the right pearl and diamond necklace, then the people who currently own it are a very successful and wealthy family – the Bellerose family. Does the name mean anything to you?'

Esther shook her head. 'No, I haven't heard the name before.'

'That's okay. Juliette was able to find it because the necklace had been registered for insurance,' Holly said. 'The only daughter, Astrid, is the public relations face of the family. They own a respected brand in the pharmaceutical and science area that goes back generations. Astrid is young, beautiful and rich.' Holly opened the folder in front of her and pulled out some colour photos of Astrid. When she came to the final one – a photo of Astrid wearing the necklace – she hesitated, then placed it in front of Esther.

Esther gasped. 'That's it! That's the photo I saw, too. She's wearing it.'

'It appears so,' Holly said. 'Juliette will explain the marking.'

Juliette nodded and pushed her auburn fringe out of her eyes. She told Esther about the symbol that jewellers often put on their work and how, in the past, many European jewellers registered it.

'Yes!' Esther exclaimed, 'I know exactly what you are talking about and I'm sure there is one.'

Juliette glanced at Holly then back to Esther. 'I hope your father didn't just use the letter "B". The Bellerose family might try and claim that as their mark.'

Esther shook her head. 'No dear, it's fine. Bohmer is my married name. My maiden name was Hirschell.'

Juliette gasped. 'I know the Hirschell name in jewellery... I'm sure it is registered.'

'Let's see,' Holly said, opening her laptop and waiting for the Antique Jewellery University page to load. 'This is so exciting, and stressful,' Holly said, with a glance to Esther. 'Are you okay?'

'I'm exhilarated,' Esther said. 'This is more progress than I've had for decades.'

'I just hope there's something there now,' Juliette said, and bit her lower lip.

'How did you come across the Bellerose name? No one else to date has,' Esther asked.

'Holly found it,' Juliette said, and Holly tried not to look panicked. How did she explain a ghost gave it to her?

She stumbled out an answer. 'It wasn't hard. Once you mentioned that the necklace was worn by a socialite on social media, I just started going through Parisian fashion shows and social media accounts...' Her voice trailed off. Technically, she had done that but hadn't found the Bellerose name or Astrid on that occasion.

The page loaded just in the nick of time and Holly typed in the registered name of Hirschell. She turned the screen so that everyone could see it and then the brand came up. A solid U and H shared a surface, interwoven, representing Esther's father's name –

Holly clicked on the logo and a list of registered jewellery pieces made by Esther's father, Uri Hirschell, came up on the screen.

'Oh my,' Esther said, placing her hand on her heart. 'My father's work and there's the Tender Heart listed. I'm sure I'd recognise some of those pieces. Not all were stolen, of course. A lot were bespoke.'

'And that's the symbol we need to find on Astrid's necklace,' Holly said, studying it.

'So... what's the plan now?' Juliette asked.

Esther and Holly looked at each other.

'We've got a few avenues,' Holly said, knowing Esther was waiting for her response. 'This has to be handled very sensitively.'

'I agree,' Esther said.

Holly continued. 'If we just contact Astrid Bellerose, there's a chance the necklace might simply disappear. The same might happen if we contact –' she glanced at her notes before continuing, '– the World Jewish Restitution Organisation or similar organisations. I'm not sure how they approach these matters.'

Esther drew in a deep breath before speaking. 'They have a process, naturally – it is meticulous and cautious as you would expect, as they do the research and file each claim for restitution. It would not surprise me, either, if the necklace went undercover then, too, if they started making queries.'

Holly nodded. 'So I think we need to establish firsthand that it is the necklace, even though we are confident it is. Let's remove all doubt by laying eyes on the marking.'

'Agreed,' Juliette said and continued. 'Then we could talk directly with Astrid and discuss the situation – gauge how she feels about it and how open she might be to accept the true owner of the necklace. What do you think?' Juliette asked.

Holly shook her head. 'I would be very surprised if Astrid would willingly give it up, even if she did hear its history. I'd also be nervous that she'd hide it and deny everything.' Holly swallowed. 'So, my plan is this: I think we should find the brand on the necklace, somehow snap a photo of the necklace and symbol if we can, then provide this information, plus Astrid's details and the photo of her wearing it, to Esther.'

'And then?' Juliette asked.

'Then Esther approaches the Restitution Agency with all that evidence and they do what they do officially.'

'I think that's safer,' Esther agreed. 'It appears this young lady doesn't need money, but the necklace may be sentimental to her if it's been handed down.'

Holly turned to Juliette. 'That will be safer for your business reputation, too, don't you think, Juliette?'

'I think you're right,' Juliette suggested. 'I'll make contact with the Bellerose family, Astrid, and say I saw the piece on social media and that I'd love to see it while I'm in Paris on business and see what she says. I've got some clients in Paris, anyway, so I can drop in and see them while I'm there. If we see the symbol, I'll try and get a photo, maybe mention that I know the work of the jeweller. See how it plays out.'

'Her reaction would be interesting, but it could get ugly,' Holly said, sitting back. She noticed that Alexander had lost interest in the discussion and vanished.

Juliette nodded. 'So shall we all go?'

Esther shook her head. 'No, I don't think my being there would be advantageous. I think you two should go if you are happy to do so and have time. I'll fund it, of course.'

'I'm very happy to do so,' Holly said, 'if you are happy to make contact, Juliette and, with your company's trading name, see if we can get a foot in the door.'

'That works for me,' Juliette said, 'but you don't need to finance me, Esther, although thank you for offering. I go over a few times a year anyway, so it can be one of my work trips.'

Holly covered Juliette's hand with her own. 'Thank you for this.'

Esther reached across the table for both of their hands. She looked weary and it was the first time Holly noticed there really was a little old lady masked behind Esther's usual energetic front. She suspected that delving into history, no matter how long ago it had been, was draining.

'Thank you both. I never thought I'd get close to seeing it again in my lifetime and now I have some hope,' Esther said.

'Imagine if we could bring it home,' Holly said, in awe. 'Wouldn't that be a wonderful thing!"

'Well, you are the finder of things,' Juliette said, 'so if anyone can, you can!'

OLD FRIENDS AND ENEMIES

he bespectacled journalist and his sidekick photographer stopped out the front of *Findlater House*. They were both panting... the rise up Findlater Lane to the house always separated the fit from the unfit, the soft from the trained! They looked soft, Alexander thought... and young. He sighed.

'They're back.'

'Who's back?' Holly's voice rose with enthusiasm as she looked up from the table where she had been working on the laptop. 'Juliette and Lucas?' she asked, as they were the last to leave the cottage earlier this morning.

'No, the ghost hunters,' Alexander said. He stood leaning against the window frame, watching them.

Holly frowned, confused and rose to join him by the window. 'Do you know them?'

'Yes, Tweedledee and Tweedledum come by every few months to try and get a story. The real estate agent sent them packing last time, so now they drop in occasionally to try and talk the tenants into letting them in. A few have in the past.'

'And what? You didn't perform?' Holly asked. 'How terribly uncooperative of you.'

'Yeah, bad me,' Alexander said, smirking. 'I want people to bugger off, not come round like the place is a tourist attraction. Can you get rid of them?'

'I'll give it my best shot,' Holly said, with a smile in his direction. 'Play along.'

She opened the door before they made their way halfway up the path. They looked surprised to see her... she wasn't a ghost. Holly suspected they were either fans of the Paranormal genre or the editor had sent them out to fill a gap in their content.

'Ah, Miss, hello,' the journalist started. He would have been early twenties if he was a day. With one slick movement, he flattened his hair and pushed his thin glasses further up on his nose.

'Hi,' Holly said. 'Can I help you?'

'I'm Gerard Clark and this is Nat Stoddart, we're from the *Best of Local News Online*. You might have seen our stories?'

Holly pursed her lips as she thought about it. 'Can't say I have, but I will from now on!'

Nat smiled. 'Thanks!' He saw the *Lost and Found* basket and glanced in.

'Do people just leave stuff here?' he asked, picking up a woollen glove.

'No, it finds me,' Holly said, with a shrug, 'so I put them there in the hope they can be reunited with family.'

Nat grinned. 'That's a good pair of sunnies. What happens if no-one claims them?'

'That's never happened,' Holly admitted. 'But if they are still there at the end of the month, I'll keep them for you.'

'Thanks.' He brightened.

Gerard cleared his throat to catch their attention and

continued on his ghost thread. 'We were hoping to talk to you about the rumours that this house was haunted. Are you just visiting?'

As they spoke, Alexander came out and stood beside Holly, his arms crossed, his expression less than impressed and his form not visible to the two young ghost hunters.

'Oh wow, I just got an increase in the waves,' Nat said, glancing at the box in his hand. He looked to Holly and explained, 'It says if there's a change in atmosphere.'

'Like a ghost had joined us?' she suggested, and shuddered. Alexander laughed beside her.

'Exactly!' Nat said. He looked around and Gerard did the same thing.

Holly responded to the earlier question. 'No, not visiting, I live here.'

'Here?' Gerard asked, surprised. 'So, have you seen anything?'

'Oh, lots of things,' Holly said. 'It's an amazing town and village.'

Gerard's face dropped. Nat continued to stare at the radar in his hand, waiting for the dial to move.

'I'm mean here, in the house,' Gerard said. 'Have you seen anything... you know, supernatural?' He looked upstairs to the windows and veranda, and back to the large windows in the living areas on the ground level.

'Like a ghost? No, thank goodness. I've heard the Sergeant can be very unwelcoming.'

Gerard and Nat stared at her. 'So you know about the Sergeant but you haven't seen him?'

'No. I heard he was really handsome so I'm a little disappointed,' Holly said.

Alexander laughed again.

'If you do see him, can you introduce us? I'll leave you my card,' Gerard said, pulling a card from his suit pocket.

'You will be the first people I call... but don't wait around for a scoop, I heard he's quite anti-social,' Holly said. 'Anyway, I'd best get back to work. Thank you for dropping in.'

'Thanks, Miss –?' Gerard asked.

'You're welcome,' Holly said, not revealing her name. 'I'll let you know about those sunglasses, too,' she said to Nat. She gave them an endearing smile and went back into the house. Holly heard the photographer say, 'The readings just dropped when she went inside. You don't think she's a ghost too, do you?'

Holly closed the door and groaned. 'Lord help us, one ghost is well and truly enough for this household."

The library was always welcoming and Holly couldn't explain the excitement that she felt on entering it. She had always been that way, ever since she was a kid. But today, she had some work to do that she didn't want Alexander seeing. Of course, he could follow her to the library but she knew he was less inclined to do that.

She saw Abby helping a few library customers and gave her a wave; Abby looked pleased to see her. Holly didn't need the microfiche today, so she settled herself at a desk with her back to the wall and a view out the window to the street and the passing parade of people and traffic. She unpacked her laptop and turned it on.

It had appeared this morning – a message on her phone from Andy Davies, Alexander's friend... the soldier who had had the Sergeant's back, allegedly. It had only been a few days since Holly took a gamble and messaged him, and she couldn't believe it when she saw his reply come up on her phone. He had to be in his late seventies and she wasn't sure how active he was online. She wanted to read it immediately but decided to get out of the house; who knew what the message might contain?

She opened it and it contained a few lines. *Hello Holly, well Alex, that's a blast from the past. I've emailed you, I can write in more detail there. Cheers, Andy.*

Fantastic, she thought, surprised he'd mastered the social media messaging at his age. *So he remembers Alexander and he's open to talking... well, maybe.* She opened her emails and as she waited for them to download, she saw Abby approaching.

'Hi Holly, I knew you couldn't keep away from us!'

'Hi Abby! You had me at "hello" and "books", Holly agreed. 'Hey, thanks for connecting me with Sebastian, he was so helpful.'

'Pleasure! Sebastian Cartwright the Third loves to be of value... I think you made his day more so than the other way around.' Abby groaned as she saw people heading to the desk again. 'Never a moment's reprieve from my checkout stamp,' she said, and smiled.

'It's the way you wield it,' Holly teased.

'Yeah, it's a skill,' Abby agreed and grinned. She left Holly and returned to the desk.

Holly checked out her emails. There was the usual bunch of junk mail that she should unsubscribe to or thought she had already; an email from her mother which she'd look forward to reading later – it was a bit of an epic in length; a sale at her favourite store in London... *good thing I'm missing that* – and there it was, an email from Andy.

She opened it. It was long and he had written it like a formal letter. Holly began to read.

*Dear Holly, well, what a surprise to hear from you and
to hear Alex's name mentioned again. Some days it feels
like yesterday when we were there in the thick of it all;
other days it feels like it was a hundred years ago. I guess
you younger people don't get that, but you will one day.
I've thought a lot about Alex over the years... he comes
and goes in my head now more than ever, as I have
plenty of time to think back over my life. Funny how
some of us get to live while others die young... it's true
what they say, you're a long time dead. Alex was a good
man, I was proud to serve with him, and he was great
company, but I confess that I never understood why he
sat on the fence. Although I suspect his missus had
something to do with that, but a mission's a mission...
commit or don't. Alex wasn't in or out, he was just there.
But that's irrelevant now, isn't it? He did his job and he
died doing it.*

*If you want to come to see me, as suggested, you are
welcome, but I'm not sure how much more I can tell
you. My memory of that night is not that great. It all
happened so quickly and, added to that, it's been nearly
five decades! I can't remember what I had for lunch
yesterday. But if you want to make the trip, I'd be lying
if I said I wouldn't enjoy the company and to show off
that I have a young lady visiting... Just kidding, I can get
in big trouble saying things like that these days, can't I?
I have two kids – both grown men now but one lives in
London and the other in Sydney, Australia, so I don't see
them much. They've got their own lives and their own
families.*

Anyway, I'm in aged care now because I can't get

*around so easily and I get a bit forgetful. My wife died
five years ago. I'm not saying that for sympathy, just the
way it is... so don't wait too long to get here in case I fall
off my perch. Best to make it a morning visit if that
works for you, too? I run out of steam pretty easily these
days.*

*My address follows and just check the website for the
facility I live in, because there are some visiting hour
restrictions and parking hassles – or so they tell me. Let
me know when you'd like to come and we can lock
something in. Okay, young lady, will leave it in your
hands. My regards, Andy Davies.*

Holly looked up and breathed out. Fantastic! At least he'll see
me. She checked out the website of where Andy lived. It would
only take her an hour or so to drive there and they were open of
a morning from 9 am to 12 noon before the lunch break. If she
left at 9 am, she could be there to have morning tea with him –
she'd take a cake from *The Cup and Saucer,* and get on his good
side.

She thought about Andy. Maybe in the flesh he'd tell her
more in detail... get caught up in the story and remember more.
She wondered who he thought had killed his Sergeant.

'I'm coming with you,' Alexander insisted when Holly read the
message to him.

'Really? Are you sure you can come that far? And how does
that work? Will you travel with me or do you just appear
there?'

'Yes, I can travel anywhere I like and I can just appear there, unless you want my scintillating company for the journey?' Alexander asked with raised eyebrows.

'I think I'll be all right. I'll listen to a podcast or put some music on.'

'Podcast? Whatever! So, when do we go?'

Holly shook her head. 'Right now, sir.'

Alexander looked pleased. 'Really?'

'No, don't be ridiculous.' She moved him out of the way of the refrigerator as she grabbed vegetables to prepare a stir-fry meal for herself. Alexander relocated to a seat at the kitchen table.

Holly continued. 'I've sent him some suggested days and times so I'm waiting on him now. Then I've got to look up the route, calculate how long it will take and when I can get away.'

'Well, give me plenty of notice, I'm very busy,' he said, and Holly laughed.

'Plus,' she said, 'I've got to work out scenarios – what to ask him, how I'll play it if he reveals nothing, or if he says he knows who – you know – knocked you off.'

'Hmm,' Alexander mused. 'You still think Ronan might have done it?'

'I do,' Holly said, 'but you don't. What will you do if Andy says he does know who did it? I'm not taking you with me if you get violent. You have to promise to stay in the background, or I won't go.'

Alexander scowled at her. 'Fine, bossy boots. Anyway, vengeance is not my role and it's not allowed.'

She turned from stirring the vegetables in the large wok. 'Promise you'll stay out of sight?'

'Yeah, yeah, I promise,' he said, impatiently.

Holly smiled at him. 'So, you're not allowed to punish,

hmm? There's an insight you let slip! But I still get my one question in return for new info.'

Alexander began to fade.

'Don't you dare!' She waved the wooden spoon at him and he laughed and reappeared in full strength.

'Go on then, ask away.'

'Why aren't you in uniform? You're in jeans and a T-shirt, but if you died as a soldier or died in a hospital bed, then why aren't you in your uniform or a hospital gown? Do you get to choose what you wear even when you are a ghost?' She turned to face him, waiting for the answer.

'Ah, very perceptive, Ms Hanlon,' Alexander nodded. 'I can wear whatever is in my imagination, and I figured jeans and a T-shirt transcends all decades and generations. Do you want to see me in uniform?' he asked, with a hint of teasing shading his tone.

She squinted at him as she thought. 'No, I think I might find that a bit sad.'

He nodded. Then, lightening the mood, he said, 'I could appear in my birthday suit.' He raised his hands as if he was about to click and action the thought.

"No!" Holly yelled.

Alexander laughed.

'You've answered the question, thanks. Leave your gear on,' she said.

She could hear him laughing after he had faded from sight.

THE HEART OF PARIS

*H*olly belted up, took a deep breath and said a silent prayer. The wheels of the plane clunked into place and the piped air always made her feel slightly claustrophobic.

Juliette studied her. 'Seriously, you're not scared, are you? Do you know how safe we are, compared to, well, driving a car?'

'I'm not scared, but it doesn't hurt just to put in a good word above for a safe flight,' she said, gazing up to the roof of the plane to indicate the heavens. 'Falling from a great height is not really the way I want to go – I'd like to die in my sleep or have a heart attack and keel over dead instantly.'

'Yeah, well, who wouldn't? So, a good word as in a prayer?' Juliette asked. 'Wow, I didn't realise you were that connected.'

Holly smiled. 'My great-aunt was a nun, she was my favourite aunty. When I was a kid, any time I travelled with her, she would say a prayer to Our Lady of the Way that we would get there safely. It was probably more a reflection on my mother's driving skills, but hey, we always got there. So thank you, Our Lady of the Way and please work your magic again for this journey.'

Juliette looked over Holly's shoulder as the plane began to level out after its ascent into the sky. Holly had the window seat, Juliette preferred the aisle. Esther had insisted Holly fly business class and Juliette had enough points to happily agree and accompany her.

'We could have gone by train. Or would you still have said a prayer?'

'Yeah, most likely.' Holly breathed out as the plane levelled off. 'I could so get used to business class. Esther was really generous.'

'Perks of the job,' Juliette agreed, and stretched her legs out in front of her. 'Look at all the room.' She continued: 'You know, I read somewhere that the odds of dying in a plane crash are like one in 200,000, but it's one in 1000 for drowning and one in 100 for a car crash.'

'That's not really great odds, but I'll take them,' Holly said, and brightened as the flight attendant approached to offer them a drink.

They requested champagne – they were going to Paris, after all – and sat back with their glasses of bubbly to talk strategy during the one-hour flight.

'I'm relieved Astrid is open to meeting us but I'm not expecting she'll acknowledge the necklace's heritage at this meeting, even if we mention the designer. But we do need to toe the line about you just being a collector keen to see beautiful pieces, rather than being a spy,' Holly said.

Juliette grimaced. 'I know. I have to be careful not to misrepresent myself, or my name in the industry – and it's a small one – will be mud. But I've basically told her the truth.'

Holly gasped.

Juliette held up her hand. 'Don't panic, not that much

219

truth. I told Astrid I saw the necklace in her online feed – true – and I had a client who was very interested, another truth. I also said I had a couple of beautiful bespoke pieces that she might like, which is true. She came back and said the pearls, as she called them, were sentimental and not for sale but she did have a few pieces she wouldn't mind an appraisal on and she'd be interested in seeing what I've got.'

'That's brilliant. And have you... you know... all the rest of what you promised?' Holly asked.

'Absolutely. That's why my company is happy to send me.' She reached down to her handbag under the seat in front of her, and grabbed an iPad. 'I've got three beautiful gold necklace and bracelet sets made by the hottest young designer in the UK, Zane Harper.' Juliette looked to Holly for a reaction. 'Everyone is after his pieces. He works with gems and pearls, too. You've never heard of him?'

Holly sighed. 'I'm so out of touch, I haven't heard of anyone.' She glanced at the images as Juliette flicked through them. 'Wow, so beautiful.'

'I know,' Juliette said, and after showing Holly she put her iPad away, but not before smiling when she saw a message waiting for her from Luke.

'So we just need to focus on finding the brand mark on rhe Tender Heart necklace, then we know it's the real thing and Esther can pursue justice, and then you can do your thing with Astrid and make some sales, hopefully,' Holly concluded.

'She's bringing her boyfriend, too, he's a musician,' Juliette said.

'Two against two. How did she come across?' Holly asked.

'I hope I'm wrong, but kind of privileged.'

'Great.' Holly sighed. 'I hope you can win her over. I've had enough tension these past few months to last for the rest of the year.'

'It's all good, let's just play it by ear. As you said, the most important thing we've got to do at this meeting is find that symbol – the brand.' Juliette clinked glasses with Holly. 'To bringing the Tender Heart home.'

'To reuniting families,' Holly agreed. She clinked and sipped her champagne. It made her think of Alexander and Meghan, then Esther and the Tender Heart, and all the lost and found items that came her way and, for just a moment, she felt like she might be doing some good in the world.

He hated to admit it, but Alexander was missing Holly.

'Bullocks', he said, wandering around the house, his hands in his pockets. It felt empty. 'Bloody crazy,' he said, shaking his head. 'I'm an idiot'.

He stopped at the front windows, glancing out just in time to see a woman and her young son claim a thin red pencil case with superheroes on it from the *Lost and Found* basket. He smiled, watching as the young lad clapped with delight on finding his pencil case and finding it still full; he opened his school bag to put it in.

Alexander shook his head. *She's a weird chick,* he thought, musing about Holly and her business of finding lost and missing items. And then he realised he was lost without her.

'I'll do something useful,' he said, to an empty room. He saw Holly's laptop on the desk – she'd taken the smaller one on her trip, the one she called a pad or something like that. Alexander opened it, turned it on and waited for it to load. A login screen appeared.

'Login? Well how the hell do I know what that is? A number, a name? For the love of God,' he said, and angrily pressed the same button to turn it off.

He stood and paced some more. *What did I do before she arrived?* he thought.

'I know, I'll go read up on Andy. Holly was going to see him, anyway.' Alexander glanced at a couple of files on her desk and finding the one with his name on it, sat down and opened it. It didn't occur to him that she might not want him to look, or that she was keeping the information from him – he was the client, after all.

There were the notes about his own death, copies of press clippings from the funeral and investigation, the photo of him and Meg taken by the gardener. It stopped him in his track as he stared at the two of them.

God, so young. Beautiful, beautiful Meg.

He flipped through her notepad; there was no information on Meg. *Did she expect I would look here? Where is she keeping that info, or doesn't she have anything yet?* He glanced at the laptop. *Bet it's in there. I should have paid more attention when she was using it.*

Then he saw the information on his mate, Staff-Sergeant Andy Davies. She'd printed out a message he sent with his suggestion to visit and the address.

'Right then,' Alexander said, taking the paper and closing the folder. 'I'll head to Andy's place and do some study of my own.' And then he vanished.

Holly recognised her immediately. She nudged Juliette and nodded in the direction of the bar where a beautiful dark-haired woman sat with a handsome guy. The hotel bar was sophisticated and private.

Astrid looked like money: her clothing, her haircut, her jewellery and her handbag said it all. Holly felt like a

Bohemian cousin allowed out for the night. Fortunately, Juliette knew how to play the game and matched Astrid's appearance dollar for dollar.

The maître d' approached them and Juliette gave their names and indicated Astrid. They were led to her table. Astrid's boyfriend rose to greet them; Holly liked that.

'You must be Astrid and Timothée,' Juliette said, extending her hand and introducing herself and Holly. 'It's great to meet with you.'

The ladies sat, with Juliette next to Astrid, and Holly beside her, next to Timo.

'It's lovely to meet with you, too,' Astrid said, speaking English with a delightful French lilt. 'We both speak English,' she said, anticipating Juliette's question.

Holly felt an odd division at the table; Astrid and Juliette were like two peas from the same pod – fashionable, sophisticated, comfortable in the spotlight. She and Timo were comfortable in their own skin, happy to remain in the warmth of their glow.

They made small talk about their journey, the weather and the environment while Holly and Juliette ordered tea and Astrid and Timo ordered coffee and a selection of dainty desserts to share.

'This is a beautiful room,' Holly said, admiring the chandeliers, plush furnishings and beautiful wallpaper.

'It's my favourite,' Astrid said.

'It is,' Timo agreed and looked a little embarrassed. 'We almost have a regular table.'

After their refreshments arrived, Juliette got down to business. She produced a number of samples of her client's work, including the bespoke work of the U.K.'s hottest designer, Zane Harper. Juliette also showed several images from her iPad.

Astrid gushed over them. 'So he could make this exclusively for me?' she said, admiring a set of gold and pearl drop earrings.'

'Indeed,' Juliette said, 'he only produces bespoke pieces.'

'Ooh, I love it. What do you think, Timo?' she asked.

Timo turned his attention to the piece and admired it as expected. He withdrew as Juliette and Astrid continued to speak.

'I'm not much of a jewellery advisor,' he said, with a grin.

'Nor I,' Holly confessed.

'I can tell,' he said. 'You are only wearing a watch. Most practical.'

'Jewellery irritates my skin,' Holly confessed. 'And I'm a little lost as a fashionista, as well. I didn't get that gene.'

Timo laughed. 'Well, that makes two of us.'

'I hear you are a musician,' Holly said to him.

'A violinist,' he confirmed.

'Professional?'

'Yes, with the Orchestre de Paris,' he said. 'I only made my debut recently.'

'Congratulations, you must be very good,' Holly exclaimed.

'Thank you,' he said, and turned his amber eyes away shyly. Holly, too, felt the connection. He was a handsome man, not showy enough for Astrid, Holly thought. He was dressed in light cream pleated pants, a crisp white dress shirt and brown brogues – very neutral but tasteful. His brown hair was neat, short back and sides and he was clean-shaven.

'I love the violin,' she continued. 'My Aunty Kate – whom I'm very close to – loves the ballet and orchestra. I have been her plus one at many a performance in London... lucky me.'

'Indeed. You don't play?' Timo asked.

'No, I play the piano, with little talent.'

Timo laughed again. 'And what is your talent?' he asked.

Before Holly could respond, Juliette interrupted.

'Holly, you must see this, it's the Tender Heart we saw online,' Juliette said, getting her attention as Astrid displayed a black jewellery case in front of her.

Astrid opened the case and Holly gasped. 'Oh, it's breathtaking!'

She felt Timo shuffle uncomfortably beside her and look around. It was an expensive piece to have out in the open and Astrid put them at risk putting it on show.

'My great-grandmother was given it on her wedding day,' Astrid said. 'It must be passed down to the first-born women in my family line. Now that my mother has passed, it's mine to mind for this generation,' she said.

Holly watched her as she spoke, so self-assured and glamorous. She returned her attention to the necklace and thought it the most beautiful thing she had ever seen.

'May I?' Juliette asked, reaching for it.

'Of course,' Astrid said.

'It is a thing of beauty,' Timo said. 'German heritage isn't it, Astrid?' he said.

'Yes,' she said, and said no more. She looked displeased at his comment.

Juliette looked at the piece closely, turning it over and admiring it. 'A beautiful design indeed.' She saw the logo engraved on the gold clasp at the top of the necklace. With a glance at Holly, she gave a barely discernible nod.

They had found Esther's Tender Heart.

WAR AND PEACE

*A*ndy must have finished his military career with a reasonable pension, Alexander thought as he surveyed Andy's modern room in the aged care complex. Not too shabby at all. Alexander thought aged care meant you'd be living in a cubicle, but Andy had a large room, with a big TV, a private bathroom and a reasonable minibar and kitchenette. Alexander also had a decent collection of wine on the shelf, which two cleaning staff were moving around and wiping as Alexander arrived. One of them shivered, feeling the chill of his entry. She looked around and suggested to her co-worker that a breeze was getting up, which her colleague thought was just fine, given the heat of the day.

So where was the old bastard, Alexander wondered. He'd sit and wait. That took all of a minute and as the ladies were finishing up, Andy entered, wheezing and leaning on a cane. He thanked them as they left. Nothing had changed; his salacious ogling of the two ladies as they walked out of his room and down the hallway to the next bedroom belied his seventy-plus years. Alexander shook his head, thinking that he himself might be dead but he'd kept his figure and knew his boundaries. He chuckled at his own joke.

Now he had to work on his subliminal thought skills; he hadn't used them for years. Well, that wasn't quite true... he'd used them to try and move tenants along from his house, but he hadn't used them to find out any serious information for a long time, maybe forever. *Shouldn't be too hard with Andy, though, given he's just been communicating with Holly. I should be fresh in his mind.* Alexander took a deep breath and began to think about their days in the army; he kept his focus on Andy.

Staff-Sergeant Andy Davies sighed, glanced to the clock and poured himself a large glass of red wine. He must be a patient with quite a few liberties, Alexander thought. Andy sat down next to Alexander; he couldn't see him.

'Steady on, mate, that stuff will kill you.' Alexander joked.

Andy took a large gulp and, sitting back, he crossed his legs, placing them on the coffee table. It was quiet in the unit; you could hear the whirl of a vacuum sweeper in the next room – the cleaners were hard at it. Occasionally, a splash could be heard from the pool outside, or a laugh from downstairs, the sound of a car coming and going, but in Andy's room, they sat quietly.

Alexander went back to work, implanting his name in Andy's memory.

Andy sighed, put his wine down and rose, walking to the bookshelf where a scattering of books and a few photo albums were displayed. Alexander waited. In a few moments, Andy selected a photo album from the shelf – the old-fashioned type, ring-bound, with a nature photo on the front. He sat back down, reached for the wine glass and took another large gulp. And then he flicked it open.

'Ah, now we're talking,' Alexander said, folding his arms

across his chest. The album contained shots of Andy's military days.

'Looking young and slim there, son,' Alexander said, and perhaps Andy had heard Alexander subliminally or perhaps he had just thought the same thing, as he smiled at the photos. He flicked through every now and then, commenting on the photos or saying someone's name.

'Jesus, look at Rod there, I'd forgotten that silly bugger,' Andy said, at the shot of himself, Rod, and a few of the other lads that had come and gone.

Andy kept turning the pages until he came to a squad shot. He turned the album on its side and studied the faces. Alexander found himself amongst the group.

'Geez, we were young, Andy,' he said.

Andy turned the page and there it was, larger than life – a shot of the two of them together in uniform and laughing. It was just before they boarded the plane, just before the mission started.

It stopped Alexander in his tracks; he'd forgotten that shot had been taken. He hadn't seen it since then.

Andy shook his head, and Alexander turned to watch his reaction.

'You silly bastard, Alex,' Andy said.

If Alexander was living, he would have held his breath. Instead, he froze, waiting for Andy to say more.

Why? Alexander thought, waiting. *Because I got myself killed, or because you didn't like me saying hello to my in-law, Ronin?*

Andy flipped the page to another squad photo. Then he flipped back and looked at the photo of himself and Alexander together. He ran his hand across his face and snapped the book closed.

Alexander watched him, trying to read if it was remorse or

guilt that had brought on the reaction. Holly would be able to ask those questions, but realistically, Alexander knew Andy wouldn't admit to anything. He may have seen more than he reported at the time and have something up his sleeve; he might have mellowed over the years and would offer up more now as he got closer to checking out of this life.

Whatever was going on in his head, Alexander wasn't going to find out just now, unless Andy drank a fair bit more of that red wine.

Now that the heritage of the Tender Heart had been established, Juliette got to work, presenting Astrid with the trendy jewellery designs and Holly could breathe again; her work was done. In truth, she just wanted to call Esther but had to wait. She did manage to get a photo, however, offering to get a shot of the two ladies with the necklace and a scattering of other designs for their social media feeds. Holly never got her head around why they could be bothered.

'I think we've been forgotten,' Timo said, turning his attention to Holly.

'Understandable,' Holly said, with a smile. 'When it comes to conversing about jewellery, I've got nothing.'

He laughed. 'Me neither.'

There was an undeniable connection between them – a current of interest and genuine attraction. A spark.

Timo continued. 'So do you get to Paris much? You know, maybe to attend the ballet or orchestra with your aunt?'

Holly thought his voice held some hope.

'I've been a couple of times, but she's a London season ticket holder. Does your orchestra tour at all... perhaps in London?'

'Occasionally, but I come to London more times with my history group.'

'Who or what is that?' Holly asked, with genuine interest.

'We're very dull,' Timo said. 'It's a group of friends from my graduation year – I studied music and history – and we go to exhibitions around Europe that excite our inner history nerd. My brother, on the other hand, follows his rugby team around Europe. I believe that is much more exciting to most people.'

Holly laughed. 'Ah, call me a nerd then. I've been known to spend hours in the museum. One day I'll travel to the U.S. and spend a week at the Smithsonian! Now, that would be exciting.'

They were so engrossed in their conversation that it surprised Holly when Astrid and Juliette excused themselves to briefly move to a table with better light. Juliette wanted Astrid to see the true colour of a selection of gems.

Holly watched them go and then returned her attention to Timo. He poured another round of tea from the pot, offering her a cup and she accepted with thanks.

Timo lowered his voice. 'You know the history of that neck-lace, don't you?'

Holly bit her lower lip and studied him. It was too risky to tell him too much. He would have to be loyal to Astrid, surely; he would have to tell her that they were here on a mission.

He nodded, taking her silence for agreement.

'It belongs with its rightful owner,' he said, with a quick glance over to Astrid. She hadn't heard him.

'Why do you say that?' Holly asked. 'Do you have some interest in this area?'

He nodded. 'My passion is history, but it's more than that. I'm Jewish.'

Holly breathed out and nodded slowly. 'I understand. I have a dear friend in my village whose father was a jeweller. He made a beautiful necklace for his bride, her mother. It was only a few years after they married – when my friend was a young girl – that their lives changed.'

'Their lives ended?' Timo asked.

Holly nodded.

'Then you must make it right,' he said. 'Bravo.'

'You will keep my secret?' Holly asked. 'I know it puts you in a very awkward position.'

He sat back and looked over at Astrid. 'No, it doesn't. We've spoken about this topic and Astrid knows my interest in it. I haven't betrayed her, I am simply aware that its ownership may not lie with her family, and she has a very wealthy family.'

'It's not about the money, of course,' Holly said. 'My friend doesn't care about financial compensation. It's all she has of them.'

'I know,' he said. 'It's her family heirloom, no one else's.'

Holly nodded. 'Thank you.'

'I've enjoyed meeting you. I hope maybe if I come to London, or rather your village, we might catch up?' he asked.

'Ah, trust me, you would have no reason to come to my village, it is very small and a little seaside town. But London, yes. It is a short drive for me. I'd love to see you play.' She opened her handbag, and pulled a business card out of her wallet. 'That's me,' Holly said.

Timo read the card: *Missing Pieces – Lost, Found and Broken.* 'I'll find you,' he said.

She nodded and gave him a shy smile. 'Good, I hope so.'

They waited until the taxi was well away from the hotel and then turned to each other.

'Oh my God!' Juliette squealed, and Holly laughed, grabbing her in a hug.

'We did it,' Juliette said.

'We've found it! I could barely contain myself,' Holly said, her face flushed with excitement. 'Thank you, Juliette, thank you. I couldn't have done it with you,' Holly said, still holding Juliette's hand.

'You introduced me to the man of my dreams, so one good favour... Are you going to call Esther?'

Holly nodded. 'Right now,' she said, with a glance to the front seat at the driver. She noted to keep the discussion in broad terms. 'I'll put it on loudspeaker.'

Esther answered after two rings.

'Esther, it's Holly and I've Juliette here with me, we're on loudspeaker.'

'Hello, my dears. So you've met her?'

Holly could hear the trepidation in Esther's voice.

'We've found it, Esther.' She heard the sharp gasp that followed.

Juliette piped in. 'We found the brand, and we photographed it. It's your mother's without a doubt.'

'Oh my,' Esther said, 'I can't believe it. For years I've been looking. I just can't believe it.'

'We nearly imploded trying to act natural,' Juliette joked and they all laughed with the tension.

'Oh, my dear girls, all these years and you found it so easily. I never thought I'd get to see it again before I died,' she said, her voice emotional.

'Do you want me to email the photo to you, Esther? Or I'll be home tomorrow if you want to come around to see it and have a cup of tea. We can start the claim phase together if you like?'

'I'd much rather do that,' Esther said. 'I just can't believe it.'

The taxi pulled into their hotel, and while Juliette pulled

out her business card to pay, Holly took Esther off speaker and exited the taxi with a wave of thanks to the driver.

'Of course, I'd love to see it through. I want to see it in your hands. Esther, it's stunningly beautiful – everything you said and more,' Holly said. 'I was quite emotional seeing it.'

'Holly, I knew from the moment you put that sign up that you were the one for the mission.'

'It was a team effort, I'm the least of the players,' Holly said, as Juliette joined her. 'If you hadn't seen the photo on her social media feed, and if Juliette didn't have the business angle, I'd still be searching.'

'No, you wouldn't, you made it happen. Thank you, my dear, thank you both.'

They wrapped up their conversation and Holly hung up.

'We have to go out tonight for dinner, Paris nightlife and real celebratory French champagne,' Juliette said.

'Without a doubt,' Holly agreed. 'Did you get much business from Astrid?'

They walked towards the lift.

'She ordered two pieces from me that are outrageously priced. I will be employee of the year,' Juliette joked.

Holly linked her arm through hers and they entered the lift. 'Riding high,' she said.

'Best feeling ever,' Juliette agreed.

'Well, that was fun,' Astrid said, as she walked with Timo to his apartment. She drew the admiration and glances of people who recognised her as they walked along. Astrid loved that.

'Nice ladies,' Timo agreed. 'What did you buy?'

'Two gorgeous pieces, expensive but worth it.'

'Dare I ask how much?' Timo's jaw dropped as Astrid revealed the price.

'Oh my God, that would be more than the average charity fundraises in a year! And you're going to wear them in your ears.'

She rolled her eyes. 'You're such a wet blanket, Timo. My family donates a lot to charity. It's not my fault that there are poor people in the world. Do you expect me to live the same way so that they feel better?'

He smiled. 'Of course not, I was just saying.'

'But you take all the fun out of it. I don't want to wear them around you now. Besides,' she continued, getting fuelled up, 'I work hard, so why shouldn't I have the occasional nice thing?'

'Sorry, I didn't mean that, really,' Timo said, trying to diffuse the mess he had got himself into. 'Of course you should have some rewards, and you'll look gorgeous wearing them. I insist on seeing them on. But now I'd like to see you with just me, tonight, for dinner.'

Astrid rolled her eyes and smiled. 'Smooth.'

Timo grinned.

They continued down the street hand in hand and not speaking. Timo wondered what they were doing together, and what an English girl in Paris was doing tonight.

HOME SWEET HOME

'$\mathcal{I}$'m home! Pleased to see me?' Holly asked Alexander as she closed the front door behind her.

He stood, arms folded, leaning against the back of the couch, his frame empty. He grinned.

'Strangely, yes,' he said. 'Can't believe I'm saying that. I even missed you!'

'Stop it right now!' Holly exclaimed. 'And to think just a few months ago when I moved in here, you couldn't get me out of the house fast enough.'

'The more important question is, how much did you miss me?' Alexander asked, and Holly laughed. She didn't answer, heading upstairs to put her bag in her room. A few minutes later she skipped back down the stairs.

'I missed you some,' she said.

'Garbage. Okay, tell me everything.'

'I'm having a wine and sitting outside to look at my garden and the waves against the rocks. Care to join me?' she asked.

'Sure. Pour me one and we'll sit in *my* garden and catch up,' he said, with a smirk.

'Did you water the garden while I was gone?' she asked, as she poured two generous glasses of white wine.

'Of course. I've always been good at following orders.' He opened the door as Holly carried the wine to their small, round, outdoor table and chairs.

'I know I've only been gone a few days but it is nice being back here. I felt like I was coming home,' she said, and breathed in the fresh salt air deeply. They clinked glasses. Holly drank. Alexander did, too, without any liquid leaving the glass.

'We had a win,' she said, and began to tell him everything.

Fifteen minutes later, a glass of wine almost gone, six passing neighbours waved to and a story recounted, Holly drew breath.

'Well, full kudos to you,' Alexander said, watching Holly with a look of pride. 'Esther must be blown away,'

'She was very emotional. It was a great trip,' Holly sighed, and smiled.

Alexander looked at her. 'Hang on, you're not telling me everything, there's more.'

'Well, I did meet a really nice French guy.'

'Did you now?' Alexander said, narrowing his eyes with suspicion. 'Is there such a thing?'

'Stop it,' she said, reprimanding him. 'You'd like him. He's down to earth and he's a musician, a violinist actually. His name is Timothée but he goes by Timo, and he visits London every now and then with his history group.'

'He sounds wild. I'll need to meet and approve of him.'

Holly rolled her eyes. 'Thanks, Dad, but you're off duty.'

'Come on, you've admitted yourself you are not the best at picking men – for the love of God, you're living with a ghost, need we say more? Besides, I met your ex-husband if you remember? Nope, I'll need to check this guy out,' Alexander insisted.

'You are so overstepping your mark,' Holly said, and shook her head.

'Call it caring. If I brought home a nice ghost girl, wouldn't you want to check her out?' he joked, and Holly laughed.

'I'd love to meet the ghost girl but just to welcome her, not to approve. I accept that you are all grown up and can make those choices for yourself,' Holly preached.

'Then clearly you aren't as worried about my welfare as I am about yours,' he said, looking like he'd had his nose put out of joint.

'That's probably because you're dead,' Holly said. 'There's not much more can happen, really.'

'Technicality, really.'

Holly swapped glasses with him and proceeded to drink Alexander's wine, that had not disappeared at all despite him having at least half a dozen sips.

'It's good to be home, though, with you,' Holly said, conceding she liked him.

'Of course it is,' he said, and smiled.

It was 9 am. Holly had been up early, had her beach run, showered and the office was open for business. It was a lovely morning – there was a crispness in the air and sunshine coming through the window in prisms of light.

Holly was expecting Esther later this morning. She opened Esther's file, updated it and closed it thirty minutes later. Then she opened Alexander's file and noticed some papers were out of order.

'Sergeant? Front and centre, please,' she called, and he appeared beside her, startling her.

She placed her heart on her hand. 'Must you always do that?'

'I must. Besides, you summoned me,' he said. 'What's up?'

'Did you go through this file?' she asked.

'Yes. I'm the client, I can go through anything.' He saw her expression. 'Can't I?'

'Well, technically yes, I suppose, but you hire me to find out information so you should let me present it.'

'Okay, I'll take that on board, Ma'am,' he said, standing straight and saluting.

She gave him a smirk. 'What did you do with it?'

'Nothing. I didn't remove anything,' he said, and sank into a chair opposite her.

'What did you do with the information you found in the file?' Holly broke down her question.

'Oh, that,' he said, and smiled, thinking she would be impressed by his initiative. 'I went and visited the Staff-Sergeant.'

'What!' she almost screamed. 'Alexander, tell me you're not serious?'

Alexander had learnt in his living years that this reaction meant he'd best tread lightly. 'Okay, I'm a little serious, I might have just dropped in.'

'Oh my God!' Holly crossed her arms across her chest and glared at him. 'Why bother with me? Why didn't you just go and do the job yourself?'

'I didn't have his address, I needed you to find it.'

'You know I was planning on talking to him. He invited me to come and see him,' Holly said.

Alexander frowned. 'Okay, back up here.' He sat down on the chair next to her desk. 'I'm clearly missing something but why are you freaking out about this? I didn't appear to him.'

'Oh,' Holly said, 'why didn't you say that? That's cool then.' She calmed down.

'Is it?' he asked, not sure.

'Yeah, that's fine. I just thought you blew it.'

'Me?' He scoffed. 'Not likely.' He saw the sceptical look she gave him.

'Oh no.' Her face turned deadly serious.

Alexander frowned and debated disappearing but thought better of it. 'What have I done now?' he asked.

'Tell me you didn't go through Meg's file, too?' She looked around her desk.

'No,' he assured her. 'I couldn't find it.'

Holly remembered she'd locked it away for that very reason. She glanced up at him.

'Ah, I forgot I was one step ahead of you,' she said, giving him one of her best smirks.

'Can't believe I'm being drilled and outsmarted by a five-foot, bossy pipsqueak,' he said, rising.

'I'm actually 165 centimetres tall – we've gone to metric, you know?' she said, with another smirk. 'So, back to Andy. What exactly did you do when you were at his place?'

'I just sat on the couch next to him and put some subliminal thoughts in his head to make him think about me,' Alexander said, 'but he didn't reveal anything.'

Holly pushed away from the desk and stood up. She walked to the front of the room and paced along the windows, looking out at the sea and rock cliffs.

'Hmm, I didn't know you could do that subliminal thing. Did you make me subliminally take on this job?'

Alexander looked truly offended. 'Don't be ridiculous! The thought never crossed my mind. But it's not a bad idea,' he said, reflecting on it. 'I guess I could have done that if you refused.'

He stopped talking, to see her glaring at him. 'Shame I said that out loud,' he said.

'Yeah, real shame. Tell me exactly what happened with Andy.' She returned and sat down at her desk.

'I suggested he think about me. After he poured himself a glass of red, he opened an album full of photos from our days as soldiers. Eventually, he flicked through to a shot of him and me, and he said something about me being a silly bastard, and that was it.'

'That was it? That's pretty lame.'

'Yeah, well, subliminal doesn't guarantee results and there was no-one there for him to talk to, or he might have spilled the beans. So you see, you will be useful, after all.'

'Goody,' she said, and gave him a smile.

He shook his head at her. 'You're developing a smart-ass attitude, Miss.'

'Yes, I picked it up from you. And it's Ms to you,' Holly said. A movement caught her eye and she glanced out to see Esther coming up the path. 'Ah, my next client.'

She moved to the door to greet Esther as Alexander returned to his frame.

VISITING HOURS

*H*olly felt she could safely boast that she was the only person to have ever driven down the motorway with a ghost beside her, navigating.

She glanced over at Alexander.

'What?' he asked. 'We're on track.' He consulted the map on his lap.

'I don't doubt that for a minute,' she said, 'but we can always use the Navman if needed.'

'That pompous twat,' he said.

Holly laughed. 'I happen to find that refined voice telling me where to go, very sexy.'

'I can do that if you need me to, just let me know,' he assured her. 'I miss driving.'

'I get that,' Holly said. 'I love driving – the freedom of just getting on the road and going. Being in charge, playing your own music... I'm always amazed you can be in a whole new town or city in a matter of hours.'

Alexander agreed. 'And the pleasure of driving a good car, there's nothing like it.'

She shook her head. 'You know, it's so weird. If anyone had said to me this time last year that I'd be driving down the motorway with a ghost to check out why he died, I would have had them committed.'

Alexander smiled. 'Yeah, you're so lucky you came to stay at *Findlater House*.

She rolled her eyes and smiled. But she agreed with him. It was amazing how her life had changed since coming to *Findlater House*. It was so rewarding to finish Esther's case today. Earlier, they had sat and filled in the forms for lodgement with the national agency who, with the law behind them, would now approach Astrid and her family for the surrender of the Tender Heart. They had emailed the files and the photo showing the brand, and then Holly had printed out a copy to mail and a copy for Esther. She just hoped the process would not take too long and Esther would be holding her mother's necklace again very soon.

Esther had invited her to dinner that weekend which she had accepted happily; especially as Luke was going to London this time to see Juliette, and Holly wouldn't have her staying over. She glanced at Alexander again. If and when he found out what happened to him and why Meghan never returned to *Findlater House*, would he disappear for good? It would be weird not having him around now. She'd come to like him, probably too much, she thought. But meeting Timo was exciting and maybe, just maybe, that might lead to something, despite their living in different countries.

It started raining and within a few seconds it was coming down hard. The wipers were working overtime. Holly flicked the lights on and slowed down. Not a good omen, she thought; definitely not a good omen for what lay ahead.

Alexander got them safely to Andy Davies's retirement village. The rain had stopped and everything looked fresher for it.

'Well, this is nice,' Holly said, looking at the gated and treed surrounds. It was private and secure and through the gates they could see elderly people sitting in the gardens, alone or with company.

'You're so polite and nice,' Alexander said. 'I think it's awful.'

Holly laughed out loud. 'Yeah, well it might be awful for you and me, but if we were in our late seventies like Andy, we might think it's grand.'

'I *am* in my late seventies,' Alexander reminded Holly. 'I'm just well preserved.'

'Yeah, well, death will do that to you,' Holly teased him. She parked under the shade of a large tree in the car park and they alighted – Alexander did so without opening his door.

'Now try not to speak to me in case I answer you and they don't let me leave,' she said, reminding Alexander – or more importantly herself – that he wasn't visible.

She went to the glass entry door and pulled but the door was locked. Holly looked around for a buzzer but before she could find one, the receptionist at the desk inside had buzzed her in. She made her way to the desk.

A middle-aged woman, with her hair pulled back into a tight bun and carrying a little more weight than was comfortable, greeted Holly. Her name tag read, *Sandra*.

'Sorry about that,' she said. 'Our residents are not locked in, but it's just a safety precaution as several of them wander... and the last one wandered almost to the next village before we found him. For an old fellow, he had some speed about him!'

Holly grinned. 'Was he sponsored?'

Sandra laughed. 'There's a thought.'

Holly continued. 'I'm here to see Andy Davies, please. I'm

a friend of a soldier he served with many years ago, he's expecting me.' Holly always gave too much information when she was nervous, and she was anxious about what was to follow, especially as Alexander had insisted on coming with her.

'Oh, Andy will be delighted to have some company. No one in here gets too many visitors, so any break to the day is always welcome. I'll call his room to announce you and then give you directions.'

'Thank you,' Holly said, and stepped back, feeling the cold air as she must have stepped into Alexander. She heard a low groan and repressed a giggle.

Sandra called, announced Holly and rose to point her towards Andy's apartment. Holly thanked her, and followed the path down a long, open, but covered walkway with nice gardens on either side. At the end, she turned left, counted three apartments along and then guessed the man standing in the open doorway was Andy and she had found the right place.

'Mr Davies?' she asked, not sure whether she should be addressing him by his regimental title.

'Andy, please, and you must be Holly, good to meet you,' he said, extending his hand. Andy greeted Holly with a look best described as lascivious; she felt like a dessert he was hoping to try later. She handed over the real dessert – the apple cake she had brought with her.

He invited her in and Holly could feel Alexander close by. She glanced around – it was a nice apartment, neat and clean and quite upmarket, all cream and neutral colours with glimpses of the garden through the windows. She raised an eyebrow as she gave Alexander a quick glance. He knew all about it, he'd been here previously.

Holly accepted the offer of a cup of tea.

'You shouldn't have brought the cake, but I'm glad you did,' he said and Holly laughed.

'Mum always said you should never arrive empty-handed,' Holly said, accepting the two butter plates and a knife.

'I'll play mum pouring the tea if you cut the cake,' Andy said. 'We could move to the garden if you like,' he said.

Holly did prefer to be out in the open but, knowing Alexander would struggle with the light if the meeting prevailed, she declined the offer.

'It's a bit of a warm one. We might be more comfortable here, don't you think?'

'Definitely,' he agreed. They sat at his dining room table opposite each other and Alexander sat next to Holly. She cut the cake and served a piece to both of them while Andy poured the tea. She expected this would be the most civilised part of their meeting once the discussion heated up.

'So you want to know about Alex. Well, that's a blast from the past,' Andy said, and gave a wheezing cough followed by an apology. 'How do you know him? You're related, is that right?'

'Not directly,' she said. 'One of my close relations was his landlady and they became personal friends.' Holly didn't want to try and explain how Alexander knew her grandmother over many decades but didn't age himself! She continued: 'So, I began researching him and the family history.'

'Nice one,' Alexander said, for Holly's ears only.

'You know, I once had a lot of time for Alex,' Andy started. He rose and went to the bookshelf, bringing back a photo album. He flipped to the photo Alexander had seen the other day, the shot of the two of them and pushed it towards Holly.

'That's us when we were young and wild,' he joked.

Holly looked at the photo of the two of them. Alexander was laughing and looked so handsome in his uniform. She smiled and touched the edge of the photo.

'Great photo,' she said.

Alexander opened his mouth to speak and Holly glanced in

his direction with a stern look. He shut it again. She couldn't concentrate if he was going to keep injecting commentary.

'There's another,' Andy said, and flicked a few more pages to a squad photo. He tapped on Alex's photo. 'That's him there.'

Holly could pick him out easily, tall and handsome in the group.

'So it is. Let me find you,' she said, and glanced along the rows. 'Ah-ha!' She pointed to a man looking very stern and sensible. Andy nodded and laughed.

'Got it in one,' Andy said. 'You know, I thought Alex was a good bloke. Then I found out that he was a plant.'

Alexander swung back in his chair, almost hitting the wall and Holly choked on her tea.

'Sorry,' she said, clearing her throat. 'A plant? Like a spy? Alexander?'

Andy nodded. 'After our first mission, I was called into headquarters and told that one of my team was a member of the IRA undercover. They didn't know who it was, but orders we were given on the last mission were intercepted by the IRA. Someone had fed them straight to their contact which is why we had so much trouble – everywhere we went, the IRA was expecting us.'

'But... Alexander?' Holly said.

'Didn't believe it myself for a long time,' Andy said, shaking his head.

'Bullshit,' Alexander said, beside her. She could feel the waves of anger coming off him.

'On our second mission, I watched all the men, and I eliminated them one by one. The only one in our squad who fitted it was Alex. His wife was a staunch Catholic, she had family in the south, and I was at his wedding, I met some of them.'

Holly stared at him, her mouth opened in surprise. 'Sorry,'

she said, coming back to the moment. 'I just didn't see that coming.'

'Me neither,' Andy said, and moved his plate forward for a second serving of cake. 'So I started again, eliminating every man as I went along. Alex was the only one with IRA sympathies.'

'What happened?' Holly asked.

Andy cleared his throat again. 'I'll make you a deal, young lady. I'll tell you what happened because there's a lot of water under the bridge now and because you're sort of related, but there are some rules.'

Holly nodded. 'Fair enough.'

'You aren't taping this or reporting it in any way?' he asked.

Holly shook her head. 'No, this is a private conversation.'

Andy nodded, narrowing his eyes at her; he'd had many years of practice at being suspicious.

'I believe I can trust you,' he said, summing her up. He cleared his throat and continued: 'The report on Alex's death said his killer was unknown.'

'Yes, I've seen a selection of the reports,' Holly said.

Andy nodded. 'If you repeat what I tell you today, I'll deny it and I'll say I can't remember what I said. I've got a bit of dementia,' he said.

'I understand. It will go no further than this room. I might tell his widow a version if you'll allow it,' Holly said.

'Well, you're an honest young lady.' He sat and thought a moment. 'Okay, given she's probably my age and who'd believe the ramblings of an old man?'

A very aware old man, Holly thought.

'Agreed?' he asked again and extended his hand to shake.

'Agreed.' Holly shook hands with him and heard Alexander groan beside her.

'I was told by my superior officers that when I find out who the mole was, I was to ensure their elimination.'

Holly gasped and Alexander stood and began to pace, unseen by Andy.

Andy held up his hand to finish. 'It was best if this mole could be on a high-risk mission and be eliminated by the enemy, or by myself in an enemy situation. I couldn't believe how easily it all came together. We're in the middle of a bombing attack and Alex is greeting one of his in-laws... a bloody republican!'

Holly breathed out. 'And you were able to "eliminate" him and make it look like an act of war by the enemy?' she asked.

Andy gave a small nod, not voicing his guilt.

She didn't know what to do with that information, neither did Alexander. Holly appreciated the honesty, but Alexander had been killed by Andy in a situation that made it look like an enemy attack. This man sitting opposite her had carried out a murder with no real evidence other than family ties.

'I was a soldier, and a soldier follows orders, no questions asked,' he said, in justification.

A soldier killed in the line of duty, but was this duty or murder? Holly didn't know what to do or what to say... Her gut instinct began to kick in – and it was telling her to feel a little worried about her own personal safety. Then Alexander's voice interrupted her thoughts.

'Be polite, thank him and get out of here,' Alexander said.

Holly nodded and stacked her plate, cup and saucer.

'I really appreciate your honesty and taking the time to see me,' she said. It was all she could muster. Holly was angry and had a thousand questions. But her mind kept coming back to Meghan's pain at her loss – the life they had missed out on together, cut short by this man.

'No need to rush off, tell me about yourself,' Andy said.

She glanced at Alexander and was saved by the bell – the phone began to ring.

'Go, go,' Alexander said.

Holly stood and grabbed her bag. 'I'll see myself out, you get that,' she said.

'Wait up, I'll just be a minute,' he said, making his way to the phone. But before he had finished saying hello, she was out of the door with a wave.

Holly felt Alexander hurrying her along. She passed by Sandra at reception and fortunately she was talking with a guest. Holly gave her a smile and waved and kept moving, Alexander pushed her along, the cold air of his presence by her side.

En route to the car, in her hurry, an umbrella, a pair of reading glasses and a small embroidery with the needle still in it, found her, but she had to whisper her apologies and keep moving. She couldn't save them today. Holly didn't waste time once she was in the car. She started the ignition and was driving out of the centre in minutes. Once she hit the road, Alexander disappeared from beside her.

Holly didn't call him back; she didn't know what to say.

Okay, she thought to herself, *he has to process the fact that his country sent him to defend its people, but then decided he was the enemy and they would kill him using a man he thought was a close friend. Now I have something to tell Meghan. I wonder what she believed happened, or what she was told, if anything?*

FOUR WEEKS LATER

*H*olly didn't hear from Alexander that night or that week, or the next week even. She didn't call out for him, either, knowing he would appear when he was ready, but she spoke to him occasionally, involving him in decisions, telling him she hoped he was working through it and she was here for him.

He did little things to tell her that he was okay and thinking of her but was not ready to talk, like putting on the lights for her when she came home late, and leaving fresh flowers in a vase in the living room. Holly felt awful for him. She wished she could help but didn't know what to do, and she knew that if she hadn't moved in and agreed to do this job for him, the whole thing would have remained a mystery, which might have been better.

Holly toyed with the idea of sending a thank-you note to Andy for seeing her. Her hands had hovered about the keyboard a few times and she knew it was the polite thing to do, but he was a killer. Sure, he was a soldier following orders but this, in her mind, was different. Alex was his friend.

Wouldn't you want to be sure before you took a man's life? Before you took him away from his wife and family and friends? Wouldn't you exhaust all options to make certain he was the mole?

Over the course of the four weeks since visiting Andy, Holly lived from day to day. She had dinner a couple of times at Esther's place, had her daily walks, watered her new garden and put the sign up in the window for new business. It usually came within weeks of each job. Holly said goodbye to Alexander and visited London for a long weekend, catching up with friends, and the following weekend Juliette stayed a night before spending two nights with Lucas; the pair were going strong.

A few weeks after her return from Paris, she got an email from Timo. He was coming to London in a few months' time and wondered if they might catch up. It was respectful and friendly, so Holly suspected he was still seeing Astrid. He did not mention the necklace or that anyone had contacted Astrid. Esther had spoken several times to the agency since the information and photos were sent... now, they waited. Holly felt like she was treading water in nearly every aspect of her life.

And then, one morning, four weeks after her visit, a message came from Andy. Holly stared at it. She took a deep breath, nervous about opening its contents. It was news that would change everything.

Dear Holly,

I'm sorry you had to depart early. There was something else I wanted to tell you but I was not sure I could say it. I don't like to do it in writing but as I am old and may not get the chance to speak with you again, I want to tell

*you the truth. About six months after Alex's death, I
found the true enemy in our squad. It wasn't Alex.
That's all I have to say.*

*Yours sincerely
Andy*

She emailed Andy back to acknowledge she had received it and
to thank him for sharing. What a huge load he had lived with
over the years, she thought. She hoped it had impacted him at
least a little, not that she wrote that. Holly printed it out and
left it on the table for Alexander to read.

Heartbreaking, Holly thought. Now, having received this, it
was time to see Meghan, but she decided just to wait another
week to see if Alexander showed himself. She was glad Juliette
was coming again to stay a night before she went on to stay with
Lucas. Holly wouldn't have been surprised if they made an
announcement about their relationship sooner rather than
later! But for now, she had an appointment, a new client and
one she didn't expect – Abby from the library. *This could be
interesting!*

She locked the house up and decided to walk to the library
as it was a beautiful day and it would only take her fifteen
minutes. She didn't see Alexander watching her through the
lounge window as she departed.

～

Alexander watched until she was out of sight. He missed Holly
but he wasn't yet ready to face her – he needed to process all
that had happened, get rid of the anger in his system. At first,

he was so angry that he wanted to destroy everything in his sight, and then, after the rage left him, he felt ashamed. He had done nothing wrong, but he had done nothing and that was the problem as he saw it. Andy's actions and the fact that Alexander was a suspect for being a mole, made him realise how much he'd been sitting on the fence.

Truth be known, he felt like he'd let everyone down. Meghan didn't want him there, it was disrespectful to her and her extended family which he had married into. Andy and his squad must have been feeling the same way if they knew there was a mole in the ranks. Even if they didn't, Andy and Alexander's superiors thought it was him. It put his loyalty in question and he'd allowed that by being wishy-washy. He should have made a stand and acted accordingly. He'd paid the price, but so had Meghan in dealing with his death, and Andy, having to deal with the consequences of acting on orders. It took him a while to accept that responsibility but he felt better for it.

He went to put some music on and saw the piece of paper on the table. Did Holly mean for him to read this? he wondered. Alexander lifted the sheet and read Andy's words: *I found the true enemy in our squad. It wasn't Alex.*

He pulled out a chair and slumped in it. It was all for nothing. Did Meghan know about any of this? Was there ever an apology, or any compensation paid to her? He closed his eyes and took a deep breath. It now added to his guilt, strangely. Because Andy had lived with this all his life, too, whereas Alexander knew that if he had just not gone... if he had done what Meghan wanted and pulled out of the mission, done something else with his life, all of their lives would have been different.

He needed to talk with Holly before she talked to Meghan, if it wasn't too late. Now, he wasn't sure if they should talk to

Meghan at all, or if it would be better to let bygones be bygones.

~

Astrid pulled a letter out of her handbag and slapped it down on the table in front of Timo.

'Did you know about this?' she asked, her eyes flaring with anger. Timo pushed his coffee aside and reached for the letter. He wasn't one for public displays of anger, and he glanced around the café to see if anyone was looking their way.

Astrid was oblivious, used to being the centre of attention. She continued. 'I got a phone call as well. They took a photo when they were here, a photo of the necklace, so there's no doubt it is in my possession.'

Timo sighed and read the letter advising Astrid that the Tender Heart necklace would be reclaimed and returned to its proper owner. He folded it and handed it back to her.

'I didn't know but I'm not at all surprised.'

'Did you invite them to Paris?' she said, studying him and watching him for his reactions.

'How would I invite them?' he said, his voice raised in surprise. 'I didn't even know them until we met that day.'

She calmed down a little.

'You seemed familiar with that other girl, what was her name?'

'Holly,' Timo answered. 'She was interesting. But no, I didn't know for sure, but I always suspected the necklace might have been stolen during the war. It's only right it should go back.'

'Insurance won't cover that. We'll get nothing for it.'

'And your family probably paid nothing for it,' Timo reminded her. 'But it's not about money, is it?'

'No,' she said. Astrid narrowed her eyes and lowered her voice with anger. 'Tell me this, Timo. If you found out that the violin that you love and that your dad bought you and mortgaged his house to buy, was stolen, would you willingly give it back with no compensation? You couldn't pay your dad back and you'd be without an instrument that you love. How would you feel about that?'

'I'd be upset and angry,' Timo agreed.

'Exactly,' she cut in.

'But,' he had her attention, 'I'd feel for the people it was stolen from because they'd feel the same way. The punishable person is the one we should all be angry at. In your case, who is that?' Timo asked.

'Well, we don't know that it was my great-grandfather. He might have bought it from whoever confiscated it, but he's no thief.'

'Of course he isn't,' Timo said, pacifying her. 'Lots of things were done in wartime that we could justify against the enemy.'

'Exactly,' she said, putting the letter back in her handbag and shaking her head.

'But the war is over,' Timo said.

A HOMECOMING

$\mathcal{I}$t was much cooler when Holly came home than it was when she left earlier. The wind chill numbed her body and the sound of the waves crashing on the rocks chilled her more. Hurriedly, she unlocked the front door and entered, shivering. She placed her bag on the desk, looked up and gave a small yelp, stepping back in fright. Alexander was sitting on a chair at the table.

'Sorry, I thought you'd be used to me by now,' he said, with a smile.

She took her hand from her heart and breathed out, then moved to sit down opposite him. 'Welcome back – and I don't think I'll ever get used to your random appearances!'

'You're cold,' he stated.

'It's chilly out there.' She stood and excused herself for a moment, raced up the stairs for a sweatshirt and returned, delighted to see him still there. She sat opposite and studied him.

'I'm so glad you're back, I missed having you around,' she said, and smiled.

'Really?' he asked, surprised.

'Of course. Are you okay?'

He sighed. 'I wasn't, but I'm getting there. I was angry at Andy, then I blamed myself for being weak and not leaving the squad when Meghan wanted me to... I've been going through it, over and over.'

'I knew you would be,' Holly said.

They sat in silence for a few moments. Holly laced her fingers to warm up, shuffled in her chair and then, realising she was fidgeting, stopped and looked at the Sergeant.

'I saw the letter you left for me,' he said.

Holly nodded. 'I can't believe it. I've been through the full gamut of emotions, too.'

He gave a grateful smile.

'So here we are then,' she said. 'Is it time to see Meghan?'

'I don't know,' Alexander confessed. 'I want her to know this, but if I put her through all the emotions I've been through this week, then is that wrong? Should I just let her live peacefully now? Did they tell her I was a mole and that's why she has never visited? Or was she just so angry at me for not getting out of the job?' He sighed. 'I'm not thinking straight. What do you think?'

'I've tried to look at this from a few different perspectives,' Holly said. 'I'm only a few years younger than you were when you died –'

'Bloody hell, I've never thought of that,' Alexander said, cutting her off.

'Weird, huh? But I can honestly say that if I lost my husband in circumstances that I couldn't explain, I'd never really rest until I found out the answer.'

'Okay,' he said, taking that on board. 'So are you saying that because Meg never came back here, it means she bought the official line?'

Holly grimaced. 'Well, we don't know what she was told, but I'd be surprised if she was told you were a mole... you'd be her hero, I imagine, if that was the case.'

Alexander made a scoffing sound.

'I'd say she was told you died in the tension that night, the crossfire. Perhaps she never thought to question it, and coming back without you was too hard.' Holly watched his reaction. 'That's how I'd feel. But I'd still want to know the truth if it was different from the version I was holding on to.'

'Even after all these years?' he asked.

'Yes. Wouldn't you?'

'I'm on the fence. What difference will it make now?'

'It's not unlike Esther's situation,' Holly said. 'She could have let that necklace go, just decided that it was history, but she couldn't because it was something that connected her to her father and mother. I bet you that Meghan will feel the same, even after all these decades. She will want to know because she has this connection with you and has probably always harboured some anger or frustration that you were there in the first place.'

'I died when I was twenty-nine,' Alexander said. 'Meghan must now be about mid-seventies,' he calculated. 'Four decades is a long time to stew.'

'She'll want to know, I'm sure,' Holly said. 'But it is entirely your call.'

He thought about it for a moment, and then agreed. 'I'd want to know.'

'So, shall I contact Meghan and let her know I've found something out and ask if I can visit?'

Alexander agreed. 'Let's do it. I guess if she doesn't want to know, we'll be the first to hear it.'

Holly nodded. 'You've never dropped in on her? Not once

since you entered that world?' Holly said, pointing towards heaven.

'I've wanted to. But...' he looked away, 'I wasn't sure I could handle seeing her again... you know.'

Holly nodded. She didn't, but she could imagine.

'You look a lot like her, you know,' Alexander said, returning his gaze to Holly.

'Do I?' Holly smiled. She had seen the photos of Meghan and thought she was lovely. She was flattered. 'So, we're both cute then?'

She smiled and Alexander rolled his eyes. 'Yeah, I walked right into that, didn't I? Apparently that's my strength.'

His comment sobered Holly.

'I'll see if I can make contact then,' she said, confirming that she was going to do it just in case Alexander wanted to change his mind at the last minute.

'I'm ready,' Alexander said.

Holly wasn't sure if calling, emailing or writing was the best idea. She tried to place herself in Meghan's shoes and decided an email or letter would be the best way to introduce herself and let Meghan react at her own pace to the shock. She decided not to message her on social media as they weren't friends and she might never see the message. Holly read back over her earlier notes on Meghan – she was now seventy-five years old, a widow and her only child had also passed away. She found the information about Meghan being the coordinator of a painting group and she looked up their website.

'Got you,' she said aloud, but to herself. She glanced around but she was alone. The painting group had an email contact and it was Meghan.

Holly took a deep breath and drafted the initial contact email.

Dear Ms Austen,

I hope you are well. Our families are distantly connected, so please excuse this out-of-the-blue email. I debated whether to call or mail and thought it might be better for you to have some time to consider my words, rather than catching you out with a phone call. My name is Holly Hanlon and once you and your husband, Sergeant Alexander Austen, rented Findlater House, *which belonged to my grandmother. I'm now staying there myself. As part of my passion for piecing together stories, I have spent some time looking into Alexander's death. My grandma thought so fondly of you both, I have heard. I imagine this email may be distressing for you, but, with the help of some very kind people, I have found out what officially happened to Alexander. It is water under the bridge, but the information might bring you some comfort, even if it may be initially distressing. Would you be open to me visiting so we can meet and talk?*
With very best wishes
Holly Hanlon.

She included her email, phone number and address, then read the email a few more times before pressing "send". And then she knew it was a waiting game.

The following morning, early, there was a knock on the door. Holly was still in her track wear after her run and looking slightly windblown. Alexander hadn't surfaced yet.

Holly answered the door and found Esther – immaculately dressed as always – standing in the doorway with her bag and a small package.

'I'm sorry to come so early,' Esther said, 'but I've just received a registered delivery, brought in person to me by a very official-looking man – it's come.'

Holly gasped. 'The Tender Heart?'

Esther nodded.

'Please, come in, come in,' Holly hurried Esther in. 'I can't believe it.'

Holly noticed the packaging was still sealed. 'Esther, you haven't opened it?'

'No. I wanted us to do it together. You've earned that, my dear, and I need to have the support.'

Holly gently squeezed Esther's arm as she placed the package on the kitchen table and the two of them leant over it.

'I feel surprisingly nervous,' Esther said, fanning herself.

'I'm terrified,' Holly admitted, 'and excited.'

They looked at each other and smiled, and then they both pulled out a chair and sat. Esther slowly broke the seal around the packaging and removed a velvet jewellery box. She placed it between them and then opened it. The creamy pearls with the pink diamond heart rested on a red velvet base.

Esther gasped.

'Oh my, welcome home!' Holly said and tears filled her eyes.

Esther removed it and held it to the light. 'The Tender Heart.'

They stared at the stunning necklace, recalling all it meant, all it represented.

'Isn't it beautiful?' Esther whispered. 'Made by my father for my mother. All I have left of them,' she said. Esther, who was usually so stoic, also teared up, her voice choked.

'May I?' Holly asked, and Esther placed it in her hands.

Holly was awestruck. 'It's the most beautiful piece of jewellery I've ever seen. I can't believe it's home with you.'

'I never thought I would live to see it come home,' Esther said, and dabbed her eyes. She accepted it back and gently placed it in the felt-lined box. She turned to Holly.

'Thank you, my dear,' she said, taking Holly's hands. Esther rose and Holly met her to embrace. Eventually, they pulled apart.

'Have tea with me and tell me everything. How it arrived, how you felt when we opened it, what you are going to do now – if you know,' Holly said, and Esther laughed.

Holly put the kettle on as Esther sat down again. Holly smiled at Alexander, who had appeared in the kitchen doorway when Esther wasn't looking, but Esther did notice Holly's glance and smile. Not much escaped her.

TIME TO MEET MEGHAN

$\mathcal{A}$fter a fun midday meeting with gothic Abby who had a quirky job she hoped Holly would take on – and she did – Holly came home to set up a file for the project. She logged into her laptop and saw two emails that excited her – one from Timo and the other was unexpected; it was from Meghan. Seeing Meghan's name in her inbox gave her goose-bumps; she looked around. After sending the email message to Meghan that morning, she had relaxed. She didn't expect to hear from her for a few weeks, maybe a month, but a response had come back that very afternoon.

Do I call Alexander or read it first? She bit her lip as she sat and thought about it. Holly decided to read it first, just in case Meghan didn't want to know about her deceased husband and then Holly could work out a strategy to break that to him gently.

She took a deep breath, opened the email, and read:

Dear Holly,

Well hello, it is a small world, isn't it? I must say your message caused an avalanche of memories and emotions, which is why I'm responding so soon – and age... at my age, one doesn't wait forever to make decisions. I am joking, of course, which you may not be able to tell given I'm typing. It's been nearly forty years since Alex passed. I can't believe it when the memories are so raw. Yes, my dear, I would be delighted to meet with you. We could talk on the phone if it were too far to come. But if you like a drive, would you care to meet me for morning tea this week or next? Perhaps we should have it at my home in case I become emotional and my make-up runs (joking again). Well, I'll wait to hear from you, Holly.

All the best
Meghan.

'Sergeant!' Holly called out – she liked to use his official title if it required his immediate action, and he appeared a few seconds later.

'What's wrong? Spider? Rubbish need taking out?' he asked, glancing around.

Holly rolled her eyes. 'Oh ha-ha, you need to take a seat.' She noticed his hesitation. 'Please, Alex, it's good, I promise.'

He slipped into a seat opposite her and leaned forward, giving her his full attention.

'I've heard from Meghan.'

Alexander stilled.

'It's okay. She wants to see me, she wants to hear what really happened to you.'

He breathed out – not that he really needed to breathe – and lowered his head to the table. Holly bit her lower lip as she watched him, not sure what to do or what to say, if anything. So she stayed silent. Alexander remained that way for just a few seconds, then sat up and looked at Holly.

'So, it means she can't know the truth, and maybe she does care, after all,' he said, and smiled just a little.

'I'm sure she cares,' Holly said. 'She said the memories were really raw. I'll read you my email to Meghan and her reply.' Holly did so and then Alexander asked her to read it again.

'When are we going?' he asked.

Holly stopped dead, a trick she'd learnt from Alexander and stared at him.

'You know those rules that we put in place when we visited Andy? The rules about not appearing, interfering, freaking out, making noises and –'

'I get it.' He cut her off. 'I promise I won't do that, not to Meghan.'

'Not even if she is angry at you, or says something you want to defend or don't want to hear? Like he was an idiot for being over there, she wanted to kill you herself, or...' Holly softened, 'she doesn't understand how you could leave her?'

Alexander glanced down as the words hit him.

'Alex?'

He returned his gaze to Holly. 'You have my word.'

'Then let's go sooner rather than later.'

It was over. Timo knew it would not last forever, he'd known that almost from the start, but he was still saddened by the end of their relationship. It had been just over a year and there had been some fun times, but he and Astrid knew they were polar opposites. More to the point, Timo could not maintain the level of adoration required to keep Astrid. He didn't want to socialise seven days a week and he didn't want to be constantly in her social media feed. He didn't want to be with someone who flirted outrageously, either to make him jealous or get a reaction, or because she just needed to feel good about herself. He loved her, but he wasn't in love with her.

He sensed she needed and wanted more, too and they were both waiting for his week away with the orchestra to gauge how they felt on his return. And on his first night back it came to a head in, of all places, her spa bath.

'You know the necklace is gone,' she said. 'You weren't here when they came to collect it, so...' Her voice drifted off as though Timo could have saved it.

'I would have been if I wasn't on tour,' Timo assured her.

She tightened her hair bun to keep her hair dry and off her neck. 'It's okay, a couple of friends came and supported me.'

Timo sighed. She hadn't asked after the tour, or if it was a success, if he enjoyed it or played well.

'So are you okay?' he asked, dutifully.

'I have no choice but to be.'

They soaked in silence for a while and finally Timo broached the subject.

'Astrid, I love you. But we both know it's not going to last. We're not really right for each other, but hell, it's been fun,' he said, with a sad smile.

He caught her unawares. Astrid liked to be the one who called things off, the one in control.

'You really want to do this now?' she asked. 'In here, in this intimate moment?'

Timo rose, strangely embarrassed now about being naked in front of her. He grabbed for the towel. 'As good a moment as any, I imagine.' He wrapped the towel around him, turned to Astrid and gave a little bow.

'Thank you, Madame,' he said, formerly, 'for being part of the fabric of my life.'

His emotional words caught her off guard. She was going to say something scathing but she watched as he went through the door. Moments later, Timo was dressed and gathering his personal items, then he left her apartment for the last time.

And within a few hours, Astrid was out with friends, her social media feed showing what a wonderful time she was having, her status changed to single.

And so, too, was Timo – single, that is.

CLOSING A CHAPTER OF LIFE

For a dead guy, Alexander was radiating a lot of nervousness as he and Holly approached Meghan's small unit in the Lilac Fields Retirement Resort. Holly had attempted some conversation along the way but Alexander couldn't focus, so eventually she let it go and they drove in silence. She pulled into the car park, parked under the shade of a magnificent large oak tree and alighted. Holly grabbed the bouquet of flowers from the back seat... one should always arrive with something, she thought.

She checked out the premises; it was a neat little place, safe and with lovely creek views. Holly wondered if lilacs would appear in the field in the right season, hence the name of the "resort". Alexander wondered what Meghan would be like now and if he could remain in the same room without breaking down.

They arrived at the front door and Holly hesitated before knocking. With a quick glance around to make sure no-one was watching them, she studied Alexander.

'Are you okay?' she asked.

'No,' he said, but nodded.

Holly frowned. 'You know the rules?'

He crossed his heart. 'You can count on me.'

She frowned, 'Okay, but I'm worried about *you*, not just about what you might do.'

He rolled his eyes and Holly smiled. *That's better,* she thought, *he's back in character.*

She took a deep breath and knocked, and then the door opened.

A dignified, trim woman with shoulder-length salt-and-pepper hair opened the door. She

was dressed neatly in a pale blue shirt and cream pants which she wore well.

'Holly,' she said, brightly.

'Mrs Austen,' Holly said, not quite sure how to address Meghan. She pushed the flowers towards her.

'Please call me Meghan, and thank you, how delightful. Do come in.' She stood aside and indicating for Holly to leave her shoes on, having no idea that she closed the door on her first husband, Alexander.

Holly almost said something, then realised, of course, that Meghan couldn't see him and in a matter of moments, Alexander stepped into the room. He was transfixed, his eyes glued to Meghan, taking in all her features and remembering them when they belonged to a young woman.

'I hope I won't embarrass you but I have to tell you, you are as beautiful now as your photo was then,' Holly said, stunned by the attractiveness of this senior woman with her creamy skin and bright eyes.

'Oh, Holly, you are very kind,' Meghan said. 'What woman would be embarrassed by such a compliment! Thank you. I'll put these beautiful flowers in water and then will you take tea?'

'Yes please, I'll help.'

The apartment was open-plan and Alexander watched as Meghan made tea and Holly put the cups and milk jug on the small table near the open door. It had a beautiful view of the gardens and creek.

They spoke about their ancestors, Holly told Meghan about the village today and Meghan marvelled at the changes and how some of the older folk were still there, especially at the nursery and library. They both relaxed – although, mused Holly, it would be hard not to relax in Meghan's warm company. Alexander, however, remained frozen, and Holly cast him a sympathetic glance.

After forty minutes of general talk, tea and biscuits, the subject of Holly's visit arose.

'I debated whether to share the information or not,' Holly admitted. 'Sometimes things are best left as they are, I imagine, but I tried to put myself in your place and I think I'd want to know.'

'I think you are right,' Meghan said. 'I truly loved Alex and it took me many years to get over his death. I was angry at him for going, angry at the circumstances, angry at the British government, the military, pretty much anyone in the firing line was the victim of my wrath,' she said, shaking her head.

'I'd be the same, I'm sure,' Holly said. She took a deep breath. 'I found out quite a bit, so please stop me anytime if you have had enough and don't want me to continue, or you need a break.'

Meghan nodded and Holly began telling her all she had unearthed – Andy's actions in finding a mole, thinking it was Alex because of his family connection, and how later he found out that he had "assassinated" the wrong man.

Meghan listened with wide-eye attention. When Holly finished, she sat back and took it all in. Alexander remained motionless beside her, as if in solidarity.

After a short while, Holly spoke. 'I'll make a fresh pot of tea, shall I?'

Meghan leaned forward and patted her hand. 'It's okay, my dear, I'm alright. I just wonder what I would have done with that information all those years ago. How I might have felt about it.'

'Did you suspect?' Holly asked.

Meghan shook her head. 'I believed what they told me... that he was lost in the battle. There were a lot of animosities, it was very complex. But I am pleased to know, Holly, thank you.'

Holly nodded and gave Meghan a small smile.

'Did you ever go back to *Findlater House*, like on your anniversary?' Holly asked, knowing full well the answer, but hoping for an explanation.

'No. Not once. Initially, I couldn't bear to be there without Alex. We had so many plans and that was where it all came to an end. We had been happy at *Findlater House*, very happy,' she said, and smiled at the memory. 'Then, as time went on, it became harder and harder to return until there seemed no point. Alex was no longer there for me, he was here,' she said, and touched her heart.

Alex drew a sharp breath beside Holly and she avoided looking his way. She wanted to touch his hand but that was impossible on a number of levels.

'I hope this meeting won't derail you, Meghan. I'd hate to leave you today and know I caused you to revisit a lot of pain,' Holly said.

'No, I'm pleased to know the truth, relieved even. Alex really liked Andy, too, considered him a friend. He would be devastated if he knew that he was killed by the hand of his Staff-Sergeant. I just wish some justice had been served.'

'It could still be,' I assured her.

'It could,' she agreed. 'But it won't just affect Alexander or me – the impact on myself and the families of everyone involved at that time will be considerable. If I were a younger woman, I'd fight the fight. Now, I'll leave the good Lord to administer justice.'

'I understand,' Holly said. She glanced at Alexander and he gave a small but discernible nod.

'Well, I'd best be going,' Holly said, 'but not before I issue you with an invitation to come back to *Findlater House*. You're welcome anytime, even just to have tea with me.'

Meghan smiled. 'Thank you, Holly. Can I offer you a small piece of advice from a woman nearing the end of her life, to a beautiful woman full of life and just beginning?'

'Please, yes.'

'For a long time I thought Alex was my great love. His death wounded me and I carried that around with me.'

Holly saw Alexander put his head in his hands.

Meghan continued. 'I carried it for so long that when I met my wonderful second husband, I didn't really allow myself to love him fully. I was scared of putting all that love out there again and the risk of the pain.' She took a deep breath. 'We had a son who passed away as well... an illness... so for the decades we were together I lived on the surface.'

Holly didn't interrupt; she had no words that would suffice.

'It wasn't until the last decade of our life together, when he first became ill, that I realised he was the love of my life, my soul mate and I had missed decades of that depth of feeling because of fear and misguided love,' she said, and then Meghan took a deep breath and brightened. 'So my dear, love with wild abandon. Love deeply every time. If you get hurt, you get hurt, but you'll never regret what you put in, only what you don't.'

Holly wiped the tears from her eyes, and in her peripheral vision she saw Alexander had disappeared.

GOODBYES AND HELLO

*H*olly drove home alone. She felt surprisingly relieved and at peace; she wasn't expecting to feel that way. She thought it would be a dramatic meeting and full of angst, but Meghan's words had empowered her. She knew, however, that Alexander might be suffering from Meghan's words. But realistically, their life together had been so short, it was only natural that Meghan eventually moved on and how wonderful it was that she had loved again.

Holly took Meghan's words on board; she would love deeply. She had briefly told Meghan about her ex-husband, but that was life and learning and, as one very clever person said, it is better to have loved and lost than never to have loved at all. And that's how she would look at it from now on.

It would be nice to be back in *Findlater House*, she thought as she drove home. She felt satisfied – two jobs finished successfully. Now she would throw herself into Abby's job. She listened to some music on her car stereo and pondered if she would see Alexander again. Meghan wasn't coming back to the house and maybe he wouldn't, either. She dreaded the thought of him just disappearing. He had kept her sane in those first few months on her own, alone.

'Come back and say goodbye to me, at least,' she whispered, hoping he would hear her. That would be painful, she admitted, but it was always inevitable and it might make her get out there more and do a bit of socialising.

As she was driving along, Holly's phone rang. She accepted the call hands-free.

'Megan, it's Timo, how are you?'

She heard his lovely French lilt and felt a rush of pleasure.

'Timo, it's so good to hear from you.'

'You're driving, can you talk safely?' he asked.

'I can, I'm hands-free. It's safe to say anything you like,' she teased. 'How are you?'

'I'm well, just back from a week's tour and preparing for a London trip.'

'Did you hit all the right notes?' Holly asked, and Timo laughed.

'I think so, and if I didn't I tried to bluff it.'

'Ah, you are way too modest, I bet you were great,' Holly said.

He laughed again, and sounded unaccustomed to praise. 'So I have some news,' he continued. 'I'm coming to London for a performance and I was hoping to catch up with you there. If not, perhaps a visit to a seaside village might do me good.'

'That would be wonderful,' Holly said. The timing was perfect and just what she needed, some good company and something to look forward to now that she was probably going to be very much alone. 'But you must stay with me. I have a lovely guest room and I'll give you the tour of the village. It should take fifteen minutes.'

Timo's laughed again. 'Great!'

'Will Astrid be coming with you? You are both welcome,' Holly asked. *Hmm, was that too obvious?* she wondered.

'Ah, no, we've broken up, so if you are happy to just give me the tour alone?' he said.

'I'd love to. I'll get my tour guide umbrella out in case you lose sight of me.' They both laughed at the image that painted.

'We might end up with a complete tour group... pick up some stragglers along the way.'

'I have been known to find things,' Holly told him.

'So, I could organise a couple of tickets for you, if you'd like to come to the London concert. Perhaps you and your aunt, or with your friend, Juliette?'

'Thank you. I am sure my Aunt would love to come with me, and then you could drive back with me if that worked out for you,' she said. Then she got serious. 'Timo, I hope the neck-lace didn't cause your break-up. I'm sorry for my role in that, if it did.'

'No,' he assured her. 'Although Astrid felt I should have been more supportive of her, I guess, but I believe it went where it should have gone – home.'

Home, Holly thought. Her new home. Later that day, as *Findlater House* came into view, she realised that she had found something else very valuable... herself.

Holly turned into her street as the last light was fading. She was hoping to have a walk on the beach just before the sunset. As she pulled up and cut the car ignition, she noticed the interior lights were on.

Alexander!

She entered, not expecting to see him there, but he was

sitting on the couch with a glass of red wine in his hand. On the table were fresh flowers.

'You're here!' she said.

'I live here,' he teased.

'That you do,' she grinned, relieved, really relieved. 'Well, I'm pleased. I wasn't sure if and when I'd see you again.' She put her handbag down. 'I'll join you for a glass of wine.' She went to the kitchen and poured herself a glass.

'Let's sit outside and watch the last of the light,' he suggested, heading to the door. Holly followed him out and they sat in their usual positions. She was aware of how odd it might look for her to be sitting there with two glasses of wine, but Holly was way past worrying about that in this quirky town.

'Big day,' she said, and clinked her glass against his. They sipped in silence for a little while and watched the red ball of the sun sink into the ocean.

'Thank you, Holly,' Alexander said.

She smiled and turned to him. 'And thank you.'

'What for?' he scoffed. 'Dragging you around the country, putting you in danger with Andy Davies, rating all your guests and scaring you half to death with my sudden arrivals?'

'Well, there's that,' she agreed, and he laughed. 'Alex, I was lost when I came here and you've been my constant friend. Made me feel safe and happy.'

He nodded.

'So what now?' she asked, fearing what he would say.

He kept his eyes focused on the ocean. 'Well, I guess it is time to go. No reason to stay now.'

'Are you okay about seeing Meghan? You don't have to talk about it if you don't want to,' Holly said, and raised her hand in a reciprocal wave to a passing neighbour on their evening walk.

He shrugged. 'You know, it's been a long time. I guess I was pretty stupid thinking that, after a mere eight years together, Meghan would live another forty-plus years pining for me. Of course she was going to grieve, deal with it, move on and find love. I'm the one who didn't move on. But I'm just glad she knows the truth now.'

'I'm glad you both do. Although I'd like to see some justice.'

They sat for a while again in silence and then they both spoke at the same time.

'You know, I –'

'Of course if it –' Alexander stopped. 'Ladies first.'

'I was just going to say that you needn't hurry away on my account, just because you have your answer,' Holly said.

'I was just going to say that if it helped for a while to have me around, you know, I'm up for that.'

'I could use some help with the business, too,' she suggested.

'Yeah. I've got some insights into that stuff you're doing for the gothic library chick.'

'Abby. Great, thanks! So, you'll stick around.'

'Housemates,' he said, and raised his glass.

'To housemates,' Holly said, and grinned, thrilled. 'Can I have one last question?'

He rolled his eyes. 'Here it comes. Yeah, I guess so, you deserve it. Go ahead.'

'Is my grandmother, Lily, happy up there?' she said, and looked towards heaven.

Alexander held up his hands to tell her to wait and slowly faded before her eyes. She waited, sipping her wine and giving a small shiver as the cool of night crept in.

Moments later, he reappeared and smiled.

'Suffice to say,' he began, 'I think all the Hanlon women are happy tonight.'

Holly laughed. 'Wonderful, thank you. Now, I was hoping

to take a beach walk to shake off the day, if I can find a bodyguard.'

Alexander jumped to his feet. 'At your service. But if that shifty guy with the dog approaches again, I'll be sending him packing. There's something I don't like about him.'

Holly rolled her eyes.

Everything was as it should be.

THE END

Dear reader,

We hope you enjoyed reading *The House on Findlater Lane*. Please take a moment to leave a review, even if it's a short one. Your opinion is important to us.

Discover more books by Helen Goltz at

https://www.nextchapter.pub/authors/helen-goltz

Want to know when one of our books is free or discounted? Join the newsletter at

http://eepurl.com/bqqB3H

Best regards,

Helen Goltz and the Next Chapter Team

You might also like:
Devilfire by Simone Beaudelaire

To read the first chapter for free, please head to:
https://www.nextchapter.pub/books/devilfire

ABOUT THE AUTHOR

After studying English Literature and Communications at universities in Queensland, Australia, Helen Goltz has worked as a journalist, producer and marketer in print, TV, radio and public relations. She was born in Toowoomba and has made her home in Brisbane.

Visit her website at: www.helengoltz.com
    Or Facebook at: www.facebook.com/HelenGoltz.Author
    Follow on Twitter at: @helengoltz

The House On Findlater Lane
ISBN: 978-4-86752-931-7

Published by
Next Chapter
1-60-20 Minami-Otsuka
170-0005 Toshima-Ku, Tokyo
+818035793528

11th August 2021

Lightning Source UK Ltd.
Milton Keynes UK
UKHW012157240821
389422UK00001B/138